PRAISE FOR DOROTHY CLARK
AND HER NOVELS

"A dynamic story of two lonely people
in a desperate search for love…riveting and
fast-paced…a fabulous story. Top Pick. 4½ stars."
—*Romantic Times* on *Beauty for Ashes*

"In *Hosea's Bride,* Dorothy Clark skillfully
lends a modern twist to the Biblical story of Hosea.
A powerful faith message is deftly interwoven with a
wrenching tale of a woman who doesn't believe she is
worthy of love. Top Pick. 4½ stars."
—*Romantic Times*

"Dorothy Clark has woven a beautiful,
compelling story of God's mercy and healing."
—*ChristianBookPreviews.com* on *Hosea's Bride*

"This debut novel…is one that will keep you turning
page after page until you all-too-soon reach the end.
The forgiveness and love [the heroine] finds
when she becomes a Christian is truly inspiring."
—*RomanceJunkies.com* on *Hosea's Bride*

DOROTHY CLARK

Joy for Mourning

Steeple
Hill®

Published by Steeple Hill Books™

This book is dedicated with deep appreciation
to my talented writing friends and critique partners,
Debby Dill and Nancy Toback, who have been with me
from the beginning on this book.
Thanks for your unfailing graciousness and encouragement.
You two are the best!

STEEPLE HILL BOOKS

Steeple
Hill®

ISBN 0-373-78542-9

JOY FOR MOURNING

Copyright © 2005 by Dorothy Clark

This edition published by arrangement with Steeple Hill Books.

www.SteepleHill.com

Printed in U.S.A.

DISCUSSION QUESTIONS

1. For ten years, Laina prayed the Lord would give her a child. It didn't happen. What are the roots of Laina's anger? Have you, or someone you know, dealt with the problem of infertility? What scriptures might help a person deal with this issue?

2. Laina has her plans made, her goals set. She is in pursuit of those goals when Billy is struck down by a carriage in front of her. Laina believes this was merely a coincidence; Elizabeth believes it was divine intervention. Do you agree with Laina or Elizabeth? Why?

3. When Billy is injured in front of Laina, Dr. Thaddeous Allen appears on the scene. How did Thad serve as an answer to one of the reasons Laina was so furious with God?

4. Laina's brother, Justin, and his wife, Elizabeth, are moved by their love and compassion to pray for Laina. Why were their prayers important? Have you had a personal experience that shows the power of prayer? What was it?

5. In the story, incident after incident lead Laina toward opening an orphanage, and then, to the fulfillment of her own deepest desires, she becomes pregnant. If you believe, as Elizabeth did, that this was God's plan for Laina, on what do you base that belief? Do you believe God has a plan for each of us? Can we mess up the plan? Are there consequences if we do? If you believe God has a plan for everyone, do you know what His plan for you is? How can you find out?

6. When Laina becomes ill and her life hangs in the balance, Thad becomes desperate, while Justin becomes frightened and frustrated. Why? What is the underlying cause of these emotions? What do these men learn from this situation?

7. Pride is a sin. How did God deal with pride in the various characters in this story?

Chapter One

New York, 1822

She couldn't stand it! Not for another minute! She had to go someplace where there were people, laughter, *life*. Laina Brighton swept her gaze around her beautiful, richly furnished drawing room, and the despair she now lived with on a daily basis gripped her anew. It was so elegant, so perfect, so *empty*. She missed Stanford. Oh, how she missed him! If only they could have had children, perhaps—

Laina wrenched her mind from her heartrending thoughts, blinked away the tears that sprang so readily to her eyes these days and walked swiftly to the doorway. Her reflection flashed in the gilt-framed mirror as she hurried past. Her steps faltered. She turned and went back to stare into the mirror. The sorrow was still there, but so was a

look of determination she hadn't seen on her face since
Stanford had died so unexpectedly nine months ago. She
whirled and yanked open the door.

"Beaumont?"

The impeccably garbed butler materialized as if from
thin air.

Laina frowned. And that was another thing—the servants *hovered.* They were so solicitous it was smothering her!

"Yes, madam?"

"I'm going to Philadelphia, Beaumont." She ignored the
quickly stifled look of shocked disapproval in his eyes—
Beaumont was a stickler for convention. "Tell Carlson to
prepare the carriage immediately. I wish to leave within the
hour."

"Within the hour? But madam, that's imposs—" He
stopped short as Laina stiffened her spine. He gave her a
small bow. "Yes, madam—within the hour. Will there be
anything else?"

"Yes. Send Tilly to my room to help Annette with the
packing." With a swish of her long black skirts, Laina
spun about and headed for the ornately carved stairway
that spiraled upward to the third floor. She glanced back
over her shoulder at her butler as she began to climb.
"And tell Hannah to prepare a food basket—enough for
two days. And—" She cleared the sudden thickness from
her throat. "And send Billy ahead to arrange for a change
of horses. I'm not stopping until I reach Randolph Court!"

Philadelphia

"Laina! What a wonderful surprise. I'm so pleased
you—" Elizabeth gasped and stopped her headlong rush

into the drawing room.

"Do I look that disreputable?" Laina forced a smile and rose to her feet. The room spun. She put her hand on the arm of the chair to steady herself.

"Laina, dear, what's *wrong*?" Her sister-in-law rushed forward and clasped her arms around her. "You're so pale—and trembling enough to shake apart. Are you ill?"

"No. I'm simply incredibly weary." Laina bit down on her lip to stop the laughter that was pushing upward in her throat. She must be hysterical. There was certainly nothing amusing— *Bother!* She blinked the sudden film of moisture from her eyes and stepped back from Elizabeth's arms. It was too easy to give in to self-pity when others were sympathetic. "I came from home without stopping."

"*Without stopping? Are you mad?*"

Laina jerked at the roar of words from the doorway. "No, dearheart—only desperate." Her lower lip quivered as she watched her younger brother hurry across the room toward her. The tears she'd been fighting welled into her eyes as his strong arms pulled her into a bone-crushing hug. Oh, how wonderful it felt to be held again! She rested her head against his hard chest. "Don't scold, Justin. I simply could not stay in that dreary, lonely house any longer. I had to come."

"I'm not scolding you for coming, Laina. Only for doing so in such a foolhardy manner." Justin slid his hands to the top of her arms and held her a short distance away, frowning down at her. "Why didn't you send word? I would have come for you. There was no need for you to make the journey alone, without care or rest. Look at you! You're all but done in from fatigue."

"I know." Laina lifted her watery gaze to her brother's handsome, scowling face. "I know it was foolish of me, Justin, but it would have meant days of waiting if— Oh!" She began to sway as the full force of her exhaustion swept over her. "I think I'd better sit down."

"You don't need to sit down, Laina. You need to sleep. Bring her along, Justin." Elizabeth spun about and started across the room.

Laina was too weary to protest as her brother scooped her into his arms and followed.

"I don't believe we need send for Dr. Allen, Justin. Laina isn't fevered." Elizabeth glanced up at her worried husband. "I think sleep is the only medicine she needs."

Laina sagged with relief as Elizabeth lifted her hand from her forehead, then gathered the last of her strength and pushed herself into a sitting position against the headboard. The bed felt too good after her long journey. She fought the desire to close her eyes, and smiled at Justin. "Elizabeth is right, dearheart. Please don't make a fuss. All I need is sleep."

"And food." Justin scowled down at her. "Haven't you been eating? Look at yourself, Laina—you're thin as a stick!"

Her heart warmed at sight of the worried frown lines creasing her brother's forehead. "You're such a loving, caring man, Justin." She wrinkled her nose at him. "Even if not a very complimentary one." She shifted her gaze to Elizabeth and forced a tired smile. "How could you ever have thought him cold and aloof?"

Elizabeth laughed. "Because he *acted* that way. How was I to know it was all a sham?" She stepped to her husband's side and rested her hand on his arm. "Laina will be fine, Justin, but we need to get the travel dust off her so she can go to bed. And that means you need to go downstairs. I'll join you as soon as Trudy and I have made her comfortable for the night."

Justin shifted his gaze to his wife, and Laina's chest tightened. Stanford had admired her, but he'd never looked at her the way Justin was looking at Elizabeth—especially after she'd failed to produce an heir for him. And now—

Laina broke off the depressing thought and watched as her brother cupped his wife's face in his hands, kissed her soundly, then lifted his head and grinned. "There! Now I've finally satisfied a desire I've had since the first night we spent together in this room—at least in part."

"Justin!" Elizabeth's cheeks flamed. "Your sister—"

"Knows I love you. Look, I've made her smile." Justin chuckled and kissed the tip of Elizabeth's finely formed nose. "I like it when you blush."

Laina sighed. She couldn't help it. Justin and Elizabeth were so much in love, so happy together. Justin glanced at her over his wife's soft golden curls. "I wish there was something we could do to ease your sorrow, Lainy."

"There is. We can let her know how much we love her." Elizabeth lifted her head and smiled. "We can share our happiness with her and we can pray for her, because the rest—the easing of her grief and the healing of her sorrow—is in God's hands."

The words were meant as comfort, but they only made her feel worse. Laina clamped her jaw together to hold back the bitter retort that sprang to her lips. She had never been on close terms with God the way Elizabeth

was, and since Stanford's death she ignored Him completely. Why not? What had God ever done for her? She
was barren in spite of years of prayers, and *now* she was
widowed and without hope of ever having a child. She
looked away lest they read her anger on her face.

"You speak truth. You're a very wise woman, Elizabeth."

Laina stiffened and snapped her gaze back to her
brother. Surely he didn't believe in God again? What had
happened to the disbelief and bitterness he'd felt after his
disastrous marriage to Margaret?

"Thank you, sir. But I am also a busy one. Now go!"
Elizabeth pushed against Justin's chest. He grinned and
tightened his grip.

The door opened.

"Oh! Excuse me, mum! I didn't…I mean…you rang
and… I'll come back."

Laina glanced at the awkward, blushing maid tripping
all over herself as she hurriedly backed out the door, and
her anger dissolved. She burst into laughter at the comi-
cal sight. It felt wonderful to laugh again.

Justin winked at her, then motioned to the maid.
"Come in, Trudy. I was only saying goodbye. I have been
ordered from the room." He gave a mock scowl and leaned
down to Elizabeth's ear. "Sometimes servants are most in-
convenient!" His whisper was loud enough for all to hear.

Trudy giggled.

Laina whisked back in time to when she and Justin
were small. They were in the kitchen watching the cook
baking and Justin leaned over and whispered, "The smell's
making my tummy hurt. I wish we could have a biscuit."
His wish was granted. Cook overheard his whisper and
slid them each a biscuit. They looked at the cookies,

looked at each other and a conspiracy was born. From that time on they'd used the whisper ploy to manipulate servants into giving them their way.

Laina chuckled at the memory. Justin grinned at her and she knew he was remembering, too. Suddenly she didn't feel so lost and alone. The tightness in her chest eased. She reached for her brother's hand. "Bless you, Justin."

He gave her hand a squeeze, then bent and kissed her cheek just in front of her ear. "It's going to be all right, Lainy—heart's promise."

This time the whisper was for her alone. It was the solemn oath they'd made to each other when one of them had been sad or unhappy after their mother's death. Laina's breath caught on a sob. Justin gave her a fierce hug, then turned abruptly and strode from the room.

"Do you feel better?"

"Much better, Elizabeth. Thank you for loaning me Trudy. The hot bath took away much of the soreness from being tossed around in the carriage." Laina adjusted the black tie at the neck of her white nightgown and sank onto the edge of the bed. She was too shaky and weak from fatigue to stand.

"Are you hungry?" Elizabeth swept her gaze over her. "I had cook make you a tray. There's chicken stew, an apple dumpling, some cheese and warm milk."

Laina made an effort. She ate a few bites of the stew, popped a bit of cheese in her mouth, then sighed and pulled her damp braid forward over her shoulder. "The food is wonderful, Elizabeth, but I'm simply too weary to eat. I'll have the dumpling in the morning." She slid under the covers and sank back against the feather pillow.

"Of course. Sleep is what you need now." Elizabeth put a few bite-size pieces of cheese on the plate with the dumpling, covered it with the napkin and placed it on the nightstand beside a glass of water. She motioned Trudy to take the tray away. "Is there anything more I can do to make you comfortable?" She pulled the red-and-cream-patterned coverlet over Laina's exposed shoulders. "Perhaps another blanket?"

"No. Nothing." Laina glanced up at the red tester above her and smiled. "Thank you for putting me in this room, Elizabeth. It will be so lovely to wake up to *color.* Everything in my house is shrouded in black." Her eyelids drifted closed. She forced them open again. "I love… color…especially…red." She frowned. Her voice sounded thick and far away. Her eyelids drifted closed again.

"Yes, I know." Elizabeth leaned down and hugged her. "Good night, Laina. It's so lovely having you here. Sleep well."

"Umm." She couldn't form a word. Couldn't open her eyes. The light against her eyelids dimmed, flickered. She heard the rustle of Elizabeth's skirts, the soft pat of her shoes against the carpet. The door opened and closed. Silence descended.

Laina gave a long sigh. At home the silence grated against her nerves. This silence was different—there was life behind it. And tomorrow she would see the children. A smile curved her lips. She cuddled the thought to her and yielded to her exhaustion.

Justin stopped pacing and pivoted to face his wife as she entered the salon. "I think you're wrong, Elizabeth. I think we should send for Dr. Allen. Laina looks *ill.*" He frowned.

"She's thin as a fence rail and weak as a kitten. And those dark circles under her eyes…" He shook his head. "One would think she'd been *punched*." He scowled. "We need Dr. Allen."

"Justin, I know it's hard for you to see your sister looking so frail, but I promise you, a good night's sleep will do away with those dark circles and cook's good food will take care of Laina's thinness and help her regain her strength." Elizabeth crossed to the settee and seated herself. "As for the rest, as I said earlier, that is in God's hands. All we can do is love her and pray for her." She smiled and patted the cushion beside her. "Why don't you come sit down and relax in front of the fire?"

"*Sit?*" Justin shook his head. "I can't simply *sit* here—I'm too agitated." He bent and threw another log on the already blazing fire, then grabbed the poker and jabbed it into place. "I wish there was something I could *do* for Laina." He gave the log another jab and shot her a look. "*Besides* pray."

"I know, dear. But at the moment all she needs is rest." Elizabeth rose and walked over to put her arms around Justin's waist. He pulled her close. She went on tiptoe and kissed his chin. "Why don't you walk to the Merchant's Coffee House, dear? You can stride off some of that frustration on the way, and talking business and politics with your friends will get your mind off Laina."

He gave her a mock scowl. "Are you trying to get rid of me, madam?"

Elizabeth laughed. "Only until you calm down a bit."

Justin's mouth twisted into a rueful smile. "I'm sorry if I'm being a bear about this, Elizabeth. I think I'll take your advice. A brisk walk is exactly what I need." He dropped a kiss on the tip of her nose, then planted one on her mouth and left the room. When she could no longer hear his footsteps, she sighed and bowed her head.

"Father God, please guide Justin and me with Your wisdom to know what is best to do for Laina. Please give us understanding of her hurt and grief, and compassion and wisdom to help her through it. And dear Lord, I pray You will lead Laina in the path of Your choosing for her that she might know peace and fulfillment. Please touch her heart with Your healing hand and make her truly happy. I ask it in Your holy name. Amen."

Elizabeth released another long sigh and blinked away the tears pooled in her eyes. She had a sudden urgent need to see her children—to look on their dear, sleeping faces. She hurried from the room, down the hall to the staircase and began to climb. How blessed she was to have a loving husband and three healthy, happy children! Her heart overflowed with thanksgiving. "Dear Lord, may You bless Laina as richly as You have blessed me!"

Laina whimpered and turned onto her side, her fingers flexing against the feather pillow, drawing it closer. It bunched beneath her hand. Her fingers flexed again.

There were children floating at her out of the darkness. Children of all ages and sizes, from babies to adolescents. Angry, crying, frightened children. She caught each child as they neared, pulling them out of the darkness and tucking them into her heart where they would be loved and protected. Her heart grew larger and larger. She was afraid it would burst, but still she gathered the children in. Her arms grew weary as she worked until at last they fell useless to her sides. No. No! She couldn't stop. She had to help the children!

A man came and stood beside her. She could feel his strength. He began pulling the children out of the darkness, and her distress eased. She tried to see who the man was, but whenever she looked, he was turned away reaching for another child. Her heart became engorged with them. How could it hold more? What would she do with them all?

Justin appeared, smiling and placing his hand on her swollen, enlarged heart. "It's going to be all right, Lainy— heart's promise." His hand turned into a purse that burst open, raining money down over the children in her heart. They began to laugh. The sound filled her with joy. She began to laugh with them.

The man took hold of her hand and suddenly they were alone. His touch made her forget how to breathe. She looked up. She couldn't see his face! Who was he?

Justin laughed.

He knew! She spun toward her brother, but he was floating away. "Don't go, Justin! Tell me! Who is he?"

"Heart's promise, Lainy, heart's promise…"

"Justin, wait!"

Laina bolted upright, startled awake by her own cry. Her heart was pounding. She clasped her hand to her chest and darted her gaze about the room searching for her brother. The dim, flickering light of the fire highlighted the objects in the room. There was no one there. She was alone. It was only a dream.

Laina shook her head and sank back onto the pillow. She could understand dreaming about Justin and children, because she'd been thinking of them when she drifted off to sleep. But who was the stranger? And what about the money? It made no sense. No sense at all. She yawned and closed her eyes. It was probably because she was so tired....

Chapter Two

It was hunger that woke her.

Laina opened her eyes, and the first thing she saw was the red tester overhead. She stared at it in confusion for a moment, then smiled as her sleep-befuddled mind cleared. She'd made it! She was at Randolph Court. Oh, glory, glory, glory!

Laina sat up and swept her gaze around the large bedroom, drinking in the sights. Someone had been in and built up the fire. It was blazing merrily, its flickering light warming the red-and-cream-patterned silk on the walls, the red, blue and green paisley fabric on the chair that sat at the side of the hearth. Oh, how wonderful to see bright colors again!

Her stomach rumbled. Laina slid from the bed, lifted the napkin-covered plate from the nightstand and carried it to the chair. The fire warmed her bare feet and the swirling colors in the paisley fabric cheered her soul as she curled into the chair's padded comfort. For the first time since Stanford's passing she felt truly hungry. She lifted the napkin, placed it on her lap and picked up the fork. The first bite of baked apple tasted delicious. She took another, then another with a bite of cheese.

Wonderful! If she hadn't had good manners drilled into her as a child, she would have smacked her lips. Laina smiled, finished the apple, then popped the last bite of cheese into her mouth.

"You're awake."

Laina gasped and almost dropped the plate as she jerked around toward the door.

"I'm sorry, I didn't mean to startle you. I was being quiet in case you were still asleep." Elizabeth smiled and closed the door. "How are you feeling?"

"Much better." Laina held up the empty plate. "My compliments to your cook."

Elizabeth's laughter washed over her like healing balm. "I hope you haven't spoiled your appetite. It's almost time for dinner."

"Dinner?" Laina stared up at Elizabeth. "No wonder I feel better. I haven't slept the night through since—" She swallowed and looked down at her hands. It was still hard to speak the words aloud.

Elizabeth bent and gave her a quick hug. "You were truly exhausted, Laina. I'm so pleased you rested well and are feeling stronger." She smiled and took the empty plate. "Do you feel up to coming down to the dining room, or would you prefer a tray here in your room?"

"No, no tray." Laina shook her head and rose to her feet. "I've had enough of being alone." She squared her shoulders, trying not to look as pitiful as she felt. "Is there time enough to see the children before dinner? I've so been looking forward to making my new nephew's acquaintance."

Elizabeth laughed and nodded. "How could I refuse such a request? We shall make time. Cook can set dinner back an hour. Now, I'll ring for Trudy while you have a wash, then she will help you dress and do your hair." Elizabeth smiled at her over her shoulder as she headed for the bellpull. "She's already set out your things in the dressing room."

"Thank you, Trudy, my hair has never looked lovelier." Laina stepped out of the dressing room and immediately spotted her newly pressed gown on the bed. It looked like a crow among a flock of cardinals. Gloom settled over her like a cloak. She walked to the bed, took the dress into her hands and sighed. "Oh, how I hate to put this dress on. I'm so tired of wearing black!"

"Then why wear it?"

"Why?" Laina shot Elizabeth a puzzled look. "Because I'm a widow, and a widow is expected to wear black."

"I know the convention, Laina." Elizabeth moved to stand beside her. "I'm only questioning your reasons for continuing to follow it when it makes you so unhappy. Stanford has been gone nine months—and this is Philadelphia, not New York. No one here will know if you take off your widow's garb a little early."

"Justin—?" Laina stopped as Elizabeth gave a firm shake of her head.

"Justin hates the custom. He says it's barbaric. He has written in his will that I am *not* to wear black if he departs this earth before me." She smiled. "He likes me in soft colors."

"*Truly?*" Laina heard the surprise in her own voice. She smiled. "Well, I can only say my brother is a very considerate and wise man." She looked down at the hated black garment in her hands. Her smile faded and she released another sigh. "Nothing would give me more pleasure at this moment than to rip this dress to shreds! But it would do no good. I have nothing but black gowns with me."

"I know…but I have others." Elizabeth laughed and hurried to the door. "Bring them in, Annie."

"Ohhh!" Laina all but swooned at sight of the different-colored gowns draped over the young maid's arms. "Bless you, Elizabeth!" She gave her sister-in-law a fierce hug, then clasped her hands in ecstasy at the array of beautiful gowns being spread out on the bed. "Oh, my! They look like a rainbow."

"God's promise of better days ahead." Elizabeth patted Laina's clasped hands, then gave a rueful glance at the gowns. "I'm afraid there's nothing red."

Laina ignored the remark about God's promise. "I know—Justin hates red." She reached out and fingered the soft satin of a periwinkle-blue gown with an overdress of cream-colored, lace-edged net. "Perhaps this one?" She shot a questioning look at Elizabeth. "Or do you think it's too—"

"I think it's perfect. It will look lovely with your dark hair and blue eyes." Elizabeth cleared her throat and turned to her maids. "Annie, go to my room and bring back my cream-colored satin slippers and my paisley stole. They look well with the dress. And Trudy, remove that black crape from around the bottom of Mrs. Brighton's petticoat, then help her into the blue gown."

She swept her gaze to Laina as the maids rushed to do her bidding. "It's fortunate we're much of a size. These gowns will do for now, if Trudy takes a tuck here and there. But you need dresses of deeper, more vibrant colors to truly enhance your beauty. And I know the very modiste who can create them for you." Her lips twitched and she looked away.

"What is it?"

Her query drew Elizabeth's gaze back to meet hers. "I can't pretend any longer, Laina. I'm so glad you agreed to cast aside your mourning attire, because your brother has already arranged for Madame Duval to wait on you tomorrow."

"He *has?*" Excitement coursed through her as Elizabeth nodded affirmation. "Well, bless his heart!"

Laina rapped softly, then rushed through the door into her brother's study before he had a chance to answer. "Justin, I'm sorry to interrupt whatever it is you're doing, but I simply had to come thank you!"

Justin dropped the bill of lading he'd been comparing against the profit statement on his desk and braced himself as Laina hurled herself into his arms. "Thank me for what?"

"For setting me free!" Laina stepped back, held her arms out to the sides and did a quick pirouette. "Do I not look lovely?"

"Beautiful." Justin's grin changed into a frown. "But much too thin." Concern darkened his eyes. "Are you certain you're not ill?"

"I'm fine, dearheart." He looked doubtful. Laina sighed. "Truly I am, Justin. It's only that I've had no appetite. Sitting alone at a dining table staring at empty chairs does not encourage one to eat well."

His face tightened. "Yes…I remember."

"Oh, Justin, I'm sorry." Laina put her arms around his waist and squeezed. "I didn't mean to bring back bad memories."

"It's all right, Laina. Thanks to the Lord's blessings, the past no longer has the power to hurt me." He kissed the top of her head, then held her a short distance away. His gaze fastened on hers. "I was remembering in regard to your circumstances. I intend to do something about them."

He sounded so certain! Hope locked the air in Laina's lungs. "What do you intend to do?"

Justin shook his head. "I don't know. I only know the first step is to pray for guidance."

The air rushed from Laina's lungs in a disgusted, disappointed snort. She stepped back. "Then I'll not hold my brea—" His finger on her lips stopped the angry words.

"Don't speak words of unbelief, Laina. They only block your own blessing." He lowered his hand to his side. "I know how you feel, and I understand. I felt the same way not very long ago. But I was wrong."

She drew breath to speak.

He shook his head. "Trust me, Laina. I'm not asking you to believe—only to be still and wait."

It was too much. She couldn't hold the anger any longer. "*Wait?* I've waited for ten years! Do you really think things will change now? Look at me! I'm barren, Justin. I'm a widow whose husband lost interest when I couldn't produce an heir. Do you think another man will marry me? Things would only end the same way."

The words spurted from Laina's mouth as fast as the tears flowed down her cheeks. She swiped the tears away and drew a deep breath. "You believe in a God who answers prayers and pours out blessings? Well, I do not! I prayed for children for ten years and I'll not waste time praying again. You believe—very well, *you* pray! And if your Lord gives me children I will serve Him all of my remaining days! Now, if you will excuse me, I have an appointment to meet your son."

With a whirl of her long skirts Laina stormed from the room. It took her several deep breaths and five minutes of pacing the hallway before she calmed down enough to join Elizabeth for their trip to the nursery.

"I'm afraid the girls are already napping, madam." Anna Hammerfield glanced toward the open door a short distance from the rocker where she had been sitting doing needlework when Elizabeth and Laina entered the nursery. Soft, sleepy baby sounds emanated occasionally from the dimly lit interior of the adjoining bedroom. The nanny smiled. "But Master James is still awake."

Elizabeth nodded. "Thank you, Anna." She turned back to face Laina. "We'll come back to see Sarah and Mary later, after dinner." A soft, beautiful smile spread across her face. "For now, we'll visit your new nephew." She stepped through the open door and led the way across the small room to the crib against the far wall.

Laina caught her breath. "Oh, Elizabeth, he's beautiful!" She smiled at the baby staring up at her and reached down to touch one small, perfect hand. "How do you do, James Justin Randolph? I'm your aunt Laina. And I'm very happy to meet you at last."

The baby gurgled, gave her a toothless smile and waved his hands in the air. Laina's heart hurt. So many emotions assailed her she couldn't begin to sort them out—except two. Hunger and anger. Those two she recognized. She knew them well. They appeared every time she saw a mother and child. She took a deep breath and forced them back into the dark, empty place inside her.

"Would you like to hold him?"

"May I?" She couldn't keep the longing out of her voice.

"Of course you may." Elizabeth lifted her son, kissed his soft cheek, then tucked a blanket about him and placed him in Laina's arms. "He likes to be rocked. The chair's over there." She nodded toward the corner. "I'll be back in a few minutes. I have to speak with Anna." She turned and walked out of the room.

Laina stared after her. What a thoughtful, caring, *unselfish* person Elizabeth was. How could she ever have thought her interested only in Justin's money? She shook her head at the sudden flood of memories, then looked down at the baby in her arms. "You have a wonderful, *wonderful* mama and papa, James Justin. And a very foolish aunt."

The baby gurgled an answer. Laina laughed, hugged him close and walked to the chair. The silky feel of his cheek against hers was more precious than anything she'd ever known. The sweet baby smell of him was priceless. She brushed her fingers through his soft, downy, dark curls and began to rock.

I was remembering in regard to your circumstances. I intend to do something about them.... The first step is to pray for guidance.

Laina tried, unsuccessfully, to close out Justin's words, but the baby's warm breath on her neck brought hope fluttering to life in her heart at thought of them. It drowned a moment later in an onrush of bitterness. Why shouldn't Justin believe in prayer? He had *his* miracle.

Thaddeous Allen glanced at the youngster on the buggy seat beside him. The too-small, tattered clothes the boy wore provided little protection against the cold March air and not even the carriage robe was sufficient to warm him. He was shivering so hard it was a wonder his bones were still connected one to the other. "You might be warmer if you crouch down on the floor in front of the seat, Sam. You'll be out of the wind down there."

The boy shot him a look full of fear and distrust. "I'm not cold."

The blatant lie wrenched at Thad's heart. "You have my word, Sam—I won't hand you over to the law."

The boy gave him a curt nod and continued to stare straight ahead, jaw set. Thad let it go. Sam was going to stay where he could watch every move and change of direction the buggy made. His fear of the law was greater than his physical discomfort. And who could blame him? Since the orphans' asylum had burned in January, the authorities had become harsh in their treatment of vagrant children, to deter them from stealing, now that they had no means of removing them from the streets.

A pang of concern shot through Thad. He'd given the boy his word he'd find a good home for him—it was the only way he could keep him from jumping out of Dan Pierson's haymow and likely breaking every undernourished bone in his body when he'd been caught stealing eggs. But who would take him in?

Thad watched as the boy shifted his thin body and buried his scratched, filthy hands deeper beneath the lap rug. The Bauers? No, Martha had developed that cough. Thad frowned. He didn't like the sound of that cough. And Martha had started losing weight. It was probably consumption. No, he couldn't take the boy there. Where, then?

Thad frowned and sifted through his patients in his mind as he tugged on the reins to turn the horse onto Arch Street. Arthur and Betsy Monroe? The names brought a shot of hope surging through him. Arthur had told him only last month that Betsy was unhappy with no one to do for since their last boy had left home. Yes! They would be perfect.

Thad slanted another look at the youngster and shook his head. The boy was so filthy you couldn't even tell the color of his hair, and Betsy was a stickler for cleanliness. *Lord, let Betsy see this boy as You see him. Let her look on him with her heart, Lord, and not with her natural eyes. Let both Arthur and Betsy see right through the dirt and grime and downright surliness to the frightened child beneath and take him into their home and hearts. Amen.*

"Look at you—skinny as a willow whip and covered with dirt and the good Lord alone knows what else! And those clothes—there's no savin' those clothes. Too small, anyway."

She was going to keep him! Thad bit back a smile as Betsy Monroe put her hands on her hips and studied the small boy standing like a lump of stone in the center of her kitchen.

"Still, I reckon there ain't nothin' wrong with you some good food, some of Ben's old clothes and a hot bath won't put to rights."

The boy jerked as if a whip had been laid to his flesh. "I heard about them bath things, an' I ain't gettin' in no water!" The words spit from Sam's mouth. He shot a panicked look at the outside door, and Thad casually stepped in front of it. The boy glared at him and swept his gaze the other way—toward the home's interior. Arthur stood squarely in that doorway. Sam's hands clenched into small fists. His chin jutted forward. "I ain't gettin' in no water—an' you cain't make me!"

Betsy nodded. "I ain't figurin' to. That's your choice, Sam. Course, nobody sets to my table or sleeps in this house that ain't respectable clean." She stepped over to the woodstove and lifted the lid from a large iron pot. The rich, tantalizing aroma of a pot roast filled the kitchen. She picked up a long fork and poked around inside the pot. The smell increased. "Ah, nice and tender!" She smiled at her husband. "Lots of rich gravy for you to sop your bread in."

Sam's stomach growled. His Adam's apple slid up and down his skinny throat as he swallowed hard.

Thad didn't blame him. His own stomach was reminding him he hadn't had time to eat today. He bit back a grin and watched in open admiration as the plump woman continued her exquisite form of blackmail.

Betsy turned her back on the boy and opened the pierced tin door of a pine cupboard. The smell of freshly baked bread wafted out. She pulled out a loaf, sliced it into thick slabs, then carried it and a small brown crock to the table.

"We'd be pleased if you'd stay and take supper with us, Dr. Allen. It's been a space since you've visited. The boy can wait there by the door till you've eaten." Betsy's eyes twinkled as she looked up at him. "Do you like apple butter or plain cream butter?"

"I might could wash my hands."

The grumbled, reluctant words were fairly dripping with saliva. Thad choked back a chuckle. Poor Sam—Betsy didn't by so much as word or deed betray that she even heard him. She went right on as if he hadn't spoken. "No matter, Doctor, we'll have both." She put a second crock on the table, then moved back to the stove, folded the hem of her blue apron and used it to lift an oblong crockery dish from the oven.

Thad's stomach tightened at sight of the dark juices bubbling their way through a delicately browned crust. Blackberry cobbler! He took a long sniff of the heady aroma riding on the rising steam.

The cobbler proved too much for Sam. He jerked forward, staring at the dessert. "I 'low as how a bath—oncet—might be a good thing."

Betsy Monroe nodded and smoothed her apron back in place. "The tub is in there." She pointed to a small room that jutted out onto the back porch. "Go strip down to your altogether and climb in. Arthur will fetch you hot water and soap. I'll set by dinner till you've finished. And mind you clean your hair and scrub behind your ears."

She stared after Sam as he trudged to the little room. "Poor young'un, seems like he ain't never had a mite of love or lookin' after, but we'll soon take care of that." She looked up and gave him a radiant smile. "May the Lord bless you for the work you've done this day, Dr. Allen. Now, take your ease—I need to go fetch some of Ben's old clothes." She swiped at her eyes with her apron and hurried from the room.

Thad pulled out one of the plank-bottom chairs surrounding the table, lowered his tall, lean body onto it and directed his attention toward the sound of wildly splashing water accompanied by grunts and groans of protest coming from the little room. A grin tugged at his lips. *Sounds as if Arthur has his hands full.*

"I ain't gettin' my hair wet! You can't make—"

Thad burst into laughter at the glubbing, choking sounds that followed Sam's pronouncement. That boy was learning about cleanliness the hard way. He rose to his feet as Betsy came rushing back into the kitchen, her arms full of clothes.

There was a flurry of splashing.

"Mercy! Sounds as if there's quite a struggle goin' on in there. I'm not sure my berry cobbler can overcome this." Betsy's cheeks dimpled as she smiled up at him.

Thad chuckled. "I think that cobbler can win out over anything. And I'm pretty sure Arthur will prove victorious in this particular battle." He nodded toward the clothes. "Why don't you give me those. I'll take them in to Sam and—" He jerked his head around as a howl of sheer fury came from the other room.

"I ain't usin' no *soap,* you *jolt-headed, da*—!" There was more splashing, choking, coughing, followed by Arthur's calm voice. "We don't use them words in this house. Here's the soap."

Betsy grinned and handed him the clothes. "Sounds like Sam's having a hard time—poor tyke." Her grin turned into laughter. "I'd better give him a double serving." She turned to the stove. Thad's mouth watered as she picked up the long fork and poked around in the iron pot again. He pivoted on his heel and headed for the little room. He'd been so busy, he hadn't eaten for twenty-four hours and he'd be horsewhipped if he wouldn't scrub Sam himself for a plate of Betsy's pot roast!

Chapter Three

"Why, Trudy, it's lovely."

Elizabeth's maid smiled. "I'm pleased you like it, mum. Will there be anything else?"

"No. That's all for now."

"Very good, mum." Trudy put the hairbrush down on the dressing table, bobbed an awkward curtsy and left the bedroom.

Laina turned her head from side to side, studying her new hairdo in the mirror. It looked wonderful. Whoever would have thought that clumsy young woman possessed such a talent? Annette could take instruction from Trudy. Laina laughed at the thought of her French maid's reaction to that scenario and lifted her hand to touch the dark brown curls that tumbled from the knot of hair at the crown of her head to her shoulders. The style would take some getting used to, but it was definitely flattering.

Laina pursed her lips and leaned closer to the mirror. Without the fringe of bangs Annette had insisted were all the rage, her face looked more…more what? Dramatic? Yes, that was it. Her eyes seemed larger, more luminous, their dark blue color striking, their long, thick lashes arresting. And her high cheekbones appeared more pronounced. Her full lips more noticeable. Oh, dear, *that* wasn't good!

Laina frowned and rose to her feet. Her mouth was too wide, and with the natural wine color of her lips it looked enormous! She sighed, snuffed the candles and headed for the door. At least she had good teeth. She was thankful for that. And for the borrowed dress. She smiled and brushed her hand over the pale green velvet fabric that whispered softly as she walked. Today she would choose the fabrics and patterns for her new gowns. After she visited with the children.

"And who is this?" Laina stared down at the huge black dog looking up at her. The monster's white-tipped tail wagged back and forth like a metronome.

"My dog—Mr. Buffy." Sarah wrapped her arms about the animal's neck.

The wagging tail increased speed. Laina laughed. "How do you do, Mr. Buffy? I'm pleased to make your acquaintance."

The dog gave one short bark and sat down. Sarah plopped down beside him, giggling as he licked her cheek. "Mr. Buffy loves me."

"I can see that."

"Doggy." Mary toddled over and patted Mr. Buffy's neck, then giggled and stuck her finger in his ear. The dog gave a shake of his great head, toppling her to the floor. She let out a startled cry and lifted her arms.

Laina scooped her up. "You're all right, Mary."

"Doggy." Mary's lower lip pouted out and she pointed an accusing, pudgy little finger at the big black brute looking up at them.

Laina laughed and squeezed her tight. "Mr. Buffy didn't mean to knock you down, precious. You tickled his ear…like this." She feathered her finger along the toddler's tiny ear. Mary giggled and ducked her head, sliding her little arms around Laina's neck as far as they could reach and holding on tight. Laina's heart swelled with longing.

"Tory."

"*Tory?*" Laina shot Elizabeth a wordless plea for help.

"She wants you to read her a story." Elizabeth laughed and shook her head. "The little extortionist asks for one whenever she thinks someone feels sorry for her."

"Oh." Laina grinned down at the toddler in her arms. "Aren't you the clever one?"

"They all are." Elizabeth rose from the rocking chair, handed her sleeping son to Anna Hammerfield and took Mary into her arms. "No story now, Mary. We have an appointment at the dressmaker's. We'll read a story later." She nuzzled the ticklish spot at the base of the toddler's neck.

Mary giggled and squirmed. "Mama." She hugged Elizabeth's neck, then twisted around and pointed down. "Doggy."

"All right." Elizabeth put the toddler down. "Watch her, Mr. Buffy."

The dog barked once and turned his massive head toward Mary. Laina felt a tug on her hand and looked down. "What is it, Sarah?"

"Do you like licorice?"

"Licorice? Why, yes, I do." The little girl beamed. Laina laughed and looked at Elizabeth. "Let me guess—a *polite* extortionist?"

"Exactly." Elizabeth grinned and reached down to rest her hand on Sarah's hair.

Laina went down on her knees and took hold of the little girl's hands. "I think I shall bring some licorice home. We could share it. Would you like that?"

Sarah nodded, gave her a shy smile, then turned and buried her face in Elizabeth's long skirt.

The afternoon sun was trying its best, but there was still a decided chill in the March air. Laina shivered. The blue velvet coat and matching "jockey's hat" bonnet she'd borrowed from Elizabeth didn't fully protect her from the cold.

"I hope you aren't overdoing it, Laina." Elizabeth's brow creased with concern. "Perhaps we should have listened to Justin and had Madame Duval come to the house. Shall I tell Daniel to return home? We—"

"No, no, Elizabeth!" Laina turned toward her sister-in-law. "It was only a momentary chill. I'm fine. And it's so wonderful to be going out among people again it's well worth a few shivers."

Elizabeth laughed at Laina's vehemence. "As you wish."

"Oh, look." Laina leaned closer to the carriage window as they rode by Twiggs Manor. "Abigail's house looks so lonely and…and sad."

Elizabeth glanced at the stately, three-story brick mansion. "It is sad. Justin hasn't decided what to do with it. He can't bring himself to sell it to strangers, so it sits empty."

"What a shame. It's a beautiful house. And the furnishings are wonderful. Abigail had impeccable taste."

"Yes, she did." Elizabeth leaned back and blinked tears from her eyes. "I still find it hard to believe she's gone from us. She was such a strong personality, the memory of it lingers."

"Strong?" Laina shot a sidelong look at Elizabeth and smiled. "Don't you mean acerbic?"

Elizabeth laughed at Laina's dry tone. "Abigail would be pleased by that description. But she was also kind, generous and very wise."

Laina recognized the sorrow in Elizabeth's voice too well. "You miss her."

"Yes…very much. I only knew her a short time, but Abigail was the best friend I've ever had. She believed in me when your brother thought me an adulteress and murderer."

Laina shook her head. "To see you and Justin together today, one would never think your relationship had such a stormy beginning."

"It was stormy, all right. Justin went around looking like a thundercloud most of the time, and I shivered and shook, waiting for lightning to strike." Elizabeth's smile died. "And then it did strike—in the form of Reginald Burton-Smythe."

She shuddered, then looked at Laina. Her smile returned. "But God turned what Reginald meant for evil to good—exactly as His word promises."

Laina held back a frown at the mention of God and changed the subject. "And now you have James Justin."

"Yes. Now we have James Justin. Another blessing from the Lord."

The smile Elizabeth gave her radiated happiness. Laina forced aside the envy that flooded through her. "And Sarah talks." She shook her head. "I can't believe she's improved so rapidly she no longer speaks with a lisp. And Mary blackmails everyone. Justin's stepdaughters, well, rather, your *new* daughters are a delightful handful."

Elizabeth laughed. "I'm afraid so. Mary is a bit like Abigail in her personality. She's very strong-minded and does not like to be thwarted." She glanced out the window as the carriage rolled to a halt. "Here we are." She smiled at Laina. "Prepare yourself. Madame Duval, also, is strong-minded."

Laina looked down at the velvet gown she had borrowed from Elizabeth. "No matter. Her designs are lovely. I shall look forward to the challenge."

"Elizabeth, look at these fabrics!" Laina followed Madame Duval into a large room and stopped dead, gazing at the bolts of cloth filling the shelves along the side walls. She glanced at her sister-in-law and laughed. "I feel like a starving man released at a feast. I don't know what to choose first." She moved forward, touching the materials, feeling the cool smoothness of satins, the softness of velveteens. But it was the colors, the wonderful splash of varied colors that enchanted her.

"Oh, I must have this one!" She paused in front of a soft sateen in a deep shade of bronze that seemed to glow with light. "And this!" She stepped to the next shelf. "Look, Elizabeth, it's the very color of spring." She pointed at the apple-green pongee in front of her and moved on to choose a midnight-blue linen as the shopgirl following in her wake placed the indicated fabrics on a large table sitting in the middle of the room.

"An' theees, Madame Brighton?"

Laina gave a soft gasp of pleasure and hurried forward at sight of the cherry-red watered-silk fabric Madame Duval pulled from a cupboard standing against the back wall.

"I have been saving theees for the right woman." The modiste looked down and ran her hand over the shimmering fabric. "Theees must be worn by a woman of style…of verve…of *élan!*" She tipped her head to one side and smiled up at Laina. "You, Madame Brighton, are such a woman. You wish a gown of theees fabric, *oui?*"

Laina smiled. Judging by the gleam in the modiste's eye, the gown would cost her a small fortune, but she didn't care. The fabric was food for her beauty-starved soul. "*Oui,* Madame Duval."

"*Bon!* And now we talk the designs for your new gowns. If you will be pleased to come with me?"

The little woman had turned all business, her fake accent evaporating, as well. Laina exchanged a wry glance with Elizabeth, then gave an eloquent shrug as they turned and followed the designer into another room.

"Would you ladies care to join me in the library for an after-dinner game of checkers?"

Laina followed Elizabeth through the dining-room doorway and glanced back at her brother. "There's no one to make a fourth."

Justin grinned and joined them in the hall. "We don't need a fourth player. I shall gain the victory over one, then take on the other."

"You believe so?"

His grin widened. "I do."

Laina grinned right back. Justin knew very well she wouldn't refuse such a challenge—they had been adamant checkers adversaries since childhood. She glanced over at Elizabeth, who had taken Justin's arm. "What is your wish, Elizabeth?"

Her sister-in-law smiled and gave her husband a saucy glance. "I wish to give this overly confident gentleman a sound drubbing."

Justin threw his head back and laughed. Laina drank in the wonderful sound, storing it in her heart to cheer her when she returned to the loneliness of her home in New York.

"And how did you find Philadelphia, Laina?"

"Different, yet much the same."

Justin smiled as he held chairs for her and Elizabeth at the game table. "Now, there's a remark I'm unable to follow. Would you care to explain?" He pulled the checkerboard from the drawer, took his own seat and grinned at them. "Which of you ladies wishes to be my first victim?"

"That would be Laina." Elizabeth laughed. "I fall prey to your skill far too often."

Justin rubbed the palms of his hands together and waggled his eyebrows, giving Laina what was supposed to be a diabolical look. "So be it! Prepare to meet your fate at my hands, fair damsel!"

Laina laughed and picked up one of the small cloth bags holding the checkers. "Do not expect *me* to swoon in terror at your threats, good sir. My fate rests in my own hands—prepare thyself!" She returned his challenge with a cheeky smile and placed her checkers on the board.

Justin chuckled and did the same.

"But to answer your query, dearheart, there are many new shops in Philadelphia. It's quite exciting to see how much the city has grown in the ten years I've been gone. But it's much the same in its cleanliness and friendly atmosphere." She wrinkled her nose. "New York does not clean its streets daily as you do here. It can become most unpleasant, especially in the heat of summer."

Justin nodded agreement. "Your move."

Laina slid a checker forward.

He countered her move. "And what is your opinion of Madame Duval?" His gaze shifted to Elizabeth and he chuckled. "My wife found her a little avaricious on their first encounter."

Laina laughed and moved another checker. "I can well understand that. There is a definite gleam in Madame's eyes. And that French accent she puts on! I'm so thankful Elizabeth warned me, or I know I would have laughed."

Laina looked down to hide the gleam she was afraid shone in her own eyes as Justin moved his piece exactly where she wanted him to. "But there's nothing fake about the designs Madame Duval creates. And the fabrics she imports are simply beautiful." She moved her sacrifice checker into place, then glanced at her brother. "It was so sad driving by Twiggs Manor today. It looks woebegone. Elizabeth said you've not decided what to do with it."

Justin nodded and made the forced jump. "I will sell it eventually—it's too fine a house to sit empty—but not yet. I'm not ready to face strangers living in Abigail's home."

"I quite understand." Laina looked away from the sorrow that clouded her brother's eyes—she saw enough of it in her own eyes every time she looked in a mirror. She shook off the gloom threatening to overtake her, jumped two of his checkers and smiled across the table at Elizabeth as Justin growled low in his throat and countered her move. "He's running from me, Elizabeth, but it will do him no good."

She moved her next checker into place and grinned when Justin groaned. "Methinks someone has walked into a trap."

Elizabeth giggled. "And straight into a drubbing!"

Thad halted the horse and stared into the darkness. Had a child run behind that building or not? He drew in a breath, then frowned and drove on. There was no sense in calling—the poor hapless children of the night were too frightened of people to answer. They either crouched silent and still in a hiding place, or crept away in the dark.

He shook his head and guided the horse onto Spruce Street. "Well, Lord, I'm sure You have a solution for this problem, but I can't for the life of me figure what it might be. The merchants are so angry over the constant theft of their wares they've little sympathy left for the children, who are only stealing what they need to stay alive. And the town council says all the available funds are going into the development of the new waterworks, so—"

"Doc! Doc!"

Thad stopped the horse and sighed as a young boy raced toward his buggy. He'd *almost* made it home. He caught a look at the boy's frightened face and guilt smote him. *Forgive me my selfishness, Lord.* "What is it, Tommy?"

"Ma's birthin', Doc. Jenny sent me to fetch you. She said Ma's in a bad way an' they need you. She said come fast."

Thad nodded and patted the seat, processing the scant information as Tommy Dodge hopped up and sat beside him. *They.* So there was a midwife in attendance. He hoped she was a good, capable woman. Of course, that would mean the problem was serious. Thad scowled and urged his tired horse into a trot, his own weariness forgotten.

Laina turned on her side, pulled the covers closer about her neck and stared at the moonlight streaming in the window. So many lovely things had happened in the past two days with Justin and Elizabeth.

Laina sighed, threw back the covers and slid out of bed. They were the best days she'd had in months and *still* she couldn't sleep. All those lovely things reminded her of the emptiness of her own life.

Laina lifted the long skirt of her nightgown, stepped into her slippers and walked to the window. Moonlight outlined the bare branches of the trees and highlighted the patches of snow in the gardens below. She wrapped her arms around herself for warmth and stared down at the scene. Everything looked desolate and barren.

She heaved another sigh and turned away from the depressing sight. She would be so glad when spring arrived. When everything came to life again. She wanted so much to feel alive again. Not on the surface, as she'd felt tonight while playing checkers with Justin and Elizabeth, but deep down inside. She was so tired of feeling like…like Abigail's empty house.

There! The thought was out. All day she'd been suppressing it. Laina frowned and walked over to curl up in the chair on the hearth. Why couldn't she get Abigail's vacant house out of her mind? She didn't want to think about sad things. She'd had enough of sadness. She'd come to Philadelphia to escape it! There had to be *something* she could think about that wouldn't remind her of her own circumstances.

Mr. Buffy. Laina gave a nod of satisfaction. Yes, that was it. She would think about Mr. Buffy. There was nothing about him to make her feel her own lack. She'd never had a pet. She leaned against the soft, padded back of the chair, stared into the dancing flames of the fire and fixed her thoughts on the big black dog.

Chapter Four

❧

"I wish you would come to church with us, Laina."

Laina looked up at her brother and shook her head. "Not today, Justin. I'm not going to make my first public appearance among Philadelphia society in widow's garb or borrowed clothes. There will be time enough for church when I have my new dresses from Madame Duval."

"But—" Justin stopped as Elizabeth laid her hand on his arm and gave a small shake of her head. A frown creased his forehead. "All right, Laina. Perhaps it's best if you wait."

"Thank you for agreeing, Justin." Laina went on tiptoe and kissed her brother's cheek, then turned and gave Elizabeth a quick hug as horses' hooves clattered against the brick paving outside. "Thank you for the help."

Elizabeth smiled at the whispered words and stepped back to slide her hand through her husband's offered arm. "We'll be back soon."

The butler pulled open the door.

Laina shivered in the sudden draft of cold air and moved to the window to watch Justin and Elizabeth descend the front steps and climb into the waiting carriage. Thank goodness for Elizabeth's intervention. Justin could be adamant when he felt the occasion called for it, and judging from his frown, he thought church was such an occasion.

Laina sighed and turned away from the window as the carriage departed. She hated to disappoint her brother, but she wasn't ready to go to church and listen to empty promises about God's blessings and answered prayer. If God answered prayers, where were the children she yearned for? If He blessed, where was the baby she longed to feel growing in her womb?

Laina's face drew taut. She uncurled her hands, which had clenched into fists at her sides, and lifted her long skirts to ascend the stairs to get her cloak. She needed to walk off her anger before Justin and Elizabeth returned. Her sister-in-law could look at her in a way that stripped away every bit of artifice.

Laina shook off the thought, strode down the hall to the red bedroom and wrenched open the door. For once the color of the room didn't cheer her. How could it? Red or black—what did it matter? Either way she was still a lonely, loveless, childless widow. And nothing would change that. No healthy man of her age would marry a barren woman.

Laina stalked to the wardrobe, yanked open the carved doors and grabbed her cloak. With a quick lift of her arm and a violent twist of her wrist, she swirled it around her shoulders, then fastened the braided loops over the self buttons, grabbed her matching coal-scuttle bonnet and rushed from the room.

* * *

Laina walked rapidly, heedless of her direction, wanting only to outpace the hurt in her heart. She was twenty-nine years old, strong and healthy. She didn't want to spend the rest of her life alone, without love. A shadow fell across her path. She turned her head, staring at the brick pillar beside her. It stood square and tall, a solid anchor for the black wrought-iron fence that marched off into the distance. Abigail's fence.

Laina scowled. Why had she come this way? Of all the places she didn't want to be right now, Twiggs Manor was foremost. She moved beyond the pillar, focusing her attention on the walkway, but she couldn't resist a strong urge to look at the brick mansion. She lifted her head and glanced at the house. Blank, dark windows stared back at her. She shivered and turned to walk on, but for some reason her feet remained planted to the spot.

Compelled by a feeling she could not identify or ignore, Laina made her way along the gravel drive. Her reluctant steps carried her over the stone sweep, up the stairs and across the porch to the front door. It was locked. She strode to one of the multipaned front windows and cupped her hands on either side of her face to peer inside. White fabric draped the furniture and chandelier of Abigail's beautiful drawing room. The carpet was rolled, the wood floor bare. There were no candles in the wall sconces, no fire burning in the marble fireplace. How sad.

Laina sighed. She could remember the wonderful lively parties Abigail had held in this house and in these gardens. Her mind's eye retained visions of people playing quoits on the lawn, chess or checkers on tables set out in the shade of the trees, dining on fabulous foods served picnic-style.

She could close her eyes and see the winter parties—people skating on the pond out back, the flickering of torches against the cold night sky, the dancing flames of bonfires where shivering servants roasted chestnuts and made hot, mulled cider for the guests. If she listened with her imagination, she could even hear the jingling bells on the horses that pulled the sleighs on rides that began at the carriage house and ended with a late-night dinner in Abigail's vast dining room. She'd met Stanford at one of those parties.

Laina stepped off the porch and looked up at the house, her heart swelling with protest. There should be warm candlelight shining a welcome from the windows, smoke pouring from the chimneys! There should be the sound of happy chatter and laughter. It was wrong to let this beautiful house sit empty and silent.

She stared at the house a moment longer, then turned and retraced her steps to the road. She would talk to Justin about selling Twiggs Manor to someone who would enjoy it. Someone who—

Laina stopped dead in her tracks, stunned by a sudden idea. Why not her? Why shouldn't *she* buy Twiggs Manor? The house needed people to bring it back to life, and she needed something to give her life meaning. There was nothing left for her in New York. She…

She was out of her *wits!* Laina snorted, shook her head and started walking back to Randolph Court. She must be going stark, raving mad from boredom. What a ridiculous notion—her buying Twiggs Manor.

Or was it?

Laina paused at the corner, pursed her lips in speculation and stepped to the wrought-iron fence to look back at the house. At least if she moved to Philadelphia she would have a goal, a purpose. She could save the three-story brick mansion from its present forlorn state and fill her life by carrying on Abigail's role as leader of Philadelphia society. It wasn't much compared to a husband and children, but at least it was something.

Laina drew her cloak close against a sudden gust of wind, crossed Walnut Street and walked south on Fifth Street. There was no problem with finances—she had inherited Stanford's sizable fortune. But her heart quailed at the thought of all the unknown legal processes involved.

Judge!

A tingle of excitement quickened Laina's steps. With Judge to handle things in New York and Justin to handle things here in Philadelphia, she—

No! Laina clenched her hands and reined in her runaway thoughts. The idea was absurd. A pathetic attempt to change a life that could not be changed. She must put it from her mind, stop railing against her circumstances and accept her future with dignity, though she'd never been good at bearing adversity patiently.

Laina sighed and turned into the brick path leading to Randolph Court. The walk had done nothing but create more questions, more distress. Would anything ever be right again?

"I'm sorry, Mrs. Brighton, Master James is asleep. So is Miss Mary. But Miss Sarah is awake. She's in the playroom having a tea party with her dolls and Mr. Buffy. Would you care to join her?"

"Would it be all right?" Laina shot an anxious glance at the connecting door to the playroom. "I don't want to intrude if she would prefer to be alone."

The plump nanny smiled. "I'm sure Miss Sarah would welcome your company—if you're willing to drink pretend tea."

Laina laughed. "I shall consume gallons of it!" She walked to the door, then lifted her hands as if holding a plate in front of her and stepped into the playroom.

"Good day, Sarah. I've brought some cinnamon biscuits for your party. May I join you until your mama and papa come home and I have to go down to dinner?"

"Oh, goody!" Sarah gave her a happy smile. "I like cinnamon biscuits."

"Wonderful. They're my favorite." Laina grinned as the big black dog sitting beside the table gave a soft "woof" and thumped his tail against the floor. "So you like them, too, Mr. Buffy. You shall have two." She walked to the small table and mimed placing a plate of cookies in the center. Bafflement took the place of amusement as she swept her gaze over the ragged-edged plates and lopsided cups that graced Sarah's table.

"Mama and me made the dishes."

"You *did?*" Laina cringed inwardly. Sarah had noticed her reaction to the dishes. She smiled, seated herself on one of the small chairs and hastened to repair her faux pas. "You did a very nice job."

Sarah beamed. "Mama showed me how. Then she tickled me. And then the mean lady came and scared me. But she wasn't really mean—she was Aunty Twiggs."

Laina choked back a laugh at Sarah's description of Abigail Twiggs and accepted the cup of pretend tea her stepniece handed her. "And did you and Aunty Twiggs become friends?"

Sarah nodded, offered Laina a pretend biscuit, then placed one on the floor for Mr. Buffy before taking one onto her plate. The dog sniffed, snorted, then crossed one paw over the other and lowered his head to rest on them. Sarah looked up at her. "Aunty Twiggs came to my tea parties in the garden. Now she's with Jesus in heaven. She got deaded."

"I see." Laina didn't want to talk about that subject, even with a four-year-old. "May I have some more tea, please? It's very good."

Sarah giggled, leaned forward and tipped a tiny yellow teapot decorated with red flowers over Laina's lopsided clay cup. "Oh-oh." She tipped her small head toward the open door, then jumped up and grabbed her plate and cup. "I have to put these away now. Mary waked up, and she breaks things."

Sarah went on tiptoe, slid the dishes on the top shelf in an alcove formed by a brick fireplace, then glanced back at Laina. "She doesn't mean to break them. She's little."

"I understand." Laina gathered the remaining dishes and placed them on the shelf as Anna Hammerfield entered the room, carrying a sleepy-eyed Mary in her plump arms.

"I hope you're not ruining your dinner by eating too many biscuits, Miss Sarah."

The little girl giggled. "They're pretend biscuits, Nanny."

"All the same." Anna Hammerfield lifted her hand higher to support Mary as the toddler twisted toward Laina and held out her arms.

"Tory."

Laina glanced at the nanny. "May I?" At the woman's answering nod, she took Mary into her arms. The toddler put her thumb in her mouth and snuggled close against her. Laina swallowed hard and laid her cheek against the baby's soft brown hair. *How could you feel joy and pain at the same time?*

"Miss Mary likes to look at pictures." The nanny glanced at Sarah and held out her hand. "Time for you to get washed up for dinner, missy."

"All right, Nanny." Sarah pulled a book off the shelf beside her and carried it to Laina. "Mary likes this one. It's about aminals."

"Thank you, Sarah." Laina smiled down at the child.

"I'll come back for Miss Mary when I've got Miss Sarah cleaned and settled, Mrs. Brighton. This one never tires of stories, but it's her dinnertime, too." The nanny tweaked Mary under the chin, then took hold of Sarah's hand and headed for the door. Mr. Buffy rose and lumbered after them.

Mary pulled her thumb from her mouth and pointed a pudgy finger. "Doggy."

"Doggy, yes." Laina smiled at the toddler and headed for the rocking chair on the hearth. "His name is Mr. Buffy. Can you say Mr. Buffy?"

Mary shook her head. "Doggy. Tory."

Laina grinned. It seemed Mary had a limited vocabulary and a one-track mind. "All right, precious. You shall have your story." She sat in the rocker, settled Mary on her lap and opened the book.

Mary pointed. "Kitty."

"Yes. A pretty, fluffy kitty. And he's chasing a butterfly." Laina glanced at Mary. "Can you say butterfly?"

The toddler's lower lip came out in a stubborn pout. She poked the picture. "Kitty."

Laina choked back a laugh. Obviously Mary was not going to tolerate instruction. "All right, Mary, we'll read the book your way." She began to rock. The toddler stuck her thumb back in her mouth and rested against her. Laina caught her breath against the sudden sharp pain in her heart and turned the page.

He'd lost her. Thad stared down at the pale, still face of the young woman on the bed. She shouldn't have died. She *wouldn't* have died if it weren't for the bloodletting. He was sure of it. Barbara Grant had been improving before her mother sent for that other doctor!

Thad shoved aside the bowl of beef broth Barbara Grant had been too weak to swallow and walked over to close the window he'd opened on entering the stifling room. No amount of fresh air would help Barbara now. Thad's mouth tightened. In truth, he wasn't sure it would have helped her, anyway. It was only one of his theories. He didn't *know.*

The door creaked open. Thad turned and looked at Barbara's mother.

"Hubert says your buggy is ready."

The woman's face was stiff with anger. Why wouldn't it be? She blamed him for her daughter's death. She thought Barbara should have been bled when she first became ill, and he couldn't prove her wrong. But Barbara had been gaining a little strength daily, until that doctor bled her yesterday morning and again last night. If Hubert had come home earlier, maybe—

Thad broke off the useless speculation and picked up his bag. "Goodbye, Mrs. Stone. I'm sorry about Barbara. She—"

"She'd be alive had you bled her and kept the windows closed so the bad humors couldn't get in!" The woman spat the words at him, then turned her back.

Thad absorbed the criticism. What else could he do without proof to the contrary? He started for the door, then stopped. Hubert Grant stood in the doorway, his lips so compressed it looked as if the taut skin around them would split. "I'm sorry I couldn't save her, Hubert."

The man opened his mouth, then promptly closed it again and stepped aside. Thad walked out into the parlor and crossed to the front door. The cold air made him shiver after the excessive warmth of the sickroom. He hunched his shoulders and walked to his buggy.

"Doc."

So Hubert had followed him outside. Thad turned to face the angry, grief-stricken husband.

The big man cleared his throat. "I wanted to say I know you did all you could, Doc. An' Barbara *was* gettin' better doin' like you said. She told me she felt stronger—that she thought she'd be gettin' up in a few days. That's why I went on my sellin' trip. But I shoulda known her mother…"

Hubert's face tightened. He made a visible effort to calm himself. "That butcher never would've got in the door if I'd been home." His wide shoulders sagged. "I don't know how I'm ever gonna tolerate seein' that woman around here, but I have to, for our kids' sake. I reckon that's my cross to bear for leavin' Barbara to her mother's mercies. But that's nothin' to you."

Hubert took a deep breath and stuck out his hand. "Thanks for tryin' to pull Barbara through, Doc. I reckon you could've saved her if she hadn't been so weak from the bleedin'.'" He pumped Thad's hand, then spun on his heel and walked rapidly toward his barn.

Thad's heart ached for the grieving man. Anger spread through him at the needless waste of life caused by the common medical procedures of the day. Why wouldn't his colleagues *listen* to him? Why couldn't they see that their patients only got weaker when they drained off their blood?

Thad clenched his jaw, shoved his bag onto the seat and climbed into his buggy, picking up the reins as his horse moved forward. It did no good to think about it. Thinking never changed anyone's mind. He needed proof. And now, thanks to Barbara Grant's mother, his proof was gone. Who would trust him to treat them according to his theories now?

Thad shook off his anger and looked around. His horse had automatically turned onto Second Street, heading for home. People were gathered in small groups on the walkway in front of Christ Church, chatting. Families were calling goodbye to friends and climbing into their carriages. Church was over. He'd missed the service again. Disappointment settled in his chest. He'd been looking forward to a good sermon.

A man nodded in his direction. Thad returned the polite greeting and urged his horse to pick up the pace. This was the part of Sunday he didn't like. It was hard watching the families go home when all that awaited him was a cold meal and an empty house. Maybe he'd go check on Martha Bauer—her cough was getting worse.

"You missed a good sermon today."

Laina glanced at her brother, laid aside her fork and reached for her cider. "I'm certain there will be others."

It was the most polite way she could think of to say she was not interested.

"Yes. But this one was stimulating." Justin cut a bite off the thick slice of roast pork on his plate and dipped it in his apple-raisin sauce. "The core message was that the purpose and result of freedom in Christ is service." He paused with the meat halfway to his mouth and glanced at her, his eyes holding a silent dare for her to question or challenge him. She remained quiet. "Does that not sound like a paradox?" He put the pork into his mouth.

Laina refused to be drawn by his question. The best way to end this conversation was to agree with him. "Yes. I suppose it does." *There!* She ignored the flash of disappointment in Justin's eyes and took a bit of mashed potatoes onto her fork.

"Ah, but it's not."

Her brother's quiet comment brought a sigh up clear from her toes. Laina resigned herself to her fate. Justin wasn't going to give up. She would hear about the sermon whether she wanted to or not. Irritation rippled through her. She stabbed a piece of meat. When had he become so enamored of God again?

"As Pastor Brown pointed out, God does not call us to the fullness of life in Him simply for ourselves, though we obviously reap the benefits of such a life." Justin leaned toward her. "Rather, freedom in Christ enables us to *become* and *do* all that He made us capable of *being* and *doing* when He created us. It sets us free from our own selfishness." He leaned back and shook his head. "It's amazing."

Laina breathed a sigh of relief. Thank heaven *that* was over. Now perhaps—

"And Jesus Himself is our example. He said, 'For their sakes I sanctify myself, that they also might be sanctified.'"

Laina tensed as Justin leaned forward again, his gaze fastened on hers. What was he doing? He knew how she felt about God! Though that didn't seem to matter. He was still droning on.

"Jesus did nothing for Himself. It was all for us. Including suffering death on the cross so we might be free to choose to live in heaven forever with Him."

A shiver ran up Laina's spine, spread throughout her body. Justin's words brought back that moment fifteen years ago when she had given herself to the Lord. She looked down at her plate to break eye contact with him. She still believed in her salvation through Jesus. It was only the other things preached from the pulpit—answered prayer, God's blessings in this life here on earth—she didn't believe. She knew from her own experience those things weren't true, and in her estimation it was cruel for those in the pulpit to give people false hope.

Anger chased the shiver away. From the corner of her eye Laina saw Justin relax back against his chair. Evidently he was through preaching at her. Good! She couldn't—*wouldn't*—listen to any more. Not even for Justin. And she really didn't want to walk away from his table.

Laina drew a deep, relaxing breath and seized the opportunity to change the subject. She forced a light note into her voice. "I had a lovely time with the children while you were gone. Sarah and I had a tea party." She looked at her sister-in-law and smiled. "Elizabeth, you must tell me the story behind those dishes…."

Thad pumped water into the trough, forked fresh hay into the rack and spread more on the floor. "All ready for you, Faithful." He opened the door and stepped aside as his horse gave a soft whicker, walked into the stall and stuck his muzzle in the trough to get a drink.

"It's been a hard day, boy." Thad thumped Faithful on the shoulder, then picked up the brush and began to groom him. For long minutes he brushed the horse, emptying his mind of the stressful events of the day, concentrating on the munching sound of the animal eating hay, the soft swish of the brush against the warm, muscular body. By the time he finished, the tightness in his chest had lessened, the tension between his shoulder blades had eased.

He smoothed out Faithful's mane and forelock, worked a tangle out of the gelding's long silver tail, then put down the brush, grabbed the old towel hanging over the stall wall and began to rub him down. The horse turned his head and gave him a gentle nudge. Thad laughed and rubbed the velvety muzzle. "Feels good, does it?"

Faithful whickered and nudged him again. "All right. All right…I'm done." Thad walked into the grain box, scooped up a measure of oats, mixed in a little bran and went back to pour it into the wood manger. "There you are, fellow. If you're lucky, we won't get called out tonight and you'll have time to eat it." He gave the horse a last affectionate pat and walked to the carriage to get his bag. His stomach rumbled.

Thad grinned and gave his flat abdomen a swat with his free hand. Its turn would come. He shut the barn door and headed for his cold, dark house. If he remembered right, there was bread left from the supper Mrs. Harding had fixed yesterday. And maybe some cheese or apple butter…

Chapter Five

❧

The children! She had to help them! Laina flopped onto her back as the children floated at her out of the darkness. Her arms flailed out into space, her hands grasping at the air. *There were too many—she couldn't catch them all.*

"Somebody help me!"

Laina jerked upright, her heart pounding. The dream was so real she swept her gaze around the surrounding shadows of the bedroom, half expecting to find children hiding in the dark corners where the moonlight from the windows didn't reach. Of course, there was no one there. She gave her head a quick shake to rid herself of the residue of anxiety the dream had left behind. How odd that it kept coming back.

Laina sighed and climbed out of bed, pulling on her new peacock-blue dressing gown as she walked to the window. Was her desire for children becoming an obsession? She'd heard of women's minds going queer over such things.

A shiver raced down her spine. Laina wrapped her arms about herself and stared out into the night. Being around Sarah, Mary and baby James these past few weeks hadn't eased her longing for children as she had expected—it had increased it. And watching Justin and Elizabeth together made her ache with a desire to experience a love such as theirs.

Laina clenched her hands into fists and glared up at the night sky. "If You're an all-powerful God, You could have answered my prayers, Lord. You could have given me children and a love like Justin and Elizabeth's. Instead You took Stanford from me." Hot tears stung her eyes. "At least with Stanford I had companionship. Now I'm alone. I have *nothing!*"

The tears overflowed and poured down her cheeks. Laina spun away from the window, her chest so tight with hurt she couldn't breathe. She swiped the tears from her cheeks and forced air into her lungs. Very well. If that was the way God wanted it, so be it! She would live her life alone.

"What a gorgeous April day!" Elizabeth spread her arms and twirled around in the sunshine. "We have come to the end of the cold, gray days of winter, Laina."

"One can hope."

"Now, that's a gloomy remark." Elizabeth shot her one of those assessing looks.

Laina cringed inwardly. She hadn't meant to let her dismal outlook slip through her cheery facade. "Pay me no mind, Elizabeth. I'm tired."

The question in Elizabeth's eyes turned to concern. "Are you still not sleeping well?"

Should she tell her about the dream? No. It would serve no purpose. Laina shook her head and walked toward the pavilion being cleaned by the servants in preparation for summer. "Better…but not well."

"I wish there was something we could do."

"So do I, Elizabeth—fervently so!" Laina forced a smile to mask the need in her words. She hated herself for feeling so helpless. "But there is nothing beyond the love and comfort you and Justin have extended by sharing your home, your children and your lives with me. You've been wonderful." She sucked in a deep breath and forced out the words she didn't want to speak. "Unfortunately, my life is what it is—and I must learn to live it. I'm going back to New York."

"*New York?*" Elizabeth grasped her arm. "But Laina, dear, why? It's only been a few weeks and we love having you with us. The children—"

"I shall miss them dreadfully! And you and Justin, as well." Tears smarted in Laina's eyes. She blinked them away.

"Then don't go. Stay with us. Please."

Laina shook her head. "I have to go back."

"Why? What awaits you in New York?"

Justin's deep voice made them both jump and spin to face him. Laina's throat constricted. "Nothing, dearheart."

"Then why…?"

"Because of that!"

Justin's gaze traveled in the direction of Laina's pointing finger. "I don't understand."

"I believe it's the new growth, Justin." Elizabeth indicated the tiny tips of folded green leaves that were breaking through the cold brown soil of the garden beds.

Justin frowned. "Is that it, Laina? The flowers? I don't understand." He took her by the arm and led her to the bench beside the path. "Now tell me, what have flowers to do with you going back to New York?"

Laina squared her shoulders and cleared her throat of the lump that was threatening to choke her. "The flowers are starting to live again. Look around you, Justin. *Everything* is coming to life again—new life after a cold, dark winter. I have to do the same." She took a deep breath and turned her head to look at him. "Don't you see, dearheart, I can't borrow your life any longer. No matter how painful it is, I have to live mine."

Justin sucked in a deep breath, squeezed her hands so tightly she thought her bones would break, then jumped to his feet and began to pace along the brick walk. Laina's heart hurt for him. It was another reason to go back to New York—she had brought him pain. She took refuge from all the hurt in anger. *Do what You please to me, Lord, but spare my brother any anguish over my situation. He trusts You.*

"All right."

She looked up as Justin spoke.

"All right, Laina, I'll accept that." He moved close to her. "But why must you live your life in New York? Why not here in Philadelphia, where you will be close to us?"

"Yes. Why not, Laina, dear?" Elizabeth took Justin's place on the bench beside her. "Surely you can—"

"I've *got* it!" Justin slammed his fist into his other palm with such force the resulting crack of sound made Laina jump. He grinned down at her. "I have the solution."

"Oh, dearheart, there *isn't* a solu—"

"Twiggs Manor!" Justin's grin widened. "I'll give you Abigail's house. That way, you can live your own life and be close to us at the same time."

Laina stared at him.

"Justin, it's perfect!" Elizabeth squeezed Laina's hand. "You will do it, Laina, won't you? You will come live in Twiggs Manor?"

"Well, I don't know…it's— *I had* thought of…" Laina shook her head. She was not making sense. She looked up at her brother.

He stared down at her. "Say yes, Lainy. It's the right thing to do."

There was absolute certainty in his face and voice. "All right—*yes!*"

Justin laughed and leaned down to kiss her cheek. "Good! Everything's going to be all right—heart's promise."

With his arms around her, she almost believed him.

A small thrill of excitement zipped through Thad as he glanced down at the letter in his hand. He hadn't expected Dr. Bettencourt's answer to his letter for at least another week. It must have come from Paris by packet. Probably on the ship that had sailed into port today. Fortunately for him, Justin Randolph's captains were a courageous bunch who outsailed the captains of other lines and vied amongst themselves for the best crossing time.

Thad tucked the missive into his waistcoat pocket, climbed into his buggy and picked up the reins. He grinned as the gelding pricked his ears, listening for instructions. "Let's go home, boy." The horse moved forward at once.

Thad relaxed back against the seat to rest while he was able. He'd had a busy morning and, if past performance was any indication, he'd have a busy evening. Most of the sailors he'd come in contact with headed straight for the waterfront grog shops when released from their duties aboard ship. In a short time, the liquor they consumed turned them into drunk, boisterous men ready to fight at the slightest provocation. That's where he came in. The sailors sober enough to walk would drag their hurt mates to his house and he would spend hours splinting broken bones, stitching and bandaging knife wounds and generally caring for the bruised and battered conditions of those still alive.

Thad sat up a little straighter and patted the letter in his pocket. At least he could try some of the new theories on the sailors. Justin Randolph was a progressive thinker who believed in Thad's theories on cleanliness and fresh air in the sickroom. It was a shame Justin couldn't convince his friends.

Thad sighed. What good did it do to correspond with the French doctors who were leading the way in practicing diagnostic medicine, when he couldn't get his patients to allow him to try the new practices on them? Why couldn't he make people believe that bleeding, cupping and blistering only made them weaker?

Movement caught his eye as the buggy approached Walnut Street. Thad frowned and glanced to his left. What was going on at Twiggs Manor? Servants were scrubbing the porch and front steps. Men were perched on ladders washing windows and cleaning the shutters. Had someone bought the place?

There was a flash of color. Thad craned his neck and looked toward the side entrance, but the large maple trees on the corner blocked his view. He caught a brief glimpse of a slender, dark-haired woman in a bright green dress descending the stairs and then he was across the intersection and the house was no longer visible.

Thad faced front again. He'd hear soon enough if he had a new neighbor. Right now, all he wanted was to get home and read his letter before someone came knocking on his door with some sort of emergency.

"Mrs. Barnes, Mrs. Brighton wants you in the parlor."

"All right, Tilly." Grace Barnes scanned the group of servants Tilly had joined in the drawing room. "Fitz, you and John carry these rugs outside and beat them clean. Tilly, dust and wax the furniture, then clean and polish the fireplace tools and fender. Sally, you clean the chandeliers."

Grace Barnes placed her fisted hands on her hips and watched as the maid began climbing the ladder with flannel cleaning rags draped over her shoulder and a bucket dangling from her hand. "Did you add a good splash of vinegar to that water?"

"Yes, ma'am."

"All right, then. When you're through with the chandeliers, do the glass doors on the corner cabinets, then wash the windows." Grace Barnes headed for the door, then turned back again. "When you've finished your tasks in here, move on to the library and do the same."

"Yes, ma'am."

The chorus of assent followed the housekeeper as she hurried out the door, across the large entrance hall and into the parlor. "You wished to see me, madam?"

"Yes." Laina looked up from the paper in her hand. "The servants from Randolph Court are here. I sent them upstairs. Please go assign them their tasks."

"Yes, madam."

"And have one of them gather all the bed curtains, linens, testers and window drapery and take them to the Chinese laundry downtown. With all we have to do, even with the loan of my brother's servants, we shall be overwhelmed if we do not make use of the laundry's services."

"Yes, madam. I'll attend to it immediately." The housekeeper turned to go and almost bumped into Elizabeth. "Good day, Mrs. Randolph." She stepped aside to let Elizabeth pass, then hurried from the room.

"Elizabeth! I wasn't expecting you to come over." Laina smiled. "This must mean Sarah is feeling better."

"Yes, she's fine. I suspect her stomach upset was caused by too much candy." Elizabeth shook her head and smiled. "And I'm certain I know the culprit. I shall have a talk with Justin tonight." She laughed and looked around.

"How wonderful to see this room restored." Elizabeth brushed her hand over the blue silk brocade fabric covering a couch placed at a right angle to the paneled wall graced by a marble fireplace at its center. The couch faced a pair of chairs with padded seats covered in blue, magenta and cream stripes. There was a piecrust tea table between the chairs. "I like the way you've placed the furniture. It's very inviting."

"Thank you. Would you care to sit down?" Laina laughed and looked about. "I'm afraid this is the only room at the moment where that is possible. And my abilities as a hostess are severely limited." She gave Elizabeth a wry look. "I can offer you a cup of tea."

Elizabeth shook her head. "Don't fuss, Laina. I didn't come to be entertained. I came to see if there is anything more we can do to help. And to see the progress you're making. I love this house. It's exciting to watch it coming to life again."

"Then would you care to join me on a short tour? I was about to take one myself." Laina smiled. "If I'm to take Abigail's place as the head of Philadelphia society everything must be perfect." She led the way out into the entrance hall, turned right and walked a short way to the dining room. "Oh, they've finished!" She stepped through the doorway, then stopped at Elizabeth's gasp.

"You've had it painted!"

"Yes. I love—"

"Color!"

Elizabeth finished the sentence for her, and both women burst into laughter.

"Do you like it?"

"It's beautiful!" Elizabeth glanced from the tureen with Grecian figures and vine border sitting on the sideboard to the alcoves flanking the marble fireplace centered in a paneled wall. "The cranberry-colored alcoves are truly striking against the green of the paneling, Laina. And they match the color on your dishes perfectly."

"Yes. It's exactly what I wanted." *No.* It would never be what she *really* wanted. Laina shoved the thought away and ran her hand along the edge of the large dining table. "I shall have lovely dinner parties here, just as Abigail did." She looked at Elizabeth and smiled. "Shall we go on to the morning room?" She turned and led the way out the door.

"Sunshine walls and window shutters the color of spring leaves. It looks like summer!" Elizabeth stepped into the smaller room and turned in a slow circle. "What a lovely room to breakfast in on a cold, gray winter's day. It would be impossible to be gloomy in this room."

"I pray you're right, for that was my intent."

"Is there something you wish, Mrs. Brighton?"

Laina turned to face Beaumont, who was standing in the doorway of the butler's pantry across the hall. "No, nothing."

Her voice sounded flat and emotionless. She forced a smile and turned back to Elizabeth. "Would you like to see the music room and ballroom? They've finished painting them also."

He was right! Cleanliness and fresh air in the sickroom were of great benefit. The tests run by Dr. Bettencourt and his associates continued to prove it. Excitement coursed through Thad. He read on. The theory of alcohol applied to wounds keeping infection at bay was proving out, as well. Hmm…

Thad folded the letter from Paris, placed it on the table beside the chair, then leaned back and plowed the fingers of both his hands through his thick, straight hair. The carefully groomed-down cowlick at his hairline sprang to life. He could feel the hair rise straight up at the roots, then flop over onto his forehead—the ends tickled the skin above his right eye. He brushed them back, to no avail.

Thad frowned and straightened in the chair. *Alcohol.* His eyes narrowed in speculation and his right knee began to jiggle up and down. If one could stop the infection in wounds…

He *had* to find a way to convince his fellow physicians at the Pennsylvania Hospital to try the new procedures.

He simply had to. And what more could he do to convince his patients to let him try the unconventional methods of treatment? He'd explained, urged, cajoled and plain out begged, and still they clung to the old beliefs.

Thad jumped to his feet as someone thudded a fist against his front door.

"Doc? Open the door, Doc!" The slurred words were accompanied by more thudding. Thad pulled his watch from his pocket. They were starting early tonight. He flipped the rug in his small entrance back out of harm's way and opened the door.

"Ya gotta help me mate, Doc. He got stuck."

A tall, thin sailor stood on the stoop squinting at Thad through the blood streaming from a jagged cut over his right eye. He was supporting a burly man nearly twice his size by holding the man's beefy arm across his shoulders. The bloodstain on the wounded man's shirt was spreading.

"Bring him in." Thad motioned for the sailor to follow, walked into his office and stepped over to the table he'd cleaned earlier. "Put him here."

The sailor propped his semiconscious mate between himself and the table, then bent and hefted him up by placing his arms around the man's knees.

"Ugh!" The wounded sailor's eyes opened. He grabbed Thad's arm and gave him a bleary-eyed glare. "Need a drink."

Alcohol! Thad's pulse picked up speed. "You need a good dose of common sense. Release my arm or you'll get no help from me." He waited till the drunken sailor complied, then lifted the blood-soaked shirt and stared at the deep slit just below the man's rib cage. He frowned, picked up the two lengths of rope draped over a nearby chair and tossed them to the seaman standing on the other side of the table.

"Tie his hands together under the table and bind his feet to the legs." Heart racing, Thad pulled the whiskey he used to help deaden pain from his doctor's bag, splashed some into a small bowl, then pulled a coil of suturing thread from his bag and dropped it into the bowl. A needle followed. He glanced at the sailor trussing his mate like a slain deer. "Tie him snug, mind you. If he moves he could do himself serious harm."

"Ain't gonna move. Been sewed up before." The sailor muttered the words without opening his eyes.

"It's not the sewing. I'm going to apply whiskey to your wound. Are you ready?" Thad positioned the bottle over the wound.

"No." The sailor opened one eye. 'S a waste o' whiskey, Doc. Lemme drink it 'stead. Arrrgh!" The seaman's body went rigid as the whiskey hit the raw flesh. His head slumped to one side.

Thad stared down at the unconscious man. Seamen were a tough lot. Whiskey poured into a wound must hurt more than he thought it would. It was something to remember. He filed the knowledge away and picked up the needle. There was a thumping at the door. He glanced over at the sailor slumped on the settle against the wall. "Open the door, please, before they break it down."

Thad glanced up from his sewing as the sailor returned with two other seamen in tow. One of them had a broken arm dangling uselessly at his side, and the other had a deep gash on his face and was missing part of an ear. He frowned and went back to his stitching. It was going to be a long and profitable night.

* * *

"Well, tomorrow you move into your new home, Laina." Justin glanced over, met his sister's gaze and smiled. "And tomorrow night you can walk in your own gardens."

"Yes." *Alone.* Laina blocked the thought from her mind and returned his smile. "And soon after, I shall have a wonderful party in those gardens. Elizabeth is helping me with the invitation list, and Madame Duval is making me a beautiful gown for the occasion." She stepped close, threaded her hand through his arm and looked up at him. "You will be very proud of me. It will be my first effort to take Abigail's place as hostess extraordinaire of Philadelphia society."

"Well, don't take on her astringent personality. You are enough of a challenge to me as you are."

Laina laughed and squeezed his arm. "Surely you're not calling me difficult?"

Justin grinned down at her. "There is no safe answer to that question. I shall ignore it." She wrinkled her nose at him. He laughed and patted her hand. "I have good news."

"Oh? What is it?"

"I had a letter from Judge today. Your house in New York has sold. You received an excellent price for it." He guided her to the left. "Since you've no immediate need of it, if you wish, I will invest the money for you."

Laina nodded. "I think that is wise. Do you have an investment in mind?"

"No. There are several to consider before making a final decision."

"I see." She tipped her head back and looked up at him. "Would the new waterworks be one of them? I am so favorably impressed with the running water in the kitchen and dressing rooms at Twiggs Manor. Surely others would be as taken with the idea." She frowned as Justin chuckled. "You find my thoughts amusing?"

He quieted and looked down at her. "No, indeed. I find them impressive. *Very* impressive. I didn't know my older sister had such an astute business instinct."

Laina stopped walking and studied his face. "Truly?"

"Yes, truly." Justin started walking again. "One of my basic requirements for a good investment is that the product or service be one that people either need or want. The waterworks is both."

"I see." She gave him a saucy smile. "Let's keep my business instincts a secret, shall we? I don't want anything to tarnish my society-leader image. But I do want the money invested in the waterworks. And equal portions of it in the new railroad company and the new freight line I've heard you speak of."

"Again, very wise investments. Expansion to the west is increasing in leaps and bounds." Justin laughed and shook his head as they climbed the steps to the back porch. "You amaze me, Laina. It shall be as you wish. I am yours to command."

"Thank you, dearheart. You take good care of me."

He shot her a sidelong look. "I thought so, but now I'm not so certain."

Laina gave him a pat on his cheek and walked through the door he held open for her.

Chapter Six

⚘

"Thank you, Carlson." Laina took her driver's hand and climbed from the chaise. "Come back for us in an hour." She glanced over her shoulder at her maid as the driver climbed back to his seat and drove away. "This way, Annette."

"Stop, you *rapscallion!*" A portly man charged around the corner and lunged for a small boy, who whirled and darted across the walk in front of her. Laina jolted to a stop.

A carriage whipped around the corner and raced down the street toward them.

"No, little boy! *Stop!*"

He paid no heed to her frantic cry. Looking over his shoulder at the man chasing him, the boy dashed into the road. The driver of the carriage hauled back on the reins, but it was too late.

A scream ripped from Laina's throat as the horse knocked the boy down and the carriage wheels, locked by the applied brake, skidded over him. She stood, frozen with horror, staring at the small inert body as the carriage came to a halt.

"Good enough for the little thief!" The man who was chasing the boy turned and walked away.

The callous words shocked Laina out of her paralysis. She ran into the street, her long skirts billowing out around her as she knelt beside the small figure. The boy wasn't moving. *Oh, God, don't let him be dead. Please don't let him be dead!* Her hand trembled as she placed it on the filthy, tattered shirt covering the child's narrow chest. His heart was beating! She released her held breath in a gust of relief.

"What's going on here, Jefferson! Did you strike down this woman?"

Laina looked up as a scowling, richly garbed man climbed from the carriage and came to stand beside his driver. "I am not injured, sir. It is the boy your carriage struck down." She looked back down at the child. She could see no signs of injury. Why didn't he wake up?

The man snorted. "Another thieving brat of the streets, no doubt. Get back to the carriage, Jefferson. We're wasting time. I've a meeting to attend." The man started around the horse pulling the carriage that had stopped behind his.

He was going to *leave?* Anger surged through Laina. She shot to her feet. "Sir?" The man turned to look at her. She swallowed back the anger and forced a reasonable tone into her voice. "The boy doesn't wake. He must be seriously hurt. Surely you do not intend to leave him lying here in the street?"

"That's exactly what I intend, madam." The man flicked a glance at the unconscious boy at her feet. "He's nothing to me."

Laina went stiff as a ramrod. "He's a *child*, sir! And *your* carriage struck him down. The least you can do is provide for his care."

"His *care?*"

The man looked astounded. Laina clenched her hands into fists and took a deep breath. "Yes, his care. Put him in your carriage and take him to a doctor."

"Put that—that *thing* in my carriage!" Fury rippled across the man's face. "I'll do no such thing." He pointed a rigid finger at her. "And you, madam, would do well to mind your own business. You're an interfering busybody!"

Laina's chin jutted into the air. "And *you*, sir, are a compassionless *pygmy* of a man with no honor!"

"*No honor!*"

Laina ignored the enraged roar and waved her hand in regal dismissal. "Be on your way, sir! I shall care for the child."

The man's mouth gaped open. His face turned purple. Laina turned her back on him and darted a look at the man climbing from the stopped carriage. At least his vehicle would protect the boy from being run over again. She dropped to her knees on the cobblestones. Would it be safe to move the boy out of the street?

"If you will permit me?" The man from the carriage knelt on the other side of the boy and took the small wrist into his hand.

Laina skimmed her gaze over the man's dark brown hair and black suit. He was neat and clean, though slightly out of fashion. "And who might *you* be?" She felt a flush spread across her cheeks as the man turned his head to look at her. She hadn't meant to sound challenging. At least the man had a modicum of compassion!

"I'm Dr. Allen." Thad locked his gaze with the woman's and spoke calmly. "Dr. Thaddeous Allen of Pennsylvania Hospital." The combative look left the woman's eyes.

"Doctor?"

There was relief in her voice. Thad nodded. "Yes, doctor." He turned his attention back to the boy. "His pulse is strong." He gently probed along the small, skinny neck and, finding no sign of injury, lifted the boy's head. There was blood pooled in the valley between the cobblestones beneath.

There was a soft gasp. Thad looked over at the woman. She'd gone quite pale. "Are you all right?"

"Yes. Pay me no mind. Help the boy."

The words were strong, but her voice quavered. Thad frowned. Judging from the woman's demeanor, she'd probably never seen blood before. He'd have another bashed head to deal with if she swooned. He dipped his head toward the black leather satchel on the road beside him. "Open my bag, please. You'll find a pile of clean cloths in there. Get me one to rest the boy's head on while I examine him for further injuries."

There, that should distract her. Thad swept his gaze over the boy's body while the woman complied. There was a roll clutched in one small hand, another smashed on the road beside him. He made a disgusted sound in his throat and jerked his head up.

"What is it? Is something broken?" The woman's voice was hushed with fear. She handed him the cloth.

"No. There's another problem." Thad gestured in the direction of the boy's hands. "These children seldom steal more than they need to survive, and this boy took two rolls." He shook his head and set to bandaging the boy's wound. "I'd guess he isn't alone. He probably has a brother or sister he's taking care of. Most likely they're sick or crippled, or…"

"Younger?"

"Yes."

"Oh, my."

Thad looked up. The woman's hand was pressed against her chest at the base of her throat. She was staring across the street. He swept his gaze over the area, but saw nothing. "What is it?"

"A little girl was peeking at us from behind that rain barrel. She ducked back when I looked her way." The woman's gaze sought his. "Do you suppose…?"

Thad's face tightened. He bound the clean pad to the back of the boy's head with another cloth. "If she hid when you looked at her, she's probably the one. Chances are—" He stopped. There was no sense in saying more. He was talking to the air. The woman was already on her way across the street. *Help her find the girl, Lord. These children can disappear even when you know their tricks. And this woman…*

Thad shook his head. He hadn't time for lengthy prayer—he had a boy to help. He ran his hands over the skinny arms and legs looking for further injury. The right ankle was swelling. Poor starving lad. He couldn't be more than five or six years old. He lifted the boy into his arms and headed for his buggy.

* * *

"Hello." Laina smiled and squatted down. The little girl squeezed back as far as she could go into the crevice formed by the barrel and the storefront. Her brown eyes were wide with fear. Tears rolled down her cheeks and quiet, indrawn sobs shook her tiny body.

Laina's eyes filled. The little girl didn't look much older than Mary. She blinked the tears away. "Please don't be afraid. I won't hurt you. I've come to take you to—" she took a chance "—your brother." She rose and held out her hand. "Will you come with me? Your brother wants to see you."

The little girl's lips quivered. She stared up at her for a long moment, then gave a brave little nod and scooted forward. Laina wanted so much to scoop her up into her arms, but she didn't dare. She reached for the tiny hand.

"Madame! You should not touch the child! The filth! The lice! The disease!"

The toddler scrunched back in her corner. Laina spun on her maid. "Now you've frightened her. Go away, Annette!"

"Madame!"

"Go!" Laina turned back as her outraged maid hurried off. The little girl had curled into a tight ball. "It's all right. I've sent the lady away. I'll not let anyone harm you." Her childhood oath popped into her mind. "Heart's promise." She smiled. "You can never break a 'heart's promise.' Now, shall we go see your brother?"

Laina held her breath as the little girl studied her face. At last the toddler crawled from behind the barrel and took her hand. Her heart squeezed painfully. The poor baby was so thin! Her hair, face and clothes were filthy, her dirty feet bare.

Anger spurted through Laina. Who cared for these children? How could she find out? If she knew their name… She looked down at the little girl walking by her side. Maybe…? It was worth a try. She took a breath. "I know how important brothers are, because I have a brother, too. His name is Justin." The toddler looked up at her. Would she be as limited in her vocabulary as Mary? "What's your brother's name?"

"Billy."

The word was little more than a whisper, but at least the little girl could talk. Excitement shot through Laina. Encouraged by her success, she tried again. "That's a lovely name. But I'll bet yours is prettier. What's your name?"

"Emma."

"Oh, that *is* lovely!" Laina led the child to the buggy, glanced at the still form on the seat, then shot a panicked glance at the doctor. "Dr. Allen, I'd like you to meet *Emma.* She's come to see her brother, *Billy.*"

She'd found out their names. Thad gave the woman a look of approval and squatted down on his haunches. "How do you do, Emma? I'm pleased to make your acquaintance." He gestured toward the buggy. "I'm afraid Billy bumped his head when he fell. He's sleeping right now. Would you like me to lift you up in the buggy so you can be with him? I put a bandage on his head."

Thad's heart went right into his throat when she nodded, and he picked her up. Her chest was so small the fingers and thumbs of his hands touched each other. He lifted her to the seat beside Billy.

"How will you take them home? Do you think she will be able to tell you where they live?"

Thad almost snorted at the whispered words. Was this woman *that* sheltered? He turned toward her and took his first really good look at her. Her fancy hairdo, elegant clothes and the maid waiting for her in the shadow of a nearby tree gave him his answer. He took a step back from the buggy and motioned her to follow. "These children have no home, madam. The orphanage burned down last January and there's no place to put them. They live on the streets."

"But, but they're little more than babies! And Billy is hurt."

"Yes. I know." The woman's voice was full of horror. At least she had a heart—which was more than he could say for a goodly number of the wealthy patrons he'd approached for help with the problem.

"Well, what are you going to do about them?" The woman's eyes shot a challenge at him—deep blue, almost violet eyes. *"Well?"*

Thad brought his focus back to the problem. "I'm not certain." He scrubbed a hand across the nape of his neck, above his cravat. "I'll try and find a home for them among my patients. At least temporarily. The boy—"

"Temporarily?" Those violet eyes flashed angry sparks.

"Yes. It's not easy to place two small children in a home." Thad frowned. "I suppose I'll have better luck if I separate them and—"

"You'll do no such thing!"

And he'd thought her eyes had flashed sparks before! Thad fought back a grin. With those flames shooting at him, he'd be fortunate if he had any eyebrows left. "Then, pray tell, what am I to do?"

"You will bring them to my house. You can treat the boy there. I'll pay all costs." The woman started toward his buggy, then stopped and looked up at him. "I shall have to ride with you. I sent my chaise home and the driver will not return for an hour."

"I'd be honored." Thad caught up to her in one long step. "And are you certain your husband and children will not object to having two ragamuffin street children foisted on them?"

The woman glanced up at him. The sparks were gone, and a deep sadness had taken their place. "I'm a widow. And I have no children."

"I'm sorry."

She dipped her head in acknowledgment, then turned and lifted a hand to summon her maid. "Annette, I am riding home with the doctor. Wait here. I'll send the chaise for you."

The maid shot a glance at the small buggy, opened her mouth, then pressed it into a thin, disapproving line and moved away.

The woman smiled up at the little girl. "Well, Emma, we are to have an adventure! The doctor is going to take us all to my house. I have a nice soft bed for Billy to rest in until he wakes up. And one for you, as well. Would you like that?"

Thad stepped closer as the child nodded. The woman placed her hand in his offered one, lifted her long skirts with the other and climbed into his buggy. She glanced down at the small, unconscious boy on the seat. "Will it do the boy harm if I move him? His head would be better protected from the jolting of the carriage if I cradle it in my lap."

This elegant woman was going to cradle Billy's bloody head against her expensive gown? Thad stared at her a moment, then nodded. "It's quite safe to move him, madam." He climbed into his buggy and glanced her way.

"Walnut Street, Doctor. I live at Twiggs Manor. Are you familiar with it?"

Twiggs Manor! So this woman was his new neighbor. He nodded and picked up the reins.

Thad hung the towel across a brass bar to dry, then turned and lifted the boy off the lounge sitting against the dressing-room wall. He'd heard of the new practice of piping running water into homes, but he'd never seen it before. Handy. Very handy. Next there'd be indoor "necessaries."

Thad grinned at the thought, then tossed over the edge of the tub the towel he'd put under the boy to protect the settee while he bathed him, and walked into the bedroom. He swept his gaze around the grand room and shook his head. Billy wouldn't know what to think when he woke up. Likely he'd be scared witless.

Thad laid the boy down on the bed and gently probed the swollen bruise above his bony right ankle. It was God's mercy Billy's legs were so skinny the ankle had wedged in between the cobblestones. The buggy rolling over it would have broken it otherwise. He pulled the covers over the small body and checked the clean bandage around Billy's head. He'd cleansed then stitched up the wound as best he could with the swelling. It was all he knew to do.

Thad frowned. His colleagues would bleed the boy, believing draining off the blood would ease the swelling and make him wake up. More likely it would kill him.

The knock on the door interrupted his glum thoughts. He went to open it. The woman stood there holding the little girl by the hand.

"May we come in? Emma would like to see her brother."

Thad looked down at the child. A grin started. He could feel it crinkling the corners of his eyes and tugging his lips upward as he squatted in front of her. She'd had a bath, as evidenced by her clean pink skin and shiny blond hair, but it was the towel draping her tiny frame that tickled him. A large red silk rose pinned two ends of it together at one shoulder and the rest was wrapped around her and held in place by a red silk sash that crisscrossed her shoulders and wound around her tiny waist. It finished in a bow with ends that trailed to the floor.

"I like your flower. I'll bet Billy will, too, when he wakes up. He's still sleeping." He glanced at the cookie in her hand. "Is that for Billy?"

"Yes. It's a cookie!" She gave him a shy smile. "I had one, too. I liked it."

Thad scooped her up into his arms and headed across the room. "Why don't you sit here—" he put her down on the bed beside her brother, then leaned her back against the soft feather pillow "—and eat that cookie, too? Billy can't eat it while he's sleeping." He looked at her drooping eyelids, shook out the coverlet folded at the foot of the bed and laid it over her. "I'm sure when Billy wakes up, this nice lady will give him a cookie."

Emma nodded and took hold of her brother's hand. Her eyes closed. A moment later the cookie fell free. Thad put it on the nightstand beside his black bag.

"*Will* Billy wake up? He's been sleeping an awfully long time. Is he going to be all right?"

Thad turned at the whispered words. The look on the woman's face as she gazed down at the children made him catch his breath. "I think so, but I can't be certain. I'll do everything I know to do for him."

"I'm sure you will, Dr. Allen. Please let me know if there is anything you need."

The woman lifted her gaze to meet his, and Thad felt something he imagined akin to a mule's kick hit him in the solar plexus. His guard went up. This woman could be dangerous to a man destined to be a bachelor. She held out her hand.

"I'm Laina Brighton. Thank you for your help, Doctor. I will be happy to pay for your services." A faint flush spread across her cheeks. "Emma wanted to bring Billy the cookie. I've no experience at such things, but I'm sure he will need broth or something instead of cookies. You've only to tell me what you require for him and I'll have cook prepare it." She smiled. "And may I offer you dinner, Dr. Allen? I'm afraid I've made you miss your noonday meal."

Thad bowed over her hand. "I'm pleased to meet you, Mrs. Brighton. And please, don't concern yourself about my meal. I frequently miss them." He looked back at the bed. "With your permission, I'll just sit here by the bed. I want to be near when Billy wakes."

"Certainly, Doctor. But you still must eat. I'll have cook send up a tray." She sent an anxious glance toward the bed. "I'll be back to see how Billy is doing, but right now I must see about a seamstress. These children need clothes." Another smile curved her lips as she looked back at him. "Though it may be difficult to get Emma to give up that towel—she was quite taken with the sash and the rose."

Thad was quite taken with Laina Brighton. He stared after her as she left the room. *Laina.* The name fit her. It was unusual, and he'd never met another woman quite like her.

These children need clothes. What did that mean? Thad scrubbed his fingers through his hair and dropped into the chair beside him. Was Laina Brighton going to keep these children? Or was this only temporary until Billy was well? His knee began to jiggle up and down as he pondered the questions.

Thad frowned and stretched his long legs out in front of him to stop the annoying movement. He couldn't believe this was merely a gesture on Laina Brighton's part. Not after the way she'd called Henry Rhodes down this afternoon for not caring for the boy.

Thad grinned and leaned back in the chair. He'd never seen the financial giant look so…so nonplussed! Not that he blamed Henry. Laina Brighton had looked magnificent—*regal*—standing there ramrod straight in her purple dress, with the sun shining on her dark curls and her eyes flashing angry sparks.

A compassionless pygmy of a man with no honor! A low chuckle bubbled out of Thad's throat. Henry Rhodes would never forget that. No one dared say such things to him. And when Laina Brighton *dismissed* him! Well, if he were a wagering man he'd be willing to bet it was the first time Henry Rhodes had ever been speechless. The look on the man's face—

A soft whimper broke off his thoughts. Thad bolted to his feet, reaching to keep Billy from moving. He was too late. The boy flopped onto his side. Thad frowned and reached down to check the youngster's pulse.

Chapter Seven

⚮

"Laina, whatever is happening? Why is Dr. Allen here?" Elizabeth rushed into the parlor, clutching two small garments in her hands. "And why do you need one of Mary's dresses?"

"Elizabeth!" Laina stopped pacing and hurried over to give her sister-in-law a hug. "How lovely you came. But you needn't have—truly. Tilly would have brought the dress to me."

"Yes. But then I wouldn't know what this is all about. I confess, I'm curious." Elizabeth handed Laina the garments.

"Oh, you brought a chemise! Thank you. I didn't think of undergarments. Look! It's such a bright, sunny yellow." Laina held up the small checked-gingham dress with matching white apron. "She'll look adorable in it!"

"*Who* will look adorable in it?"

"Emma."

"And who…?"

Laina laughed. "This will go faster if I simply tell you what happened. But I must hurry before she or Billy wake."

"*Billy?* Who is—?"

"Billy is the little boy who was struck down by a carriage." Laina pulled Elizabeth down beside her on the blue brocade couch. "When I went to market this—"

"*You* went to market?"

Laina nodded. "I wanted to see what was available for the garden party. Anyway, as I started down the street a little boy—Billy—darted into the road. He was being chased by the stall owner from whom he'd stolen two rolls."

"Billy's a *thief!*"

Laina lifted her chin. "He's a young boy who is trying to keep himself and his little sister alive."

"I see." Elizabeth's gaze fastened on her raised chin. "And Emma is Billy's sister?"

"Yes." Laina shot her an exasperated look. "Elizabeth, do stop interrupting, or I'll never finish before the seamstress arrives."

"The seam—?" Elizabeth snapped her mouth closed. "I'm sorry. I'll refrain from interrupting again. Please continue."

"Well, that's actually about all there is to tell." Laina rose and walked over to peer out the front window. Where *was* Carlson? Surely he should have returned with the seamstress by now. "Billy didn't see the carriage coming, and the driver, who was going much too fast, couldn't stop. The horse knocked Billy down. He hit his head on the cobblestones and went unconscious. The carriage ran over his legs."

Elizabeth gasped. Laina whirled to face her. "Exactly! And the owner of the carriage was simply going to leave the child lying there in the street! I told him I would care for the boy and sent him on his way. And then, while Dr. Allen—"

"Doc—? Sorry." Elizabeth clamped her mouth shut again.

Laina frowned. "Am I not making sense? Dr. Allen arrived on the scene and examined the boy. It was he who noticed the two rolls and realized the boy was not alone. And then when I saw the little girl peeking at us from behind the rain barrel we decided she must be the one the other roll was for, so of course I went to get her." She drew a breath. "And when Dr. Allen explained about the orphanage burning down and these children having no home but the streets…well, there was no choice but to have him bring them here. And I certainly couldn't put their filthy, tattered clothes back on them after their baths."

Elizabeth stared at her.

"Well, *could* I?"

"No. Of course not." Elizabeth gave a little shake of her head. "That explains the dress, the seamstress and Dr. Allen's buggy out front. How is Billy now?"

"He's still unconscious." Laina rubbed her thumbs over the soft cotton fabric of the small dress in her hands. "I'm concerned for him."

"Yes. I can see you are."

Elizabeth sat studying her, and Laina was afraid her sister-in-law saw a lot more than the worry on her face. She had a feeling Elizabeth was looking straight into the secret places of her heart. She drew a deep breath and offered a source of distraction. "I'm sorry, Elizabeth, I've been rude. I haven't even offered you tea." She headed for the bellpull next to the door.

Elizabeth shook her head and rose. "Not today, Laina. I have to be on my way. Why don't you take that dress up to Emma and look in on Billy?" She smiled and gave her a hug. "We can have tea anytime. Right now you have other things to tend to, and so do I. Justin is bringing home some business associates for dinner and I must get ready." She stepped to the door. "Send Tilly if there is anything more you need. I'm pleased to help. And don't worry so, Laina. Billy will be all right." With a wave of her hand, she left.

Laina drew a deep breath. She loved Elizabeth dearly, but sometimes her sister-in-law made her uncomfortable. How could she believe with such certainty Billy would improve? She shook her head, looked down at the dress in her hands and headed for the stairs. Beaumont would inform her when the seamstress arrived.

"He was awake?" Laina glanced up at the doctor. He was taller even than Justin—her head barely reached his shoulder. She looked away. He made her feel small, a sensation she was unaccustomed to, being taller than most of her friends.

"Not fully awake, no. But he did turn over and moan. And that's a good sign."

Laina shot him a perplexed look. "Forgive me my ignorance, Dr. Allen, but I've no experience at this sort of thing. How can it be good that Billy is hurting?"

Thad shook his head. "You mistake me, Mrs. Brighton. Billy's pain isn't good, his awareness of it is. It means his mind is working."

"I see. That makes sense. Still..." Laina brushed a strand of soft blond hair off the bandage on Billy's forehead. "What a brave little boy he is, caring for his sister when he's not much more than a baby himself. Oh!"

Laina jerked her hand back as Billy moaned and rolled onto his back. Tears welled into her eyes. "I hurt him!" She looked up at the doctor. "I'm so sorry. I—"

"You didn't hurt him, Mrs. Brighton. He's coming back to consciousness." Thad gave her a warning look. "You may want to leave. He will probably be sick."

Laina's stomach churned at the thought. She took a breath, blinked the tears from her eyes and shook her head. "No. I'll stay. If I'm to have the children, I must learn how to care for them."

She was going to keep them! Thad nodded approval. "It seems Billy is not the only one here who is brave."

Laina gave a nervous little laugh. "I'm not brave, Doctor. I'm a coward. My stomach is even now rebelling at the thought of that unpleasantness. I'm not sure I will manage to remain."

"Which makes you very brave, Mrs. Brighton. Anyone can do something that doesn't bother—"

A retching sound scraped across his words. Thad grabbed the washbowl he had waiting on the nightstand, put it on the bed and gently turned Billy onto his side. He tightened his arm around the boy's bony shoulders as his thin body tensed and tried to release the contents of his stomach.

"Don't you hurt Billy!"

Thad twisted his head toward the little girl on the bed and a small fist struck him on the ear. Another hit his shoulder. He ducked his head to protect his eyes.

"Emma!" Laina rushed to the other side of the bed and pulled the enraged toddler away from the doctor. The child twisted about in her arms and grabbed a fistful of his hair. "You leave Billy alone!"

Laina gasped, forced open the small hand and pulled it tight against her chest. "Emma, the doctor is not— Ouch!"

Laina yanked her hand away, staring in disbelief at the teeth marks across its back, then again imprisoned Emma's grasping hand in hers. "This is *not* the way a young lady acts, Emma. Now, stop fighting and *listen* to me!" It was her mistress-of-the-house voice.

The toddler froze.

So did Laina. Had she spoken that sternly to a *child?* She didn't follow the thought further. "Dr. Allen is not hurting Billy, Emma. He's helping him get better." The child quieted and stared up at her. Laina smiled. "You can help Billy, too, by being a good girl and letting the doctor do his job. You want to help Billy, don't you?"

The toddler's lower lip quivered. She nodded.

Laina's heart swelled. "Of course you do." She gave Emma a quick hug, then smiled down at her. "I have something for you. Look." She freed one hand and held up the dress she'd dropped on the bed. "Billy will be so happy to see you in a pretty new dress." She filled her voice with excitement. "Shall we put it on?"

Laina unpinned the rose, then undid the sash that held the bunched-up towel in place and pulled the garments over Emma's thin little body. "Oh, my!" She stepped back and clasped her hands together in front of her. "You look so pretty, Emma."

"She certainly does." The doctor put the bowl back on the night table and reached for the little girl. "You look like a drop of sunshine. I think I'll call you Sunshine."

Laina laughed as the doctor lifted Emma over his head and whirled in a circle. The little girl squealed and grabbed for his wrists.

"Put her down!"

Billy! Laina gasped as the young boy tried to raise himself up and grab his sister.

"Ugh!"

"It's all right, son. Don't try to move. I'm putting your sister down." The doctor kept his eyes fastened on Billy as he lowered Emma to the bed. "Be careful not to bump Billy, Emma."

The toddler nodded and crowded close to her brother.

"How do you feel, son?"

Billy's eyelids lowered. He jerked them open again and groped for his sister's hand. "You stay here, Emma! Don't let go of my hand, you hear?" His eyes closed.

Emma rose on her knees to peer down at him. "Billy? We're in a big, big house, Billy! And the nice lady gave me soup and cookies! She gave you one, too. Do you want your cookie, Billy? They said I could eat it, but I didn't. I saved it for you. And I have a new dress…. Billy?"

"He's gone back to sleep, Emma. He's very tired. You can tell him about your dress the next time he wakes up."

Laina couldn't take her gaze from the doctor's face. He had a wonderful smile, but it was his gentle expression as he spoke with Emma that touched her heart. He obviously loved children.

Someone tapped softly.

The seamstress. *Finally.* Laina turned with a swish of her long skirts and hurried to answer the door. "Please come—" She stopped, frowning at sight of the empty hallway. There was no one there but her maid. "What is it, Sally?"

"Beggin' your pardon, ma'am, but there's a lad saw the doctor's buggy. He says there's been an accident and his da needs the doctor bad."

"The doctor?" Panic rushed over her. Laina whirled to face the bed. What about Billy? She didn't know how to take care of him! She struggled to put on a brave face as Thaddeous Allen picked up his black bag and strode to the door.

"It will be all right, Mrs. Brighton. If Billy wakes, keep him quiet. Don't let him move around much. If he feels up to eating, give him light broth only, a few swallows at a time." He smiled down at her. "No cookies yet."

Laina's cheeks warmed. That teasing remark was meant to make her feel better. So much for a brave face—he'd seen right through her. She nodded and gave up the pretense. "You will come back, Doctor?"

"Yes. As soon as possible. If it's not too late." He stepped into the hall.

Panic struck again. "The time doesn't matter, Doctor. Please stop back. Beaumont will let you in. I will be here with Billy." She called the words after him as he rushed down the hallway toward the stairs. She'd never felt so inadequate, so inept, so *scared.* She lifted her chin a notch as he glanced back at her.

"Very well, Mrs. Brighton, I will come back no matter the hour." He disappeared down the stairwell.

Laina closed the door and sagged against it. Now what? A moan and the sound of retching gave her her answer. She took a deep breath and hurried to the bed.

Thad rushed down the elegant staircase to the large entrance hall and strode quickly toward the white-faced boy standing by the door. "What is it, Johnny? What's happened to your father?" He pulled open the door and led the way out onto the porch.

"He's hurt bad, Doc. He was cuttin' hay and the scythe slipped. He's bleedin' somethin' fierce."

Thad nodded and ran for his buggy he'd parked in the shade beneath one of the trees that lined the drive. Gravel spit from under the wheels as Faithful leaped forward. Thad dropped his bag onto the seat and picked up the reins. Good old Faithful—he always knew when it was an emergency.

He braced himself as Johnny sprinted by on his horse and raced off down Walnut Street. A moment later Faithful charged into the same turn. The buggy skidded sideways in the loose stones of the drive, then righted itself as the gelding chased after Johnny.

"Two street children! What does Laina know about caring for children?" Justin scowled. "There's no time to talk to her about it now. I'll go over in the morning." He glanced into the mirror and lifted one hand to flick the frill at his neck. "I don't like this, Elizabeth. I don't care if it is the latest style from Europe. I'd rather wear one of my cravats."

"But Justin, you look wonderful in it. Here, put on your new suit coat and see how nice it looks." Elizabeth held the black wool jacket out to him. "I'm not so sure you should speak against the children being in her home, dear. Laina was like her old self when I spoke with her this afternoon. I haven't seen her so animated since she arrived in Philadelphia."

Justin shrugged into the jacket and buttoned it. "Even so, she can't have street orphans living with her." He tugged at the bottom of the jacket that hit just below his waistline in front. "No waistcoat, Elizabeth? I'll have to keep this thing buttoned all night!" He swept his gaze over his image in the mirror. Patent leather shoes with gray spats, light gray, shadow-striped trousers and the frill that filled the space between the square-cut lapels of the black swallowtail jacket. He gave a disgusted snort. "I look like a dandy."

Elizabeth smiled at the grumbled words. "Dandies do not wear black, dear. And you're far too masculine to ever be mistaken for one. You're a very handsome man, my husband." She went on tiptoes and lifted her face for a kiss.

Justin lowered his head and obliged, then grinned at her. "All right, I'll wear the new suit. But don't think you fool me with your feminine wiles. I'm onto you, you saucy wench!" He pulled her close against him.

Elizabeth laughed. "You may be onto me, but my feminine wiles still work."

"Umm, indeed they do." Justin lowered his head again. He touched his lips to hers, withdrew, then came back and claimed hers fully. Elizabeth put her arms about his waist and held on. When he finally lifted his head, she was trembling—but then, so was he. He burrowed his face into her golden curls.

"Justin?"

"Hmm?"

"Please don't discourage Laina's having those children in her home."

Justin drew back and looked down at her. He knew that tone. "Why, Elizabeth? Laina told you the boy's a thief."

"Yes. But she also said he's only a young boy trying to take care of his little sister." Her eyes clouded. "Sometimes things are not as they appear, Justin. We know that better than anyone. Think of the things we once believed about each other. The truth was so very different." She laid her hand against his chest and looked deep into his eyes. "How do we know these children are not the answer to the prayers we've been praying for Laina?"

A quietness settled over him. Justin stared down at her. "I believe you're right." He shook his head. "You amaze me, Elizabeth. You're so wise. I should have thought of that."

She tossed him one of those pert smiles he loved. "Methinks you would have if you hadn't been distracted, good sir."

Justin took her hand and placed it on his arm. "Let's go downstairs and prepare to meet our dinner guests, Mrs. Randolph…before I forget myself entirely and tell Owen to send them all home when they arrive."

Where was the doctor? Laina was hard put not to wring her hands. Billy was becoming increasingly restless and she was supposed to keep him quiet. What should she do? She winced as the young boy moaned and flopped onto his right side, his hands grabbing at the covers.

"Emma?" Billy's eyelids twitched. His hands groped through the air. *"Emma?"*

Of course—she should have known. Laina gently pulled the sleeping Emma's hand from beneath her feather pillow and placed it in Billy's. His fingers curled around it. He quieted.

Laina gave a sigh of relief, straightened the mussed cover over Billy and walked to the open window. She was exhausted. Having children was harder than she had imagined. Of course, one usually started with a baby, not with a young injured boy and his little sister.

Laina leaned against the window frame and closed her eyes. What a day! She'd gone to market to see what was available in order to plan her garden party and come home with children. Never in her wildest dreams could she have imagined such a thing happening.

She had *children!*

The truth struck her like a hammer blow. Laina popped her eyes open and stared at the two blond heads visible above the blankets that covered the two small bodies. They were orphans. No one wanted them. No one would take them from her. She would be their mother!

You believe—very well, you pray! And if your Lord gives me children I will serve Him all of my remaining days!

The angry challenge she had flung at her brother rang through Laina's mind. Her pulse raced. Had Justin picked up the gauntlet she had thrown down? Were Billy and Emma an answer to Justin's prayers?

Laina couldn't stop her gaze from rising to the moon-lit sky any more than she could stop the furious pounding of her heart. Did God really hear and answer prayer? How could she know? She frowned, staring at her hand, which she'd lifted to place against the glass. She was letting her emotions carry her away. She knew. It was all simply a coincidence.

"Mrs. Brighton?"

Laina gasped and jerked around toward the door.

Thad gave her a polite nod. "I'm sorry. I didn't mean to startle you. When you didn't answer my tap on the door, I thought you were probably asleep. I was going to sit with Billy." He stepped into the room and walked to the bed. "Has he wakened again?"

"Yes. Twice. Though not fully." She walked over and faced him across the expanse of bed. "He hasn't been sick. He simply retches and then goes back to sleep."

"That's to be expected." Thad set his black bag on the nightstand. "He has no food in him. It's hard to be sick with an empty stomach."

"Of course. I should have thought of that." She looked down at Billy. "I'm afraid I'm not very good at this."

Thad looked her way. "You're doing fine, Mrs. Brighton. Most women in your position have their nannies tend their sick children. Or hire a nurse."

"Truly?" She lifted her gaze to his.

He nodded. "Of course, I realize you haven't a nanny available to you as yet."

Her violet eyes flashed. "I would be here in any case, Doctor."

Thad fought down the urge to smile. "I'm certain you would. I didn't mean to offend, Mrs. Brighton."

Even by the light of the single candle she had burning on the nightstand, he could see the soft rose color spread across her cheeks. "Forgive me, Doctor. I didn't mean to be waspish. I—"

"Where's Emma?"

Thad looked down into brown eyes that were burning with fear and defiance. "She's sleeping on the bed beside you, Billy. No, don't move!"

His warning was too late. Billy jerked to his side. "Ugh!" The boy's hand grabbed for his head, then fell limp against the pillow. His eyelids slid closed.

Thad lifted the boy's wrist and counted his pulse.

"Is he all right?"

He could barely hear her whisper. "Billy's going to be fine, Mrs. Brighton." Thad gave her a reassuring smile. "He was fully conscious a moment ago and that's an excellent sign. We've only to wait. The time between his waking moments will shorten, and each time he will be cognizant a little longer. What is needed is to keep him from moving so violently. That could cause him harm."

Laina Brighton's face paled. She bent, turned Emma on her side and placed the child's small hand in Billy's. "He's such a brave little boy. Even in his illness his concern is for Emma. He's afraid for her. He stays quiet when he feels her next to him." She straightened and took a deep breath. "Thank you for coming back, Doctor. But I'm keeping you from your rest. I'll have Beaumont see you out."

"With your permission, I'll stay, Mrs. Brighton. I want to be here when Billy regains consciousness, and I have a feeling it won't be long."

She gave him a look of pure relief. "I'd be very grateful if you would stay, Doctor." A frown creased her forehead. "I'm afraid cook's long abed, and I have nothing in the way of refreshments to offer you, except…"

She glanced at the sleeping children, then lifted something from the nightstand and held it out toward him. "Would you care for a cookie?"

Their soft laughter rose and mingled over the bed between them.

Chapter Eight

Laina jerked and opened her eyes. How long had she been sleeping? She rose quietly, lifted her arms above her head and stretched up on tiptoes to work out the kinks, then yawned and stepped over to look out the window. Dawn was painting a new day on the horizon. What a gorgeous pink color. She opened the louvered shutters that covered the lower sash, lifted it to let in the refreshing morning air and glanced down at the formal gardens below. The early light illumined the leaves on the trees, bathed the hedges and flowers in its rosy glow and outlined the statuary and tables. The gardeners and painters had been working from dawn to dusk for weeks, and everything was in readiness for her debut party.

Laina gave another delicate yawn and rested against the window frame watching the sunrise. Elizabeth was coming today to help her finish the invitations. She'd have to send word to her not to come. There would be no garden party—at least, not now. Perhaps after Billy was better and he and Emma were comfortable in their new home. A smile curved her lips. She shook her head. How quickly one's life could change.

She pushed away from the window, fluffed her curls with her hand, smoothed her skirts and hurried to Billy's bedroom. The doctor was bent over Billy, holding the struggling boy still. Laina pushed the door wide open and hurried forward to offer help.

"I'm a doctor, Billy—Dr. Allen. You were hurt when a horse and carriage ran you down. You cracked your head on the cobblestones when you fell and I had to stitch it up and bandage it. That's why you can't move quickly. You'll hurt yourself."

Laina listened to Thaddeous Allen's calm, soothing voice, watched some of the fear leave Billy's eyes. The doctor needed no aid from her.

"I'm going to take my hands away now, Billy. Remember, you need to stay still." The doctor straightened. "Tell me how you feel, son."

"My head hurts." There was belligerence in Billy's tone. His hand tightened around Emma's.

Thaddeous Allen nodded. "That will be better in a few days if you do as I say."

Billy glared up at him. "I got no money to pay you."

"I want no money, Billy."

"Then what?" Fear burst full-blown into Billy's eyes. "You ain't hurtin' Emma! You ain't *touchin'* her!"

Laina gasped. What sort of life did this little boy lead? She jerked forward and instinctively reached for his free hand. "No one's going to hurt you *or* Emma, Billy. Not *ever.* I promise!"

The little boy yanked his hand away and glared at her. "Who're you?"

"Don't be mean, Billy. She's the lady that gave us a cookie!" Emma rubbed her eyes still filled with sleep and looked at her brother. "An' she gave me soup. An' a pretty new dress. See my dress, Billy?" She rose to her feet, tottered on the uncertain footing of the soft feather mattress and plunked down on her behind. She giggled, then looked down at her lap and sobered. Her lower lip trembled. "Where's my pretty dress?"

The words ended in a sob that wrenched at Laina's heart. "Your dress is here, Emma." She picked up the folded garment and hurried around the bed. "I took it off when you went to sleep so it wouldn't wrinkle. Do you want to put it on so Billy can see it?"

Emma's tears stopped. Her face brightened. She smiled and nodded. Laina helped her stand on the bed, then slipped the dress on over her chemise. "There you are."

"See, Billy?" Emma tried to turn toward her brother, and promptly plopped onto her behind again. She giggled and bounced up and down.

"Ugh."

"Emma, you mustn't bounce. You'll hurt Billy's head." Laina snatched her off the bed. "Are you hungry?" She smiled down at her. "Shall we go have breakfast while Dr. Allen is caring for Billy?"

"She's not goin' anywhere with you!" Billy made a grab for Emma, groaned and fell back on the pillow.

"Stay still, son." Thaddeous Allen reached for the boy as he started to retch.

Emma burst into tears. "I want to go, Billy. My tummy's hungry."

Laina hugged the little girl. "Hush, Emma. You shall have your breakfast." She looked down at the young boy in Dr. Allen's arms and tears welled in her eyes. "I'm sorry, Billy. I promise you Emma will not leave this room until you are better. She will have her meals right here on the bed beside you, on a tray. Please don't worry about her." She lifted her gaze. "I'm sorry, Doctor. I didn't mean to upset him."

He nodded his understanding while checking Billy's pulse.

Laina drew in a long breath, blinked the tears from her eyes, moved to the bellpull at the head of the bed and gave it two quick yanks. At least *this* she could handle. She knew how to plan meals. She formed a quick menu in her mind. An omelet, potatoes, toast with jam, bacon, ham, tarts…and chocolate! Had Emma ever had hot chocolate? A smile touched her lips.

"Mrs. Brighton?"

Laina turned toward the doctor. He was winding a clean bandage around Billy's head. The boy's face was pale, his lips compressed. To keep from moaning? Nausea swirled in her stomach at the thought of the young boy's pain. She swallowed hard. "Yes, Doctor?"

He glanced up at her, then went back to his task. "I only wanted to remind you these children are not accustomed to eating large meals or rich foods. It would be best to keep Emma's breakfast simple. Perhaps oatmeal, or toast with a bit of apple butter."

Laina's shoulders sagged.

"I want a cookie."

The doctor looked up at Emma and burst out laughing. He tied off the bandage, lowered Billy's head gently to the feather pillow and straightened. "I stand corrected, Mrs. Brighton, at least as far as this one's stomach is concerned. She may have oatmeal *and* a cookie." He tapped the tip of Emma's tiny nose. She giggled and ducked her head. He grinned and tickled her ear. "But Billy must have only a thin gruel. Nothing solid until his nausea subsides."

Laina nodded and looked up at him. "I understand, Doctor." She gave Emma a hug, handed her to the doctor and went to answer the soft knock that announced her maid had answered her summons. She gave her orders for the children's breakfasts as Dr. Allen had instructed, added another of eggs, ham and toast for him, then hurried to her room to prepare for the day.

"Do hurry, Annette! I have to get back to the children before the doctor leaves."

"*Oui,* madame." The maid slipped another silver hair comb into place to hold the thick knot of hair on top of Laina's head and stepped back. "I am finished."

"At last!" The fabric of Laina's apple-green dress rustled softly as she rose and started for the door. "Come along, Annette. And bring my hairbrush."

"Your hairbrush, madame?"

"Yes, and that piece of white satin cording. You can use it for a bow in Emma's hair." Laina stopped by a chair to pick up the soft cotton undershirt and matching drawstring pantaloons the seamstress had made for Billy.

"But *madame.* Surely you are not asking me to attend that—?"

Laina straightened at the shocked, offended tone in her maid's voice. "That is exactly what I am asking, Annette." Her voice cooled. "Must I make it an order?"

The maid's body stiffened. "I am employed to be *your* maid, madame. Not to tend to *street urchins*. If I may inquire, how long are they to remain?"

Laina fastened a cold gaze on her maid. "They are *children*, Annette. *My* children, not street urchins. This is their home now and for always."

The maid's features hardened at the rebuke. "Then I wish to resign my position and return to New York, madame. I cannot stay in a house with thieves."

Laina stiffened. She walked back to the dressing table and picked up her hairbrush and the piece of satin cord while counting to ten and waiting for her temper to cool. "You're right, Annette. You cannot stay in this house."

She hadn't waited long enough—her voice was trembling with anger. She looked up at her maid's shocked face. There was a hint of trepidation in Annette's eyes. Had she thought she would throw the children out in order to keep her?

Laina turned back toward the door. "Pack your things immediately, Annette. Carlson will take you to the Liberty Inn. You will find public conveyance for New York there." She walked to the door and opened it. "I will leave the wages due you with Mrs. Barnes."

Laina closed the door with a satisfying yank and stormed down the hallway. Were there others in her employ who felt as Annette did? Fresh anger shot through her at the idea. She would have a meeting with Beaumont and Mrs. Barnes as soon as possible to find out. She

wanted no such people in her home. She was still smol-
dering when she reached what she already thought of as
Billy's bedroom. She drew a calming breath and quietly
opened the door.

"So Dr. Simon let me take care of it all by myself. That
little fox pup was my first patient. I kept him in a cage in
the woodshed."

Laina stopped, staring at the tableau before her. Thaddeous Allen sat in the wood chair facing Billy, who rested
back on pillows propped against the headboard. The boy's
eyes were closed, but there was an alertness about him
that suggested he was listening to the doctor's story. There
was no doubt about Emma's interest. She was perched on
the doctor's knees, staring up at him out of wide brown
eyes, the fragment of a cookie in her small hand. They
looked like a family.

Laina's anger dissolved before an onrush of such intense
desire to have a family of her own that it left her shaking.
She slipped back out into the hall through the still-open
door and sagged against the wall, gulping back a lump in
her throat that threatened to choke her.

"Did ya make his paw get better?"

"I sure did, Billy."

"I wanna see him."

Laina smiled through the tears blurring her vision and
concentrated on the voices coming from the bedroom.

"I'm afraid that's impossible, Emma."

"Why?"

"Because I found the wounded baby fox when I was
only a lad, not much older than Billy is now. And when
his paw was healed I took him back to the woods and let
him go."

"Why?"

Laina's smile widened. She blinked the tears from her eyes. *Why* was one of Mary's favorite words. It seemed Emma was very fond of it, as well. She took another deep breath and pushed away from the wall. She'd be all right now. She stepped to the door, listening to the doctor's answer.

"Because the fox was wild. He belonged in the forest with his fox family."

"I gots a family."

Laina's heart stopped, then beat furiously. A *family?* Would she have to give up Billy and Emma? The thought was unbearable, even after this short time.

"You do?"

The doctor sounded surprised…wary. She held her breath, waiting for Emma's answer.

"Billy says we're a family and we gots to take care of each other."

Laina's breath came out in a gust of relief. She looked down at the undergarments crushed in her hand, shook them out and walked into the bedroom.

"Billy's right, Emma." Dr. Allen smiled at the toddler on his lap. "It's very important for family members to take care of one another."

The little girl beamed up at him. "You taked care of Billy." She wiggled down off his lap and ran to Laina. "An' you taked care of me." She dashed back and scrambled up the bedside steps to look at her brother. "We gots lots of family now, Billy!"

The boy's eyes opened. "They ain't family, Emma. It ain't the same thing."

"It is so!"

Billy blinked his eyes, then shut them tight. "No, it ain't, Emma. You got to be born to family." He grabbed her hand. "An' that's only you an' me."

Laina's chest tightened. Billy was trying to sound tough, but he only sounded lost and alone. She moved to the bed. "It doesn't have to be that way, Billy. Sometimes people become a family in their hearts."

She didn't dare say more. Couldn't say more. There was another lump in her throat that wouldn't permit the passage of words. When she could speak, she lifted her gaze to the doctor's face. The approval in his eyes made her pulse quicken. She flushed with pleasure. At last she'd done something right! The heat in her cheeks increased as the doctor dropped his gaze to them. She thrust the undergarments she held toward him. "These are for Billy. Can you move him enough to put them on him?"

"Yes, indeed." The doctor's gaze rose to meet hers for a moment, then dropped to her hands. He took the garments from her and began to undo the buttons at the shoulders of the shirt.

Laina expelled the air in her lungs and held her hand out to Emma. "I have a pretty bow to put in your hair. Let's go to the dressing room while the doctor gets Billy dressed and I'll get you cleaned up and ready for the day."

What had she forgotten? Cook was informed of the children's special menu needs. The seamstress was installed in a third-floor bedroom making them clothes. Oh, there was so much left to do!

Laina folded her hands and tapped her steepled forefingers together. The children needed so many things. Shoes and stockings. Books and drawing supplies. Paints!

And toys. She closed her eyes and tried to picture the nursery at Randolph Court.

The children needed their own rooms, with common space to play and a room for study. Yes! Laina opened her eyes and looked at the young boy asleep on the bed. Billy was old enough to begin lessons. She would have to arrange for a tutor. And a nanny for Emma. Not to mention a new lady's maid for herself. A frown creased her forehead.

Laina glanced over at the little girl, who was standing on tiptoe to look out the window. Emma must have a doll, and dishes for tea parties. Laina looked back at the bed and cast through her memory to the toys Justin had played with. Tin soldiers with horses and wagons. Balls and—

Laina jumped at the soft knock on the door. At least it hadn't wakened Billy. She hurried to open it.

"Beggin' your pardon, ma'am, but did you want me cleanin' the room?"

"Yes, Sally. But quietly, please. Billy's injured and must rest." Laina stepped aside.

The young maid entered with her bucket of cleaning supplies and smiled down at the little girl, who rushed up and stopped in front of her. "And who are you, little miss?"

"I'm Emma." The toddler stared up at the maid. "Who are you?"

"My name's Sally, Miss Emma." The maid walked a slow circle around the little girl. "My, aren't you the fancy one, with your pretty yellow dress and a shiny white bow in your hair?"

Emma nodded. "I gots a…a…this, too!" She lifted her dress to show off her chemise.

"Ain't I told ya to keep yer dress down, Emma!"

"Billy! You must stay still." Laina hurried to the bed as the boy flinched with pain.

Emma's lower lip quivered. She let her skirt drop into place. "I wanted her to see it, Billy."

Sally dropped onto her knees. "It's a fine shift, Miss Emma. But a lady always keeps her dress down."

Emma's eyes widened. "Oh."

"It's good you have Billy to teach you things like that." The maid rose and began dusting.

"What are you doing?"

Laina smiled. Emma's questions were starting.

"Making the room nice and clean."

"Why?"

Laina listened for the maid's response while she walked to the dressing room to get a facecloth wrung out in cold water. She'd heard a cold cloth helped headaches.

"Because it makes the room prettier and nicer to live in."

"Oh."

Laina grinned. She could tell by Emma's voice there was more to come. She got the facecloth and walked back to the bed.

"Can I do it, too?"

She glanced over as Sally shook her head. "No. That wouldn't be right, Miss Emma. You're a guest, and guests don't clean." The maid smiled at the crestfallen toddler. "Why don't you play a game while I clean? Would you like that?"

Emma gave a vigorous nod, ran over to the bed and climbed to the top of the bedside steps to look at her brother. "Let's play pretend." She looked up at Laina. "Do you want to play with us? You could be our pretend ma."

Laina nodded and cleared her throat. "I'd love to play pretend with you and Billy, Emma."

"I'm too tired to play."

Laina's heart sank at Billy's gruff words. She smiled at the disappointed little girl. "Perhaps when Billy is feeling better." She folded the cloth and bent to place it on Billy's head.

He glared up at her. "Whatcha doin'? What's that?"

"It's a cold cloth. It will help to make your head stop hurting." She hoped that was the truth. She'd no experience of headaches. He watched, a wary look in his eyes, as she laid it on his forehead. At least he let her do it. She held back a sigh, pulled a light blanket over him and looked down at Emma. "Would you like me to tell you a story while Billy rests?"

Emma nodded. Laina lifted her into her arms and seated herself in the chair. Why had she offered to tell her a story? Whatever would she say? Emma couldn't relate to her childhood.

The little girl squirmed into a comfortable position on her lap and looked expectantly at her. Laina searched her memory for an appropriate tale, but nothing came to mind. Panic set in. She'd have to make up something as she went along. She took a breath and began. "Once upon a time there was a little girl who had a big brother. They lived together…in a tree in the woods."

Where had *that* come from? Laina glanced over at Billy. He'd closed his eyes, but it was obvious from his expression he was listening. She took another breath and continued. "The little boy was brave and strong. He took very good care of his little sister." She looked down as Emma nodded. Well, *that* was good. Now what? She glanced at the window. "One bright summer day the boy and girl went for a walk...."

Thad yawned and closed his notebook. As always, he'd had a few successes and a few failures to record. And more questions than answers about procedures to jot down. Poor Mrs. Tibbins. There had to be something that would help her aches and pains, but the best he could advise was a cooked-onion poultice on the joints that hurt most. The moist warmth seemed to ease her discomfort a little.

He frowned down at his desk, reached out and placed the stopper in the inkwell, laid his pen in its pewter box and closed the top. It had been a long day. He'd wait until tomorrow to write Dr. Bettencourt and inquire how he and the other doctors of the French Clinical School treated the disease that deformed joints and caused eventual crippling. Maybe he'd also ask how they felt about washing their hands before and after treating a patient. He was sure it helped prevent the spread of disease. At least, he'd found it so in his own practice. That's why he bathed every night when he came home, even if he was so tired he could barely pump the pails of water.

Thad scrubbed the end of the towel draped around his neck over his still-damp hair, then picked up his candle and headed for the stairs. He ought to look into getting water piped into his house the way it was in Twiggs Manor. He'd never seen anything so handy. But the cost...

He shook his head, climbed to his bedroom, tossed the towel over the back of a chair to dry and blew out the candle. Moonlight poured in the window, highlighting his bed. His *lonely* bed.

Thad scowled. Now, where had that thought come from? He'd long ago accepted the toll his profession exacted on his personal life. What else could he do? It was God's will for him to be a doctor. Why else would God have provided him with his gifts? And there was little time, and even less money, in a doctor's life to court a woman, let alone marry and raise a family. It wouldn't be fair to them.

Thad shrugged off the yearnings that never quite left his heart and flopped onto his bed. It was too bad there hadn't been a candle burning in Billy's bedroom when he'd driven past Twiggs Manor tonight. He'd wanted to check on the boy—though he was receiving excellent care.

A grin spread his lips. Every time he thought of Laina Brighton, the image of her standing in the street calling down Henry Rhodes flashed into his mind. He pulled a cover sheet up to his bare chest, laced his hands behind his head and rested back against his pillow. He'd never seen anyone as pretty as Laina Brighton. Those beautiful dark blue eyes of hers fascinated him, the way they changed so quickly with her emotions. He'd seen them dull with sadness, bright with amusement, soft with compassion and flashing with sparks in anger. How would they look warmed by love?

Thad jerked his mind from the thought, snapped his eyes open and turned onto his side to stare out the window. A scowl creased his forehead. He couldn't afford to let his mind wander down that path. Even if it was harmless speculation, it was dangerous ground for a man destined to remain a bachelor.

* * *

How could one feel tired, inept and exhilarated at the same time? Laina shook her head, pulled the blanket over Emma's exposed arm and went to curl up in the soft padded chair on the hearth.

Moonlight streamed in the windows, adding a silver cast to the bayberry-white plastered walls and slate-blue paneling of the bedroom. She sat for a moment admiring its beauty, then smoothed the fabric of her long skirt over her legs and leaned her head against the padded draft protector, thinking back over the events of the day. Billy seemed to be relaxing a little. He was a tad less suspicious and wary of her every move, and he no longer frowned and flinched away when she changed the cold cloths on his forehead. He had even accepted her help when he became too tired to feed himself. She was definitely making progress with him.

Laina glanced at the children asleep on the bed and smiled. The made-up story about a boy and girl living in the woods and a lady finding and caring for the little boy when he hurt himself falling out of a tree helped. She didn't know where the sudden inspiration for the story had come from, but she was grateful for it. And for the improvement in Billy's health. He was staying awake for longer stretches of time. That had to be a good sign.

She sighed and closed her eyes. She wanted to ask Dr. Allen about that and a hundred other things. Why hadn't he come to check on Billy tonight? Should she send for him in the morning? A smile curved her lips at thought of seeing him again.

Laina frowned and opened her eyes. She mustn't let herself become dependent on Dr. Allen. He was a very nice man—handsome, too, with his dark hair and brown eyes—but Billy was not his only patient. He had many others who depended on him, not to mention his own life to live. Even doctors had a life.

That thought gave her pause. Laina gave a soft sigh and rose to walk over to the window. She hadn't considered the doctor's private life before. Did it include a wife and children?

Chapter Nine

❧

"Laina! Owen told me I'd find you here in the nursery. I'm sorry I was out when you arrived." Elizabeth hurried across the room and gave her a hug, then glanced down at the paper on the table. "What are you doing sitting here all alone? Didn't Owen tell you the children are outside in the playhouse?"

"Yes, he did." Laina smiled up at her sister-in-law. "I'm taking advantage of their absence to make a list of their books and toys. I have nothing for Billy and Emma to play with, and I'm not certain of what I need." She swept her gaze over the abundance of little-girl toys and sighed. "I'm afraid there's nothing here for Billy, except a ball."

Elizabeth laughed. "Not yet. James is too small for toys."

"Yes." Laina frowned. "Has Justin returned? He can tell me what toys a young boy wants, and what books are appropriate for him. I want to speak with him about hiring a tutor and a carpenter, as well." She glanced at another paper. "I'm unfamiliar with the craftsmen and artisans of Philadelphia, Elizabeth. Perhaps you could suggest a good cabinetmaker? I'll need appropriate furniture. And artists to—"

Elizabeth burst into laughter. "Why don't you bring your lists downstairs to the library, Laina? We'll have tea. I think this is going to take some time."

"A carpenter?" Justin scowled and set his cup back on his saucer. "Is there a problem at Twiggs Manor?"

Laina shook her head. "No, dearheart. I want the third floor turned into a nursery."

"A *nursery!*" Justin shot a look at his wife. Elizabeth gave a small warning shake of her head. His scowl deepened. He looked back at Laina. "Why do you want a nursery?"

"Why, for Billy and Emma, of course." Laina gave her brother an exasperated look. "They can't very well play in the drawing room."

"No. I suppose they can't." He fixed an assessing gaze on her. "I wasn't aware this was to be a permanent change in your life, Laina. I thought you were keeping the children only until the boy was healed of his concussion."

"Truly?" Laina lifted her chin. "And then what would you have me do? Cast them out into the streets again?"

Justin's left eyebrow rose. His lips twitched. "Now, there's the Laina I know and love."

She flushed and softened the sharp tone of her voice. "I'm sorry, Justin. But surely you know the Cherry Street Orphanage is gone and there is no place for these children to live."

"Yes, I remember when the orphanage burned, but I've only recently become aware of the extent of the problem that created. I assumed the children were placed elsewhere." Justin studied her for a moment, then reached for a raspberry tart. "So you intend to keep these children for your own?"

Laina lifted her chin a notch higher. "Yes."

"And have you asked them how they feel about that?"

She stared at him, feeling rather like one of those hot-air balloons that had suddenly sprung a leak. "No. I've not asked them." Emma would be delighted. But what about Billy?

Justin nodded. "Perhaps you should do so. Before you make all these changes."

There was compassion in Justin's voice and eyes. Laina took a deep breath and looked down at the lists on the table in front of her. What if Billy said no? Emma would go with him. She couldn't force them to stay. And he was already so much better.... Her stomach knotted. She drew another deep breath and gathered the lists into a pile.

"Laina?"

"Yes?"

"I said *perhaps.*" Justin's hand covered hers. "I believe the children will agree to stay. I only think it's wise to ask them how they feel about the matter before you continue making plans." His grip tightened. "I don't want to see you hurt."

"I know, dearheart." Laina forced a smile to her lips and looked up at him. "I shall do as you suggest. I'm far too impetuous for my own good. Now I must go. Sally is with the children, and I don't want to leave them alone too long." She rose and stepped around the table to give Elizabeth a hug. "Thank you for tea. And thank you for your advice, dearheart." She stepped into Justin's opened arms, rose on tiptoe to kiss his cheek and walked to the door.

"Laina."

What now? She turned back to face her brother. His eyes were…well, not exactly twinkling with amusement, but close to it. A small warning bell went off in her mind. "Yes?"

A grin spread across Justin's face. "If those children say yes, and I believe they will—" his grin widened "—we'll see you in church on Sunday."

Her vow. She'd forgotten about it. Laina froze. A dozen protests rushed to her lips, but every one of them died in light of her promise. There was nothing to do but agree. She nodded and hurried from the room.

Church. Now see what her rash words had let her in for! Laina scowled and watched the toes of her shoes appearing and disappearing from beneath her long skirts as she hurried up the drive toward the front porch. When would she learn to control her temper? She—

"Whoa there!"

Strong hands gripped her arms and steadied her as she caromed off a hard body. Laina caught her balance and looked up.

Thaddeous Allen grinned down at her. "If you're in a race, you've left the field far behind." He made a show of sweeping the area behind her with his gaze. "You're a sure winner, all right. There's nary another racer in sight."

Heat climbed into her cheeks. "I'm sorry, Dr. Allen. I didn't see you. I was…thinking." His gaze brushed over her flushed cheeks and locked with hers. Her breath shortened. Time seemed to stop. It started again when he nodded and looked away.

Laina sucked in air as he released his grip on her arms and stepped back. She looked down and brushed at some imaginary lint on her skirt, ascribing the odd sensation to her agitated state. "Are you coming or going, Dr. Allen?"

"Coming."

She nodded and took a firm grip on the railing to help her up the porch steps. Her legs felt wobbly. She must have expended too much energy in her rapid walk home from Randolph Court. "I think you'll be pleased with Billy's progress." Laina glanced up at him. "His nausea has abated."

"That's good news." He smiled. "And I'm always pleased when a patient improves, no matter the degree of progress."

"Of course." Laina hurried forward as the front door was pulled open. *Trust Beaumont to be watching for her.* She led the way across the entrance hall to the stairs and started to climb. Thank heavens the strength had returned to her legs.

She stole a look at the doctor over her shoulder. Would he think her irresponsible for leaving Billy and Emma? "My maid Sally is with the children. They were napping and I had to speak with my brother about a few things I need for them. I've been away from Philadelphia for ten years and I'm not yet familiar with the shops and craftsmen."

Laina clamped her mouth closed. She was babbling. Suddenly having children was playing havoc with her usual poise and self-confidence, not to mention her manners. Her private life held no interest for Dr. Allen.

"I believe your brother once mentioned that you and your husband resided in New York. Does Philadelphia compare favorably with that metropolis?"

Laina winced inwardly at the polite inquiry. Obviously the doctor's good manners had prompted a response to her inane prattling. "I believe so." She started down the hallway to Billy's room. He fell into step beside her. "Philadelphia is the smaller of the two, of course. It's also much cleaner. And more friendly, in my opinion."

He gave a polite nod and reached to open the bedroom door. Laina almost jumped as his arm brushed against hers. She frowned. Her nerves were more tightly strung than she'd realized.

"...I'm thinking of an animal on a rug, that curls up so very snug."

"I know! I know! A dog!"

Laina smiled and forgot about her taut nerves as Emma blurted out her answer to Sally's riddle.

"It ain't either. It's a cat." Billy's voice was full of an older brother's disdain. "Dogs can't curl up like cats do."

"They can so!"

"No, they can't!"

"Can so!"

An argument! Laina stepped into the room. "You must be feeling better, Billy."

Both children stared at her in surprise.

Sally rose and bobbed her head.

Laina dismissed the maid, then held out her arms as Emma scrambled down the bedside steps and ran to her. "Billy says dogs can't curl up like cats!"

"Billy is older, Emma. You should listen when he tells you something. He's right about cats. They can curl right up into a warm snuggly ball!" She caught herself before adding *the way you do under the covers in bed at night.* Emma had no experience of warm cozy blankets. Anger toward all the people who had turned a blind eye to these children's needs shot through her. She pushed the anger away and walked to the bed.

"And Billy, perhaps the next time you are teaching Emma something, you can be a little more gentle in the way you speak to her." Laina smiled down at him. "She seems to have a bit of a fighting spirit." She winked at him, hugged Emma, then took a chance and gave in to her longing to kiss the toddler's smooth little cheek.

Emma's eyes widened. "What's that?"

She didn't even know what a kiss was! Did Billy? Had no one ever shown them love? Tears smarted at the backs of Laina's eyes. She blinked them away and smiled. "That was a kiss. And here's another." She kissed Emma's cheek again. "And this is a hug." She squeezed the little girl tight against her.

Emma giggled. "I can do that!" She threw her thin little arms around Laina's neck, kissed her on the cheek then leaned back and looked at her. "I wanna kiss Billy, too. I won't hurt his head—heart's promise." She pointed a little finger straight at her. "You said you gots to do a heart's promise, so I will."

Laina couldn't speak. Her heart was so full she could barely contain her joy. She nodded and lowered Emma to the bed. The little girl crawled to Billy's side, carefully kissed his cheek, then rose onto her knees and peered down at him. "That's a kiss, Billy. Do you like it? I do."

The young boy pressed his lips tightly together, closed his eyes and gave a tiny, almost imperceptible nod.

Laina turned away to hide the tears she couldn't control.

"Don't move your head, son." Thad stepped up to the bed, pressed his fingertips to Billy's wrist and counted his pulse, giving everyone a little time to gain control of their emotions, including himself. It worked. Out of the corner of his eye he watched Laina take a deep breath, wipe the tears from her cheeks and turn back toward the bed. A frown knit his brows together. When had he stopped thinking of her as Mrs. Brighton? He shoved the thought away and looked back down at Billy. "How are you feeling today, son? Is your head better?"

"Some." Billy opened his eyes. "She put cold cloths on it."

Thad followed the boy's gaze to Laina. Worry clouded her eyes. Those incredible eyes, glistening from her tears.

"I hope that was all right? I've heard cold cloths help headaches." Her voice was soft, hesitant, concerned.

Thad nodded. Relief replaced the worry in her eyes. He tore his gaze away from her face and focused his attention back on Billy. "And what about your stomach, son? Do you still feel sick?"

"When I move my head quicklike."

"Yes. You have to remember not to do that." Thad pulled the covers back and examined Billy's leg. The bruise was fading. He covered him up again. "Does it bother you when you eat?"

"Nah. Eatin's all right."

"Good." Thad refrained from looking back at Laina. "Have your cook add some soft vegetables to Billy's broth tonight, Mrs. Brighton. But no meats yet. He can have breads, too."

"And a cookie!"

Thad grinned and tweaked Emma's nose. "Yes, Sunshine, Billy may have a cookie." He looked down at the boy. "How's that sound, son?"

"All right, I guess."

Billy's voice was gruff, but there was a distinct shine in his brown eyes.

Thad turned to Laina. She was looking at Billy, her blue eyes luminous, a half smile curving her wine-red lips. Full, soft-looking lips. His pulse did a mad sprint. He scowled and cleared his throat. "I'll return tonight to see how Billy tolerates the food, Mrs. Brighton. Good day."

"Good day, Dr. Allen."

The sound of her soft, cultured voice followed him as he left the room.

The sunshine had disappeared. A storm must be brewing—it was too early for nightfall. Laina placed the empty supper trays on the nightstand, glanced at the children resting on the bed eating their cookies and walked over to look outside.

Dark clouds hung in layers across the early-evening sky, blocking the sunlight. Laina took an appreciative sniff of the rain-scented air and lowered her gaze to the trees being whipped into a frenzied dance by the rising wind. How should she ask Billy and Emma about staying with her and being her children? Were they even old enough to understand all it would mean?

Rain spattered against the windowpane and made tiny pools on the exposed sill, announcing the storm's arrival. She pushed the nagging questions aside and reached to close the window. Lightning glinted across the sky, staying her hand. Thunder rumbled across the heavens.

"It's lightnin', Billy!"

Laina whirled at the panic in Emma's voice. The little girl was pressed as close as she could get to her brother's side, her face buried in his undershirt. "Emma dear, there's nothing to be afraid—"

There was a loud crack as lightning streaked to the earth, darting its brilliance into the room. Thunder rolled, blocking out all other sound save Emma's scream.

Laina spun about, slammed the window shut and yanked the curtains across it. Lightning flashed again. She ran to the other window and repeated the process, then rushed to the bed. Emma was sobbing. She reached for the little girl, then froze as her gaze fell on Billy's face. His lips were quivering and he'd gone pale as the sheet he rested on.

Lightning sizzled to earth again, the white brightness visible even through the curtains she'd drawn. Billy jerked. Emma wailed.

Laina yanked the ties that held back the blue bed curtains, climbed inside the dark cocoon they made and pulled both children into her arms. They were trembling. She leaned back against the headboard and cuddled them close. "Shh, Emma, don't be afraid. I'm here. You're all right. Shh…shh."

"She's sc-scared cause she's a girl an' she's little. An' 'cause lightning hit the sh-shed we was sleepin' in one night an' it catched afire. Bobby and Joe burned up." Billy shuddered.

Laina gasped and tightened her hold on him. "Well, Emma doesn't have to be afraid anymore. You'll never sleep in a shed again! *This* is your home now. I want you and Emma to stay right here with me. I'll take care of you and Emma. You won't ever have to pretend you have a mama again—I'll be your mama." She looked down at the young boy trying so hard to be brave. "Do you understand me, Billy? You're going to stay here with me and we'll be a family in our hearts. I'm not *ever* going to let you go!"

He jerked back, staring at her.

Laina took one look at the shock on his face and could have cut out her tongue. What had she done? Would he grab Emma and run away as soon as he was able? "Billy, I—" She stopped, aghast, as tears rolled down his cheeks.

Billy threw himself against her shoulder, sobs shaking his thin body. "Everybody always only…only ch-chased us away."

"*Oh, Billy.*" Laina squeezed the crying boy against her. She tried to take a deep breath to calm herself, but her chest was so tight with anger it was impossible. She laid her cheek against his, promising herself no one would ever hurt him or Emma again. But what about all the other children who lived alone on the streets? How many of them were frightened or cold and wet because they had no place to shelter from the storm? How many of them had never been kissed or hugged? Tears slid down her face and dampened the bandage on Billy's head. Who would help those children?

"Good evening, Dr. Allen." The butler gave him a polite bow. "Mrs. Brighton wishes to see you in the parlor. If you will follow me?"

What was this about? Thad frowned, followed the butler down the length of the entrance hall, then stepped forward as Beaumont bowed him into the room. Laina Brighton was pacing back and forth, an intent look on her face. "You wished to speak with me, Mrs. Brighton? Is there a problem with Billy?"

Laina whirled to face him. "No. Yes! That is, not anymore." She gave him a radiant smile. "The children have agreed to stay with me."

"That's wonderful!" Thad grinned at her excitement. "I'm happy for you, and for Billy and Emma. They are blessed to be in your care."

"Thank you, Dr. Allen. You're very kind." She took a deep breath in an obvious effort to curb her emotions, and walked toward him. "Please come in. I have many questions to ask you."

Thad moved into the room, set his bag on a chair and fixed a curious gaze on her. "What sort of questions?"

"About the orphans roaming the streets."

Surprise lifted his brows. "I'm not sure I have any answers for you, Mrs. Brighton. But I'll do my best. What specifically do you want to know?"

"Everything! Please have a seat." She moved to the couch. "I'm afraid I have no spirits in the house. May I offer you tea or coffee? Or perhaps cider?"

"Nothing, thank you." Thad seated himself in one of the chairs opposite her.

Laina nodded, gave him a polite smile and folded her hands in her lap. "Then I shall come straight to the crux of the matter. You seem very familiar with the plight of these children, Dr. Allen. May I inquire how you learned about them?"

"By observation." He enlarged on his answer. "I constantly traverse the streets of Philadelphia on my way to and from my patients' homes, Mrs. Brighton. It would be difficult *not* to know about the orphans."

Her eyes flashed with angry sparks. "It seems others are quite able to ignore what is before their eyes, Doctor." The index fingers of her folded hands straightened and tapped against one another. "And do you have contact with many of these children?"

Thad studied her face. She looked ready to do battle. "As many as I'm able to entice out of hiding."

Her gaze sharpened. "And how do you do that?"

"Any way that I can. Usually by promising I will not turn them over to the authorities, but will find them a home."

"But I thought—?" She stopped, staring at him. "Where do you find homes for them?"

"Among my patients." Thad blew out a breath and ran his hand through his hair, frowning as his cowlick popped free. "But the truth is, I'm running out of people both willing and able to provide for a child. Most of my wealthier patients refuse them." He brushed at the lock of hair falling on his forehead.

"I'm appalled, but not surprised. Not after what Billy told me earlier." Laina shot to her feet.

Thad rose and stood by his chair, following her with his gaze as she began to stride about the room. She was clearly angry, but there was something more...

"He said everyone always chased them away. That he and Emma slept in a shed and lightning struck it!" She whirled to face him. "It caught afire. Can you imagine their fright? And no one helped them! How can people be so uncaring about these children?"

"I don't know that they're *all* uncaring, Mrs. Brighton. A few are, of course—"

"Like that wretched man whose carriage ran Billy over!" She stared at him, her eyes daring him to disagree with her. He didn't. He nodded and looked away. He had to. Her rigid posture, raised chin and clenched hands made him want to smile. Laina Brighton was a fighter of the first order, at least as far as children were concerned.

"I've done a lot of thinking since talking with Billy, Doctor." Her voice had gone quiet-serious. Thad looked back and met her steady gaze. "These street children must have a home, and I intend to see that they get one. I want to start an orphanage."

"An orphanage!" Thad gaped at her, astounded by her pronouncement. He didn't doubt her sincerity—there was total conviction in her voice and unwavering determination on her face. But surely she didn't understand the vast and varied components of such a project, let alone the prejudice she would be up against. He gave a low whistle and ran his hand through his hair again, weighing his words. "Mrs. Brighton, I appreciate how you feel, but an orphanage is a tremendous undertaking."

"I realize that, Dr. Allen. And I don't fool myself that I can do it alone." She hurried over and stood looking up at him. "I intend to enlist the aid of others, including my brother…and you."

His face went slack with shock.

Laina Brighton pulled herself to her full height and locked her dark blue eyes on his. "I would like you to be one of my advisers, Dr. Allen, as well as physician to the children when the orphanage is opened. Will you accept the positions? I'll pay for your time, of course."

Thad stared down at her, trying to grasp the concept of a society woman such as Laina Brighton running an orphanage. She had a heart for the children, but… But *what?* Did the rest matter? Workers could be hired. Problems could be solved or circumvented. Her heart full of love for the children was most important.

Excitement coursed through Thad. He had failed in his attempts to garner support for these street children from the wealthy members of Philadelphia society, but perhaps they would rally behind one of their own. Maybe Laina Brighton *could* succeed. He inclined his head. "I shall be happy to accept both positions, Mrs. Brighton, on one condition."

A wary look sprang into her eyes. "And that is?"

Thad smiled. "I shall serve without recompense. I care about these children, too."

"But that's wonderful! Thank you so much for accepting, Doctor." She clasped her hands in front of her chest and gave him a happy smile. "And as we shall be working together, Dr. Allen, please call me Laina."

"I shall be pleased to do so…Laina." He made his voice stronger, more businesslike. "If you will call me Thad."

She dipped her head. "Very well…Thad." She took a quick little breath. "And there's one thing more before we go upstairs to check on Billy. Should you happen across any more children in need and have difficulty placing them with loving families, please bring them to me." A shadow of sadness darkened her eyes. "I may not be able to provide them with a father—" she took a deep breath "—but I can give them love and a comfortable home." Another smile curved her lips, chased the shadow from her eyes and shot straight to his heart.

Thad nodded and reached for his bag as an excuse to turn away. He was suddenly, *undeniably* certain he'd just made a huge mistake—it was not wise for him to spend time with Laina Brighton.

Chapter Ten

It felt odd sitting in the Twiggs pew—the *Brighton* pew now—while Justin and Elizabeth occupied the Randolph pew in front of her. Laina smoothed a fold in the skirt of her dress, ignored the urge to adjust the large decorative comb in her hair and stared at the pulpit, concentrating on its design, disregarding the pastor's sermon about God's blessings. *Blessings?* There was no husband sitting beside her. No baby she'd prayed ten years for!

Laina suppressed a frown and slid her gaze sideways, seeking distraction from her sour thoughts. Her lips curved into a smile as she watched covert glances being exchanged between a young man and woman obviously more interested in each other than in the pastor's message.

Laina came to herself with a start as the congregation rose as one. She hurried to stand and bow her head as the minister intoned his closing words. At last! Now she could go home to Billy and Emma. She tossed her lace shawl around her shoulders, picked up her reticule and stepped into the aisle, joining the flow of people heading for the door as Justin made space for her.

The line stopped. Started. Stopped again. *Bother!* What was causing the delay? She tapped her foot in impatience, willing the people ahead of her to move on.

"Relax, Laina." Justin's warm breath swept across her cheek as he leaned forward and whispered in her ear. "It's only people saying goodbye to the pastor. You'll be out soon."

She glanced over her shoulder at him. "Not nearly soon enough, dearheart!"

The line moved forward again.

They were next! Laina looked longingly at the door. Justin's hand gripped her elbow, tugged her aside. "Sir, perhaps you remember my sister, Laina Brighton? She's recently moved back to Philadelphia from New York."

The minister smiled. "Of course I remember her. One does not forget someone as lovely and lively as your sister, Mr. Randolph." He took her hand. "Welcome back to Philadelphia, Mrs. Brighton. I was certain that was you in the Twiggs pew." His smile faded and a look of compassion warmed his eyes. "I heard of your husband's passing. I hope you were encouraged by today's sermon."

"Thank you for your kind words, sir—oh!" Laina jolted forward, bumped by a man squeezing by her in the press of people. The pastor caught her arm and steadied her.

The man turned and gave a curt bow of his head. "Excuse me, madam, I didn't mean to— *You!*"

Laina glanced up. Anger stiffened her spine. "I see you make a habit of running people over, sir!" She shifted her gaze back to the minister. "Today's sermon about God's blessings may have been meant to encourage, Reverend Brown, but in my opinion *some* members of your congregation would be better served by a message about learning to do for others less fortunate. They have already learned well how to amass blessings unto themselves!" She gave the man a pointed look, nodded politely to the pastor and stormed out the door beside him.

"I'm sorry I embarrassed you, dearheart. I shouldn't have stalked off and left you to deal with that situation, but that horrid man makes me so angry! When I think that he was going to drive away and leave Billy lying injured in the street, I simply…well…I lose my composure."

Justin snorted.

Laina paused as they turned the corner at Walnut Street and gave him a rueful look. "Was Pastor Brown angry?"

"I think dumbfounded would be a better definition." Justin looked down at her. The corners of his mouth twitched. "He's not accustomed to the members of his congregation telling him what to speak on, especially when they've been away for ten years and have only just returned."

Her cheeks heated.

Elizabeth shook her head. "Justin, stop teasing her."

He looked down at his wife and grinned. "All right, but she deserves it. Watch that rough spot in the brick." He took them each by the elbow and guided them around it. "Everything is smoothed over, Laina. I told him what prompted your outburst and he was very understanding. In fact, he intends to speak with Henry Rhodes about his callous disregard for a child's well-being." His grin returned. "I'd like to be there for that meeting."

"Well, I wouldn't." Laina gave a haughty toss of her head and started up the gravel drive to her house. "I hope I never see that heartless *pygmy* of a man again! Now, let's forget about him and have our dinner."

"I must say, Laina, the house looks wonderful." Justin propped his elbow on the mantel and grinned down at her. "Even I can appreciate the job you've done decorating it."

"Thank you, dearheart. I'm pleased you like it."

"I think it's beautiful." Elizabeth smiled and swept her gaze around the drawing room. "Look at these wonderful vibrant colors! I would never have the courage to use them together."

Laina set her empty cup on the piecrust tea table. "No one who knows your story can accuse you of a lack of courage, Elizabeth." She laughed. "I think perhaps *boldness* is the more accurate description of my decorative talents. Subtlety is not my long suit."

"How true."

Laina grinned at Justin's dry comment. "That being the case, dearheart…"

"Uh-oh."

She wrinkled her nose at him. "I shall tell you I had an ulterior motive for inviting you to dinner—not that your charming company isn't reason enough." She took a deep breath. "I've decided something must be done about the orphans living on the streets of Philadelphia." She glanced at Elizabeth, then fastened her gaze on

Justin. "I want to establish an orphanage, and I want you both to help."

"What?" Justin jerked erect. "Establish an orphanage! Laina, you're going too far. I know you're fond of these children you've taken into your home, but—"

"How can I help, Laina?"

Justin's mouth gaped open. His gaze darted to his wife's face. "Elizabeth, what are you saying? She can't—"

"Yes, dear, with the Lord's help, she can. And I believe this is the Lord's will for Laina." Elizabeth's voice was firm, her gaze steady on Justin's. "I believe this is the answer to our prayers for her and that we should help her any way we can. We have been blessed by the Lord, Justin. Don't you feel as I do, as Laina said to Pastor Brown, that it's time to share the blessing?"

Laina couldn't help smiling, even if Elizabeth *was* talking about the Lord. She'd never seen her brother look so unsettled. He stared at Elizabeth for a long moment, then took a deep breath and slowly nodded his head.

Excitement spurted through Laina. Did that mean he would help her? She wiped the smile from her face as he turned back to her. "All right, sister of mine, what do you want me to do?"

She was stunned by the rapid capitulation. She had expected, at the least, a lecture, if not outright refusal. Laina shot Elizabeth a look of gratitude and hurriedly gathered her thoughts. "I want you to be one of my advisers."

She rose and rushed to hug Justin. "I know I can't do this by myself, dearheart. I need you." She went to hug Elizabeth. "I need you both. Thank you so much for agreeing to help me."

Laina pulled a list from her pocket and went back to her chair. "I've written down my thoughts. The first thing, of course, is to find a suitable place." She glanced up. "I thought you might know of one, Justin. It must be large, of course—at least four floors. And have a vast lawn to allow for expansion, for kitchen gardens *and* for the children to play." She stopped as Justin shook his head. "What is it?"

"You're wrong, Laina. The first matter is funding. You'll have to pay for this property."

She gave him an exasperated look. "I'm aware of that, Justin. I intend to use the money from the sale of my house in New York instead of investing it. That should be ample. If it's not, I'll use some of the money Stanford left me." She frowned at him. "Justin, *do* stop shaking your head in that negative way or we'll never get this list covered."

"If you want me to stop shaking my head, Laina, you'll have to be more reasonable in your thinking." He held up a hand to forestall her protests and walked over to take a seat beside her at the tea table. "Stanford named me to oversee the fortune he left you, because he trusted me to keep it intact and increase it. I'll not let you toss it away on this venture."

She surged to her feet, glaring at him. "Justin Davidson Randolph, if you think you—!"

"Sit down, Laina." He grasped her arm and tugged. She plopped back onto her chair. "If you want this orphanage to succeed you must think of it as a business."

She jumped to her feet again. "Children are *not* a business!"

"No, they're not. But caring for them in large numbers takes a vast amount of continuous funding the same as running a business does." He looked at her. She sat. He nodded and continued. "Providing a building for orphans to live in is only the first step." He ticked items off on his fingers. "You have to furnish the rooms and hire staff. You have to provide food, clothing, medical care, schooling and a hundred other things for the children."

"Yes, but I have—"

"No, Laina, you don't." Justin covered her hand with his. "I know you feel strongly about these children, but you have to be sensible. Your fortune would be sufficient to purchase the property and get it established, but the remainder would soon be eaten up by the day-to-day cost of maintaining it. You need financial backing—and that means support from the city or from private donations." He squeezed her hand. "I know you're disappointed you can't rush ahead with this, Laina, but if you want the orphanage to prosper, your first step must be establishing financial support." He smiled at her. "So use some of that emotional fire you're expending on me to garner it."

Laina stared at him, then jumped from her chair and threw her arms around his neck, almost toppling them both to the floor. "You see, dearheart, I *told* you I needed you. You're so calm and sensible! You can carry our case before the city fathers." She glanced at Elizabeth. "And we shall have to plan several small dinner parties and invite potential financial supporters. Oh, and intimate teas for their wives!"

She looked back at Justin. "We'll need your help with the guest lists—you know, those wealthy enough to help." She smiled. "Meanwhile, I need the name of that carpenter I inquired about. As I'm sure you could tell by my presence in church this morning, Billy and Emma agreed to stay and be my children!"

Laina rose from the chaise, pulled her dressing gown on and walked to the bed to look at the sleeping children. Her children. She couldn't believe it, couldn't grasp it. She'd waited so long. And now she was going to start an orphanage.

I believe this is the Lord's will for Laina. I believe this is the answer to our prayers for her.

A chill raced down her spine and prickled her flesh at the memory of Elizabeth's words. Laina closed her eyes and hugged herself against the chill. God's plan for her. An answer to their prayers. Another chill chased through her body.

Laina opened her eyes and crossed to the window, looking up at the starlit sky. Elizabeth was always so certain when she spoke about God. But Elizabeth wasn't barren after ten years of prayers for a baby. As far as she was concerned, it was all a coincidence. There was no way to know.

Laina frowned and walked back to the chaise. Elizabeth reminded her of Grandmother Davidson—she was always reading the Bible, and Grandmother Davidson had said many times that the answer to every question or situation in life could be found in God's word.

Laina pursed her lips. If that was true, then the Bible should tell her if God heard and answered prayers. Then she would know if He had a plan for her life. Determination rose within her. She was going to find out the truth. She closed her eyes, searching through her memory for where she had seen Abigail's Bible. She recalled it resting on the fruitwood table at the end of the couch in the library. She'd left it there for effect—and to keep Justin from asking where it was.

A twinge of guilt pricked Laina's conscience. She ignored it and glanced at the bed. The children would be all right for the few minutes it would take her to run downstairs and get the Bible. She stepped into her slippers and hurried from the room.

There! Laina checked the children, settled herself comfortably in the padded chair and pulled the candle she'd lit closer. She would start with Psalms. She rather liked the poetic quality of them.

She lifted Abigail's Bible into her lap and reached to open the cover. There was a tiny gap in the pages. She frowned. Something was stuck in there. She thumbed through to find whatever it was, went too far and started back. A piece of folded paper was wedged near the spine. She took it out and opened it, scanning Abigail's shaky, but familiar handwriting.

Dear Gracious Lord,

I don't know how much longer I will be aware or have the strength to pray, so I am writing out my prayer for Justin and Elizabeth and placing it here, in Your word, beside the appropriate verse, James 5:16.

I have spoken with Justin and Elizabeth, but they will not yield and I am too weak to do more.

Dear Lord, override their stubborn pride, I pray. Their love for each other is strong and beautiful, and I know they belong together, for I see Your hand in their beginning. Have Your way in their lives, my Lord, have Your way. I ask it in Your holy name.

* * *

Laina's vision blurred. How beautiful! She was glad Abigail had lived long enough to know Justin and Elizabeth had admitted their love for one another and become a true husband and wife. But was it an answered prayer?

Laina wiped the tears from her cheeks, blinked them from her eyes and glanced at the paper—*appropriate verse, James 5:16.* She looked down at the page and read the verse. "Confess your faults one to another, and pray one for another, that ye may be healed. The effectual fervent prayer of a righteous man availeth much."

Laina stared at the page. She read the verse again trying to absorb it, to change her way of thinking. It was difficult to do when she had doubted for so long. She looked over at the bed, at the children sleeping so soundly. *Her* children. The answer to her years of prayers?

Laina sighed, folded Abigail's note and tucked it back where it had been. Try as she might, she couldn't make herself believe that. If God was answering her prayers she would have a baby growing in her womb. *That* would be the true answer—to have the child of a husband who loved her growing in her womb, and that would never happen. But she shouldn't hold it against God. It wasn't His fault her prayers went unanswered. She asked too much.

She sighed and closed her eyes. "Forgive me, Lord, for being angry with You. For turning my back on You when I didn't receive an answer to my prayers. I'm sorry, Lord. Please forgive me my impatience and selfishness." A sense of peace enveloped her. She suddenly felt light, as if a weight had been lifted from her. How odd.

Laina lifted the Bible to the table beside her, blew out the candle, then rose and walked to the bed to look at Billy and Emma. She couldn't get enough of looking at them. It didn't matter that her prayers hadn't been answered. She would settle for this. These children were enough. She brushed a curl off Billy's forehead, leaned down to kiss the spot she had bared, then kissed Emma's cheek and pulled the covering sheet over them both. How many children had no bed to sleep in, no one to tuck them in or kiss them good-night? No one to take care of them if they were ill or hurt?

Laina straightened and crossed to the window. She stood looking out into the night, her heart aching for all the homeless children roaming Philadelphia's streets trying to find a safe place to sleep. What if Elizabeth and Justin and Grandmother Davidson and Abigail were right? What if God *did* answer prayer the way the Bible said? The fact that *her* prayers went unanswered didn't mean it wasn't so. Maybe it was only for some people.

Laina caught her breath at that thought. Surely God would care about the children. She closed her eyes. "Dear Gracious Lord, I don't know if it is Your will for me to start an orphanage. I confess I don't understand about such things. But I do know these children of the streets have no home and no one to care for them. Please, *please* help me to start an orphanage that will meet their needs. Please bring it to pass, heavenly Father, for I ask it in the name of Your Son. Amen."

Laina opened her eyes and walked back to the chaise. Whether the prayer was answered or not, it made her feel better to ask God's help for the orphans. She shrugged out of her dressing gown and slid beneath the covers. Maybe now she could sleep.

* * *

"Very nice, Miss Benson. You're very talented." Laina met the older woman's gaze in the dressing-table mirror. "How many years were you with Mrs. Thorndyke?"

"Seven, madam."

Laina nodded. She liked this woman Elizabeth had sent to interview as a possible replacement for Annette. She was neat and clean, pleasant and well-spoken. And her qualifications were certainly in order. But how would she feel about the children?

Laina rose and turned to face her. "Miss Benson, I have recently taken two young street children under my charge. The boy was injured when run down by a carriage as he was fleeing from the shopkeeper from whom he'd stolen two rolls—"

"The poor lamb!" Cora Benson flushed and stood a little straighter. "I beg your pardon, Mrs. Brighton. I didn't mean to interrupt."

Laina smiled. "That was the very reaction I was hoping for, Miss Benson. Please don't apologize for caring about the children." Her smile widened. "The position is yours, Cora. I'll have Carlson take you home to get your things and when you return, Mrs. Barnes will show you to your room."

"My, there is certainly a lot of activity going on around here." Elizabeth glanced at the gazebo being built at the end of the stone path, then swept her gaze over the men uprooting one of the formal gardens a short distance away. "Is that where the playhouse is going?"

"Yes. And the swings will be in that large oak tree. Excuse me, Elizabeth." Laina stood. "Billy, Dr. Allen said you mustn't run. Please *roll* the ball with Emma." She took her seat on the garden bench again. "It's so hard for Billy to stay quiet when he feels so much better. And there's no bandage on his head to remind Emma she must still be careful with him."

"It's been almost two weeks now—how much longer will it be before Billy is pronounced fully recovered?"

Laina shook her head. "I don't know. But I'm sure it will be soon. Thad checks on him every day."

"Thad?" Elizabeth's eyebrows rose. "Who is Thad?"

"Dr. Allen." Laina waved away a buzzing fly. "His name is Thaddeous, and as he will be one of my advisers as well as physician to the children, we decided it would be expedient to use first names."

"Expedient. I see."

Laina felt like squirming under Elizabeth's steady regard. She looked down, smoothed a wrinkle from her skirt and changed the subject. "Miss Tobin is wonderful with the children. She's an excellent nanny." She looked up and smiled. "I can't thank you enough, Elizabeth, for your help in finding people to fill all these positions. I'm so grateful to you and Justin. I'd have been lost trying to locate carpenters and other workers here in Philadelphia."

"It's our pleasure, Laina." Elizabeth glanced toward the third-floor windows of the house. "How's the nursery coming along?"

"More quickly than I imagined—and not as fast as I'd hoped." Laina laughed and smoothed back a tendril of hair that had come loose in the soft, warm breeze. "I'm a little concerned about putting Billy and Emma in separate bedrooms. They've never been apart." She sighed. "I'm hoping the special toys and furniture in the rooms will entice them to agree."

"I'm sure it will work out, Laina. They're lovely children. And they respond beautifully to your love and care."

"Do you truly think so?"

"I do."

"But they sometimes argue, and I'm not certain what to do about it. I'm sort of feeling my way along this path of motherhood." She gave Elizabeth a rueful smile and glanced at the children. "Billy can be bossy, and Emma... well, Emma can be very...opinionated."

Elizabeth laughed. "Emma and Billy have had no opportunity to learn proper social behavior living on the streets. Stop worrying. They'll be fine now that they're with you."

Laina stared at her. "I am worrying, aren't I? I didn't realize..." She gave a little shake of her head and laughed. "I'm not accustomed to feeling this way, but then, I've never been so unsure of myself. Thank you, Elizabeth, for sharing your wisdom. You're a wonderful encouragement to me."

"You're welcome, Laina. And here's another bit of advice I'll share with you. The next time you feel anxious over Emma's opinionated behavior, think of Mary." She grinned. "That should make you feel better."

Laina burst into laughter. "Ah, yes, Mary, the little extortionist. I'd forgotten."

"What's this? My daughter an extortionist? Surely you are mistaken." Justin grinned as he came down the stone walkway to join them. He waved to Billy and Emma, then bent and kissed his wife and gave Laina a hug. "I have news."

"What sort of news, dearheart?"

"Well, first, during the last two weeks I have talked with several members of the city government. They all say there is no money available for an orphanage at this time. It seems private funding will be our only resource."

Laina's heart sank right to her shoes. She straightened her shoulders. "Very well. Then we shall acquire private supporters." She looked at Justin. "You said *first*. What is the other news?"

"It's about a possible property for the orphanage." He held up a hand as Laina sucked in her breath and clasped her hands in front of her chest. "I said *possible*, Laina. This place came to mind as soon as you told us of your plans, and I've been doing some quiet investigating."

"*And?*"

"Patience." Justin grinned and took a seat in one of the chairs placed at right angles to the bench she and Elizabeth sat on. "Laurelwood is located on Vine Street. It's a large stone home of three full stories with dormers in its mansard roof and plenty of land on either side for future additions. There is spacious acreage in back with existing gardens and lawn area."

"It sounds perfect!" Laina jumped to her feet and hugged Justin. "May I see it? Who owns it? When do we buy it?"

"Not so fast, Laina. There's a problem."

"A *problem*." She sank back onto the bench beside Elizabeth. "What is it?"

"The property is entailed." Justin frowned. "A rather unusual entailment that might in the end work to our advantage."

"I don't understand." Laina folded her hands in her lap to keep from shaking the information out of him. Patience had never been one of her strongest virtues. "If it will work to our advantage, why is it a problem?"

Justin shook his head. "You have a knack for ignoring words like *might*, Laina. I said it *might*, in the *end*, prove advantageous. Simply put, the entailment states the property is to go to any of the deceased owner's German male descendants, ranked by age, who may submit a claim within one year from the date of her death. In lieu of any proven descendant coming forward, the property is to be sold to the highest bidder, the sum payable to her attorney. There is a proviso, however. The property may be used as a residence only—no business may be set up there. And—" he smiled "—the proviso further states Laurelwood is to go to the prospective purchaser with the greatest need."

Laina stared at him. "But that's wonderful! I see no problem. Who has a greater need than these children? Unless…" She frowned. "Is an orphanage considered a residence?"

Justin nodded. "It is."

"Then the problem is a descendant?"

"Possibly—yes. None have appeared thus far, but there are still six months left until the one-year anniversary date of the owner's death."

"Six months!"

Justin's mouth twisted into a wry smile. "And there is the other problem, my dear sister—your impatience." He leaned back in his chair. "The waiting period will give us time to work on securing funding."

"Funding." The word was bitter in her mouth. Laina looked at Billy and Emma, who had stopped playing with the ball and were sitting in the shade of a tree watching the workers tear up the garden. "I know you think I'm being rash and impulsive, but I'm not. At least, not for myself." She shifted her gaze back to Justin. "Six months is a very long time when you're young and alone and hungry."

"I'm turning her over to the law, I tell you! I'm sick of these children stealing from us! Why, it's not safe for my wife to put pies out to cool on our own porch!"

"I understand, sir." Thad looked at the skinny, pale-faced, tight-lipped girl in the furious man's grip. She was frightened to death. He lifted his gaze to the man's face. "But if you'll allow me to take her in my charge, I give you my pledge she'll never have to steal food to eat again."

"I don't know…"

"Look at her, sir. She's starving. I know. I'm a doctor."

"A doctor?" The man lifted a respectful gaze to him.

Thad pressed his advantage. "Yes. Please have mercy, sir. Wouldn't you want someone to show your children mercy if they were starving and had to steal to survive?"

The man scowled, looked down at the girl, then thrust her arm that he was holding toward Thad. "Take her, then! But see she never steals from me again!"

"You have my word, sir." Thad grasped the young girl's elbow and rushed her toward his carriage before the man changed his mind.

"Let me go!"

Thad tightened his grip as the girl tried to pull away. "Stop fighting me. The man is watching. Do you want him to turn you over to the law?"

She lifted a defiant face to him. "I'm not getting in your carriage. I'll not be alone with you."

Thad gaped at her. Her voice was cultured, though quivering with fear. He swept his gaze over her. Her clothes were soiled and torn, but of high quality, her face and hands dirt-smudged, but basically clean. He caught a glimpse of movement out of the corner of his eye and shot a look back at the porch he'd half dragged her away from. The man was coming down the steps, a deep scowl on his face.

The girl followed the direction of his gaze, gasped and jerked around toward the carriage. "Your hand, sir."

She was obviously used to riding in carriages. Thad helped her to her seat, then climbed to his own. Faithful lurched forward, pulling the buggy out into the street.

"You may let me off at the corner."

Thad glanced at his young passenger. Her features were delicate, though pinched with fear, her stature small, her posture correct. Her hair was tangled, but he could tell she'd made an effort to groom it. This was no ordinary street child. "Look, Miss…?" He waited, hoping for a name. There was none forthcoming. She merely clamped her lips together and looked away. "I don't know what has happened to so frighten you of men, miss, but I assure you you're safe with me. I'm a doctor. I help people, I don't harm them."

Tears shimmered in her eyes. She bit down on her lower lip and clasped her hands tightly in her lap. She looked about twelve, maybe thirteen. Thad's hands tightened on the reins. He'd like to get hold of whoever had caused such fear. He nodded toward the seat between them. "Open that bag. You'll see I'm telling you the truth. It's my medical kit."

She stared at him for a moment, then pulled the bag close to her on the seat and opened it.

"Don't take out the cloths. I want them to stay clean."
He smiled down at her. "I believe cleanliness is important
to healing, though my colleagues don't agree with me."

He guided Faithful onto Walnut Street while the girl
was looking into the bag. "I have a friend, a lady friend—
her name is Mrs. Brighton. I think you would like her."
The girl lifted her head, and her nostrils flared as if sniff-
ing danger. Thad kept his voice calm. "She helps children
in trouble. I know she'd welcome you into her home if
you'd care to stay with her awhile. She lives a few houses
down this street. Shall I take you there? You can, at least,
have a wash and a good meal."

Lord, help her to know she can trust me. He sat looking
straight ahead, praying. He could see her studying him,
trying to decide what to do. *Please let her agree, Lord.*

At last she nodded. "Very well, I will go and meet your
friend." Her little chin rose. "And then I shall see if I wish
to stay or leave."

Relief surged through Thad. *Thank You, Lord.* He guided
Faithful into the drive leading to Twiggs Manor.

Thad was waiting for her in the parlor with a young girl.
Perhaps she was to have another child. Laina hurried into
the room, and her heart jumped right into her throat
when she saw the dirty, disheveled condition of the girl
sitting on the couch. She darted a look at Thad.

He gave her a polite nod. "Mrs. Brighton, I have
brought you a guest for tea." There was a warning look
in his eyes, the slightest emphasis on the word *guest*. He
was acting odd. She turned toward the girl, masking her
confusion as he continued his introduction. "I'd like you
to meet Miss…"

"Altman. Audrey Altman." The young girl rose and made her a perfect curtsy. "It's so kind of you to agree to receive me on such short notice, Mrs. Brighton. I apologize for my appearance. I…" The girl's lips quivered. She squared her shoulders. "I have fallen on hard times."

Why, she couldn't be more than eleven or twelve! Laina squelched her desire to rush over and take the girl into her arms. Instead, she took her cue from the girl's own demeanor and acknowledged the apology with a polite nod of her head. "I'm pleased to meet you, Audrey. Please sit down." She looked toward Thad, blinking rapidly to clear the gathering tears from her eyes. "Will you join us for tea, Dr. Allen?" The girl stiffened. Why?

Thad shook his head, gave her another look she couldn't read and picked up his bag. "I'll leave you ladies to your tea. I have a patient to check on." He gave a polite bow and left the room.

Laina stared after him. What did he expect of her? What was she to do now? She yanked the bellpull to summon Beaumont, then took a deep breath and turned back to Audrey. The girl was rubbing at a smudge of dirt on her hand. "Audrey."

The girl looked up, tears trembling on her lashes. Laina's heart broke. She rushed over and knelt in front of her. "Why don't we forget about tea and go upstairs so you can have a warm bath? I'll have cook make a tray and you can eat something while you soak. Would you like that?"

Audrey caught her quivering lower lip in her teeth and nodded.

"Good." Laina rose and held out her hand. "Come along with me. I have some lovely rose-scented soap you may use."

* * *

Elizabeth put down her hairbrush and looked over at Justin, already resting in the four-poster bed they shared. How blessed she was to have such a loving husband. And now perhaps Laina would be blessed, as well. She smiled. She might have been wrong when she'd imagined Laina and Henry Rhodes as a match, but— A giggle burst from her.

Justin opened his eyes. "What's so funny?"

Another giggle escaped her. "I was thinking about Laina and Henry Rhodes."

Justin propped himself on one elbow and grinned. "I could almost feel sorry for Henry. I've been on the receiving end of my sister's ire." He shook his head. "She's a tigress when angered."

"Aren't we all?"

"I suppose." Justin's eyes twinkled. "I remember our first night together at the Wetherstone Inn."

Elizabeth laughed. "In my defense, sir, I thought you had *designs* on me."

"You weren't far wrong. That's what so irritated me." Justin grimaced at the memory. "Honor is a weak defense against love."

"I don't agree." Elizabeth rose, walked to the bed and sat beside him. "You treated me honorably, and you loved me."

"Indeed I did. I was *attracted* from the moment I first saw you. But I began to *love* you when you decided to walk stocking-footed into the snow in a mistaken effort to please me."

Elizabeth's heart melted at the love in his eyes. "You never told me that was when you fell in love with me."

"I should have." Justin's voice was soft. He leaned over and kissed her.

She returned his kiss, then smiled when he came up for air. "Do you know when I began to love you?"

He went back on his elbow and propped his head up with his fist, gazing at her. "No. When?"

"The next day, when you gave me the moccasins."

"Really?"

Elizabeth smiled at his surprise. "Oh, Justin—" she threw her arms about his neck "—sometimes it frightens me to think how close we came to losing one another."

He pulled her tight against him.

"Oh!" She pulled back and looked up at him. "I wanted to tell you something!"

"What?"

"I think the Lord is answering another of our prayers for Laina."

"*Laina?*" His mouth twisted into that crooked grin she loved so much. "I wasn't expecting that." Her cheeks heated at the look in his eyes. "I love your blushes." He kissed the tip of her nose, then leaned back, tucking his hands under his head. "All right, what about Laina?"

Elizabeth smiled down at him. "We've been praying the Lord would bless Laina with a love like ours and I think He's answered our prayers. I think she and Dr. Allen are falling in love!"

"*What?*" Justin jerked to a sitting position. "Are you sure about this?"

"Well…I'm not positive. But she calls him Thad, and won't look at you when she talks about him, and he calls her Laina, and stops by every day to *check* on Billy." She giggled. "Anyone can see the boy's doing fine. He doesn't need a doctor's care any more than we need more stars in the sky."

Justin laughed. "Sounds like love to me. I remember making up excuses to be with you. How long do you suppose he'll keep that poor boy fettered as an excuse to see Laina?"

Elizabeth gaped at him. "Do you think that's what Dr. Allen is doing?"

Justin shrugged. "I can't say. I only know I loved you so much I would have done so, as long as it didn't hurt the child."

"Oh, Justin, I love you." Elizabeth scooted back into his arms and kissed him. His arms tightened about her, and all thoughts of Laina and Dr. Allen fled her mind as he returned her kiss.

The children floated at her. She grabbed them as they neared, tucked them into her heart. Her heart grew larger and larger. The man came and helped her. He caught the children and handed them to her. She looked up to thank him.

Laina shot to a sitting position in bed, her heart pounding. The stranger in her dream was Thad! She shook her head trying to rid herself of the image, but it clung like a burr to her consciousness. She took a long, slow breath to calm her racing pulse. It was *happening*. The dream was coming true. Thad was bringing her children and she was taking them into her heart and— *Oh, my!*

Laina's nerves tingled as she recalled the next part of the dream. *The man took her hand—she couldn't breathe.* And that man was *Thad?* Oh, she was being absurd! That would never happen. Why, for all she knew Thad was married with a family. And the whole thing was silly, anyway. What about Justin and his hand turning into a purse that rained money down on the children in her heart? That wasn't happening and— *The funding!* Justin was searching for financial support for the orphanage!

Chills chased up and down Laina's spine. She threw back the covers, stepped into her slippers and pulled her dressing gown on. *Did* dreams come true? Because if the dream was coming true, then Justin would get the funding they needed for the children. They would be able to start the orphanage.

Laina started pacing, thrilled at the thought. As for the other—that was foolishness. She'd never been breathless at a man's touch, not even Stanford's, and she never would be. Not now. She paused by the window, the memory of the moment she'd collided with Thad outside the house staying her steps. She'd been short of breath then—and weak in the knees, as well. Of course, that had been caused by her rapid walk home from Randolph Court… hadn't it?

Laina yanked the sash of her dressing gown tighter, whirled away from the window and hurried from her bedroom. She would go check on Billy and Emma and make sure Audrey was all right. That should bring her back to her senses. She'd had enough of this silly dreaming!

Chapter Eleven

"May I be excused, Mrs. Brighton? I'd like to go to my room now."

"Of course, Audrey."

The young girl looked at Elizabeth and smiled. "I'm pleased to have met you, Mrs. Randolph." She rose, made a polite curtsy and left the room.

"My word, Laina, she's lovely! Absolutely lovely."

Laina laughed. "You look astonished, Elizabeth."

"I *am* astonished." Elizabeth shook her head. "How did such a gently reared child come to live on the streets?"

Laina's face tightened. "Last night I finally managed to get Audrey to tell me her story. Her mother died last winter, leaving Audrey's inheritance in her stepfather's safekeeping. When the interment was over, her stepfather's grown son made improper advances to her and when Audrey told one of her mother's friends, the stepfather berated her for a troublemaker and brought her to Philadelphia, from New York, and placed her in the Cherry Street Orphanage."

Laina's fingers clenched on the handle of her teacup. She put the delicate china down before she broke it. "Audrey received nothing of her inheritance, of course, and when the orphanage burned to the ground, she—along with the rest of the orphans—was left to fend for herself. She's been on the streets ever since."

"The poor child! How well I understand her story." Elizabeth shook her head and sighed. "I've been blind to the plight of these orphans, Laina." She dabbed her mouth with her napkin, then placed it back on her lap and straightened. "I'm so thankful the Lord revealed their need to you and that you're giving us this opportunity to help them. What you said to Reverend Brown was true—those who have been blessed of the Lord should share the blessings with those less fortunate. And I'm sure there are others who will feel the same way." Her eyes darkened with determination. "I think we should start planning those dinner parties and teas right now. These children have suffered long enough."

"I couldn't agree more." Laina pushed the tea things aside, then rose and hurried to the walnut secretary in the corner for pen and paper.

"It's a *house*. An' I gets to play in it 'cause it's my size."

Thad grinned down at the toddler in his arms. "May I play in it, too?"

Emma giggled. Her shiny blond curls swung back and forth as she shook her head. "You're too big. Ain't he, Mama?"

Laina stumbled, caught her balance thanks to Thad's quick grasp on her arm, and looked up to meet Emma's bright brown-eyed gaze. *Mama.* Her throat constricted around a lump so large she had no hope of speaking. She looked at Thad in mute appeal.

He tweaked the tip of Emma's tiny nose. "Very well, Sunshine. If I can't fit in the playhouse, I shall swing with Billy."

"I can swing, too." Emma twisted in Thad's arms and looked down at her brother. "Can't I, Billy?"

"Yeah. Long as ya hang on tight." Billy looked up. "Right, Mama?"

Laina's heart swelled to the bursting point. She blinked back a rush of tears and nodded.

Thad cast a look her way, reached down and ruffled Billy's hair, then lowered Emma to the stone walk. "Why don't you two run ahead and swing? We'll be along in a minute."

"Goody! Come on, Billy!" Emma broke into a run, squealing as Billy caught up and passed her.

Laina took a deep breath. "Thank you for the rescue." The words were soft, shaky.

Thad turned toward her. Their gazes met. The look in his eyes made the lump come back to her throat bigger than ever. "That's the first time they've called you Mama, isn't it?"

He was so understanding, so gentle! Thad's face wavered beyond her teary gaze. Laina caught her trembling bottom lip in her teeth and nodded.

"Why don't we sit down for a moment?" Thad took hold of her elbow and started for the bench beside the path.

Laina's breath shortened. She followed him, refusing to lift her free hand and pull at her collar as she wanted to do. She sat and tried to suck in air, but her lungs felt too small.

He took her hand. "Relax, Laina." His thumb stroked back and forth across her skin.

Everything got worse. She couldn't breathe at all. Her heart fluttered. Panic set in. Laina yanked her hand away and grabbed for her throat.

"Lie down." Thad jumped to his feet, gripped her shoulders and pushed her to a reclining position on the bench. "Take small breaths."

It was his doctor's voice, calm and authoritative. Laina closed her eyes to the sight of him hovering over her and followed his advice. It helped. After a minute her breathing returned to normal. The panic ebbed. She opened her eyes and sat up, staring down at her hand. It was still warm and tingly from his grasp. "I'm sorry, I don't know what came over me." She squared her shoulders and looked up at him.

Thad studied her face. "I think, perhaps, your heart was simply overwhelmed with love for a moment and it manifested itself in an attack of breathlessness."

Laina nearly swooned. *Overwhelmed with love because of his touch?* Heat surged up her neck and spread across her cheeks.

"I fully understand, of course." Thad looked toward the swing. "Billy and Emma are wonderful children."

Of course! Her breathless state was because of Billy and Emma calling her Mama. It had nothing to do with Thad's touch. Laina didn't know whether to shout with relief or scream with frustration. She would have realized that immediately if it hadn't been for her ridiculous dream planting foolish ideas in her head!

Her face cooled on a gust of relief. She took a deep breath, smoothed back her hair and rose to her feet. "Shall we go on, Thad? I do want your opinion of the safety of the playhouse before they continue with its construction." She shook out the long blue-on-blue embroidered skirt of her dress, tugged its blue-and-cream-striped spencer into place and started down the stone path.

"I find nothing to fault, Laina." Thad glanced up from the drawings he was studying. "The playhouse is bright and airy—" he grinned at her "—and the right size. And this furniture looks sturdy and well able to withstand the play of exuberant children."

She laughed at his reference to Emma's earlier claim to the playhouse and poured him a cup of tea. "Then I shall have the carpenters continue their work on the playhouse and have the cabinetmakers begin on the furniture immediately." She looked across the table. "Cream and sugar?"

He shook his head and laid the furniture drawings aside. "Cream only."

Laina added it to the tea, handed him his cup and saucer, then poured tea for herself. "I'm very grateful to you, Thad, for taking the time to advise me on these things. I want everything to be right for the children." She put cream in her cup and stirred. "But I do apologize for taking up your time. I know I'm keeping you from your home."

"No need to apologize, Laina. I have the time." He chose a biscuit from the selection arrayed on the tray she held out to him and put it on his plate. "Faithful is stabled for the night and I've left word with my neighbor where I can be found in case of an emergency."

"Your neighbor? What of your wife?" The words simply popped out. Laina flushed.

"I'm not married."

"Oh."

"You sound surprised." Thad took a swallow of his tea.

"I am surprised—and rude." Laina forced herself to look at him. "Forgive me, please. I didn't mean to pry. I simply assumed…" She clamped her lips shut, refusing to enter the morass of embarrassing explanations she was heading toward.

He nodded and grinned. "Assumptions can be dangerous." His grin faded. "You learn that early in the medical profession."

Laina held back a sigh of relief and pounced on the change of subject. "May I ask why you chose to become a doctor?" She shot him a look. "Don't answer if you'd rather not."

Thad took another swallow of tea, then put his cup down and looked at her. "I don't mind. The choice was made for me. My parents and my older brother died in a yellow fever epidemic when I was a toddler and—"

"You're an orphan?" Laina blurted out the words on a surprised gasp. "No wonder you're so compassionate with the street children."

Thad stared at her, a shocked look in his eyes.

Laina's cheeks warmed. "I'm sorry, I seem to have forgotten my manners tonight. I didn't mean to interrupt. Please continue."

Thad gave his head a little shake, then blew out a breath and rubbed the back of his neck. "It seems odd now that you've pointed it out, but I've never thought of myself as an orphan before this moment. I suppose that's because the doctor who tended my family took me home to his wife and they raised me as one of their own."

A smile tugged at the corners of his mouth. "I followed Dr. Simon around like a puppy. I suppose it was inevitable that his love of medicine would rub off on me." He sobered. "But mainly, I grew up determined to help people so they didn't lose their families as I'd lost mine. Unfortunately, it doesn't always work that way." He scowled down at the table. "I still take it as a personal affront when I lose a patient."

"That must be terribly hard." Laina added a bit more cream to her tea. "You're very brave to continue."

Thad lifted his gaze to meet hers. "That sounds noble, but the truth is, bravery has nothing to do with it." He sat forward in his chair. "There's a great need for competent, learned doctors, and that need has to be met. That's why I went to France to study, and learn their new progressive approach to medicine."

He reached up and plowed a hand through his hair. His cowlick popped up, dangling a dark lock of hair onto his forehead. He brushed it back. It fell forward again. He frowned and swiped at it once more. "There are far too many untrained, uneducated practitioners who do a great deal of harm, and as a result spread distrust and disdain for the medical profession among people."

His hand clenched into a fist on the table. "And then there are those doctors who will not change. Who will not listen to new ideas or solutions to conditions that have plagued people for years! Who are so concerned with being *right*, they—"

He stopped, sucked in a deep breath and gave a wry grimace. "Sorry. I tend to get carried away on the subject of medicine." He brushed at his hair again. "I didn't mean to lecture."

"Don't apologize, Thad. I find what you say interesting." Laina pulled her gaze from that lock of hair her fingers were itching to smooth back in place. "You're very passionate about your profession."

Thad gave a small snort. "I'd better be—it's stolen all else from me." His tone was resigned.

Laina shot him a puzzled look. "All else?"

"A wife…children—" he gave her a lopsided grin "—an ordered existence."

"And why is that?"

His grin faded. "Because of the nature of the profession. Sickness and emergencies happen any hour of the day or night and a patient's needs must come first." His gaze locked on hers. "That leaves little time for family life, and even less time for a social life."

He shrugged and reached for his plate. "Not that much social life would be possible, anyway—doctors are ill paid. All of which means there is little to offer as a marriage partner. Hence, no wife and no children."

Laina studied Thad as he took a bite of cookie. "And believing that, you have never considered quitting medicine for another profession?"

He took a swallow of tea. "I'm only human. I've thought about it. It's not possible for me."

"You're very dedicated."

Thad shook his head and set his cup back on his saucer. "It's not dedication, it's belief. I believe practicing medicine is God's will for me." He lifted his gaze to hers. "You don't quit on God."

The words pierced her heart. Laina stared at him. "Some of us do." She couldn't stop the words any more than she could stop the tears stinging her eyes. "I turned my back on God for those very reasons. I wanted children more than anything and I asked God every day for the ten years of my marriage to give me a baby. He never did."

Laina blinked back the tears, lifted her chin and forced out the hated words. "I'm barren. I'm sure—as a doctor—you're familiar with the condition." She made an effort to curb the bitterness in her voice. "And then God took Stanford from me. My husband was twenty years older than I, but still, it was quite unexpected. Suddenly I was without a mate and without hope of ever having children." She lifted her chin a notch higher. "My faith in God's power faded. Until recently."

"The children?"

"Yes. Justin and Elizabeth believe they are an answer to their prayers for me." She looked away from the compassion in Thad's eyes. Where was the recrimination for her lack of faith? She forced a light note into her voice. "How can I remain angry and distant from a God who gave me Billy and Emma and Audrey?" She frowned. "That is, if He *did* give them to me. I'm still not convinced it wasn't all a coincidence."

Laina looked up. "I'm trying to discover—by searching through the Bible—if God truly does answer prayers. And if He does, why mine have been ignored." She sighed. "It's a big book."

Lord, guide her to Your truth. Thad nodded and cleared his throat. "It is indeed." He swallowed the last of his tea, put his cup down and rose. "It's getting late—I'd better be going. Thank you for the cookies."

"Thank *you* for your help."

He nodded and headed for the door.

"And thank you for bringing Audrey to me. She's a pure delight, though unnaturally quiet."

Thad stopped and turned back to face her. "Quiet? In what way?"

"In every way. She prefers to be alone. I'm sure you noticed she didn't make an appearance earlier this evening." Laina tossed her napkin down on the table and rose. "I've been letting her spend her time in her room, hoping that will change once she becomes accustomed to being with me. I wanted to give her time to learn to trust me. Is that the right thing to do? I don't want to *force* her to be with me."

"What of meals?"

"She's asked for a tray in her room." Laina walked over to stand beside him. "Am I wrong to allow her to eat alone?"

Thad looked down into Laina's concerned blue eyes and wished he had his doctor's bag with him so he had something to do with his hands. He scrubbed one through his hair and focused his attention on the girl they were discussing. At least, he tried to. "I think you're wise to let Audrey come to trust you. However, trust is given when we learn someone is trustworthy. She won't learn to know you by spending all her time alone."

"Yes, I see." Laina nibbled at her bottom lip. "What should I do?"

Thad yanked his gaze away from her mouth. *Dear Lord Jesus, I can't think straight. Help me get out of here, Lord.*

"Well…" His right knee began to jiggle. He began to pace the room. It was easier on him to be at some distance from Laina. He turned and came back her way. "You said Audrey's well mannered?"

Laina nodded, her dark, softly curling hair rippling with reflected light. It looked soft and silky, and he knew it smelled like roses. Thad pivoted back in the other direction and drew in air through nostrils flared like a racehorse's.

"That being the case, as a first step I believe you should require Audrey to take supper with you in the dining room. It's a reasonable request and it will give you a chance to be together in a pleasant atmosphere." He turned and headed for the door. Their gazes locked. His pulse sprinted. "It will give her the opportunity to come to know and love you as Billy and Emma do."

As I do.

The thought jolted him clear to the soles of his feet.

"An excellent idea, Thad. I'll do as you say." Laina smiled at him. "Perhaps you could join us for supper tomorrow night and ease us through our first meal together? It would be very helpful to have you with us. Would seven o'clock suit?"

Thad stared at her, listening in his mind to the sound of the door to his escape slamming shut. He had given his word to help her. *What price honor?* He held back a self-disgusted snort and nodded. "Barring an emergency, I will be here tomorrow night at seven. Don't wait supper if I don't appear—I'll be otherwise engaged with a patient."

He gave her a polite bow, stepped through the doorway into the entrance hall and hurried outside to take a deep breath of cool night air.

"Look, Mama, I gots my own bed!" Emma ran to the chaise, hiked her soft cotton nightgown above her knees and climbed under the covers. "See the pretty flowers?" She patted the quilted coverlet. "Nanny said they're roses.

An' they're *pink*. I *like* pink." She gave a little bounce. "An' Billy's qu-qu—"

Laina smiled down at her excited daughter. "Quilt?"

"Yes! Quilt." Emma bounced higher. "Billy's quilt is *blue!* An' *this* is blue." She touched the wood paneling behind the chaise, then patted the sheet beneath her. "An' this is *white*." She jumped to her feet and reached for Laina. "I remembered my colors you teached me!"

Laina scooped her into her arms and hugged her tight. "Yes, you did. I'm very proud of you. I'll teach you more colors tomorrow." She glanced over to where Billy sat curled up in his cotton undershirt and pantaloons, watching them. There was a book in his hand. The chair dwarfed him. She smiled and walked over to him. "Is that your new numbers book?"

He nodded and held it up for her to see. "Nanny Tobin teached—" he flushed "...*taught* me 'em up to twenty."

Laina widened her eyes and gave a little gasp. "Twenty! You can read numbers all the way to twenty! Why, Billy, that's wonderful! I'm proud of you." She freed a hand and cupped the back of his head. The ridge of his scar stretched underneath her fingertips, bringing to mind the day they had met. *An accident that disguised a blessing?* "Will you say your numbers for me tomorrow?"

"Yeah. I mean...yes." He beamed up at her.

Laina smiled, leaned down to drop a kiss on top of his blond curls, then straightened and used both arms to hold Emma. The toddler had already gained weight. Her cheeks were round and rosy and her little arms and legs no longer felt like sticks. As for Billy...

Laina looked down at the young boy who was the son of her heart. His face was pink with health and there was a slightly embarrassed but oh-so-happy look in his shining brown eyes. *Was* their meeting a blessing, an answer to prayer? Or simply a case of happenstance, of one need meeting another? Did it really matter? She'd be eternally grateful either way.

Laina hugged Emma, then ruffled Billy's hair. "It's bedtime for you two. Let's go sit on the bed and I'll read you a story before I tuck you in for the night."

"Goody! I like stories."

Laina laughed. "You like everything."

Emma's face clouded. She shook her head. "I don't like lightnin'."

"Yeah." Billy nodded agreement. "But it's all right if Mama climbs in bed with us and tells us stories." He hopped up the bedside steps, flopped down on his stomach on top of the blue quilt, then propped his chin on his fisted hands and looked up at her. "Would you *tell* us a story tonight, Mama? Would you tell us the story about the little girl and boy that lived in a tree, and how the lady took them to live with her when the boy got hurt?" A slow flush spread across his cheeks almost as wide as his grin. "I like that story."

"Come in."

Laina opened the door. Audrey was seated at the writing desk by the window.

"Leave the cocoa on the nightstand please. I'll drink it later."

Laina laughed and stepped into the room. "I have no cocoa, Audrey. I've come to say good night."

The girl dropped the pen she was holding and rose to face her. "I'm sorry, Mrs. Brighton. I thought you were Sally." Her cheeks were pink with embarrassment.

"An understandable mistake." Laina smiled and moved toward her. A drawing of a young girl playing a violin covered the piece of paper Audrey had been working on. Laina halted, staring down at it. "Why, it's you, isn't it? That's a very good likeness." She glanced up at Audrey. "May I?"

"If you wish."

Laina picked up the paper. There was another under it covered with drawings of violins. Something stirred deep in her unconscious. She stared at the drawings, grasping for the vague, elusive something.

"I'm sorry for wasting your paper and ink, Mrs. Brighton. I promise I won't do it again."

There was an undercurrent of fear in Audrey's voice. Because of treatment at her stepfather's hands? Laina's emotions swung from pity to anger. She ignored them both—neither would profit the girl. She looked up. "This is your bedroom, Audrey, and everything in it is for your use. When the paper and ink are gone they will be replaced."

She pulled the candle closer, studying the drawing in her hand. "You have a gift for portraiture. I knew immediately this was you." She picked up the other paper. *Something about music...* "Violins interest you. Do you play?"

"I did."

The words were soft, bitter. Laina looked up, all other thoughts fleeing her mind as she focused on the girl. "What happened?"

Tears sprang into Audrey's eyes. "My violin was a valuable one. When Mother died, my stepfather sold it."

There was deep pain in the girl's voice. Laina drew a calming breath. She would love five minutes alone with that greedy, brutal stepfather. "I'm sorry, Audrey."

The girl nodded, blinked her eyes and looked away, her stiff posture rebuffing any attempt at comfort.

Laina laid the papers back on the desk. "Are you comfortable here, Audrey?"

There was an audible intake of breath. "Yes, Mrs. Brighton. The room is lovely. Green is my favorite color."

So polite. So wary. Who could blame her? "I'm pleased you like it." Laina made a mental note to have the seamstress start on a green dress for Audrey tomorrow. It would look beautiful with the girl's auburn hair and hazel eyes. And the one she'd already ordered made out of the bronze sateen would be flattering, as well. It should be finished tomorrow. She smiled, anticipating Audrey's pleasure, then took a breath and plunged. "Dr. Allen is coming for supper tomorrow evening, Audrey. We'll dine at seven." She looked up. "I'm looking forward to your company at table. Please be downstairs on time."

"But, but I'm only twelve years old!"

Laina's heart soared. It was the first spontaneous, *childlike* thing Audrey had said since she arrived. She looked at the girl's shocked face and dismissed the protest with an elegant wave of her hand. "I don't stand on ceremony with Dr. Allen, Audrey. He's a friend." She gave her a warm smile and walked to the door. "Good night, dear. I hope you have pleasant dreams."

Laina stepped into the hallway, pulled the door shut, then leaned against it and grinned. At last Audrey had looked and acted exactly what she was—a twelve-year-old child. There was hope after all.

Thad finished writing the daily notes in his medical journal, rose and stretched his arms up and out to the sides. It felt good. He rotated his shoulders and neck, loosening the taut muscles, then closed his office door and headed upstairs. Of their own volition his legs carried him to his bedroom window. It faced north. Toward Walnut Street and Twiggs Manor. Toward Laina.

I'm trying to discover—by searching through the Bible— if God truly does answer prayers. And if He does, why mine have been ignored.

Laina's words flowed into his mind. Thad plowed his fingers through his hair, then tugged the window open and drew in a long breath of the fresh night air. The light note Laina had forced into her voice hadn't fooled him for a moment—there was a world of hurt beneath it. It had taken all his self-control not to go around the table and take her into his arms.

Thad shook his head and forced the image from his mind. If he started thinking that way he'd drive himself crazy. He leaned on the sill and looked up.

"Lord, please help Laina to discover the truth she seeks. Help her to understand that what You do for one, You do for all. Answer even the silent cries of her heart, I pray, and cause her to recognize Your hand of blessing in the answers she receives. I ask it in Your holy name. Amen."

Thad stood staring at the starry night sky a moment, then lowered his gaze and looked north again. Foolishness. He couldn't even see Twiggs Manor through the intervening buildings and trees.

He turned from the window and walked over to flop down on his bed, his heart and mind full of Laina. He tried to block her out, but failed miserably. He scowled, punched his feather pillow into shape and rolled onto his side, away from the window.

It didn't help.

Thad growled and flipped onto his other side, tired but unable to sleep. Thoughts churned in his mind. He'd never had this problem before. He'd always been able to overcome any attraction to a woman by concentrating on his work and putting up a defensive wall around his emotions until the attraction died. But Laina Brighton was another story. She had burst into his life and lodged in his heart from the instant he saw her standing in the street protecting an injured child. He had no defense against her, because what he felt for Laina—right from that first moment—was a lot more than mere attraction. She was magnificent! *Regal!* How could he not love her?

"Arghhh!" Thad threw the covers back and surged to his feet. Tired or not, he might as well go downstairs and write his answer to Dr. Bettencourt's last letter—he wasn't going to sleep, anyway.

Chapter Twelve

❦

"Good morning."

Justin jerked his head toward the door. "Good morning." He rose to his feet as Laina entered the morning room. "You're up and about early."

"Yes, I am." She laughed. "Having children changes one's lifestyle." She gave an elegant little wave of her hand. "Sit down, dearheart, and finish your breakfast."

"Will you join us?"

She glanced at Elizabeth and shook her head. "I've already eaten. But I will have a cup of tea."

Justin came around the table and held a chair for her.

She smiled her thanks. "Forgive me for coming so early and interrupting your meal, but I have a small emergency."

"An emergency?" Justin paused on his way back to his own chair. "What is it?"

"I have no violin."

His brows knit together. "I beg your pardon?"

"Don't frown, dearheart." Laina reached over and took a piece of buttered scone from his plate as he seated himself. "I went to the music room this morning and discovered I have no violin." She broke off a bite of scone and popped it into her mouth.

"Laina, that is *not* an emergency. However, that *is* my scone." Justin gave her a mock scowl and lifted the cover of the bun warmer to get himself another.

She wrinkled her nose at him. "Yes, dearheart, it is. And a very good one, too. I like the raisins in it." She laughed as he shook his head and reached for the butter. "But back to my emergency. I discovered last night, quite by accident, that Audrey plays the violin." Her face tightened. "At least, she did until her beastly stepfather sold hers."

She stopped to smile at Owen, who had appeared and was placing dishes in front of her. He smiled back and poured her tea. "Anyway, Thad said I should have Audrey come down to dinner instead of eating alone in her room and so, of course, I invited him to supper tonight, and then—" She bit off her words. "What does *that* mean?"

"What does what mean?"

"That look you exchanged with Elizabeth."

"It means I love my wife." Justin laid down his butter knife. "Continue with your story." He took a bite of sausage.

Laina glanced at Elizabeth, who was stirring honey into her tea. But wasn't she concentrating on it a little too much? Laina frowned and turned her thoughts back to her purpose for coming. "Where was I…" She took a sip of tea, then steepled her fingers and tapped them together. "Oh, yes—the drawings."

"What drawings?"

"Of the girl playing the violin. When I saw Audrey's drawings—"

"Audrey drew the girl playing the violin?"

"Yes." Laina shot Justin a look. "Dearheart, *do* pay attention, please. The sketch is a very good likeness. I recognized Audrey immediately, so I asked if she played the violin and she told me she did until—well, I told you about the stepfather selling hers."

Laina frowned and took another sip of tea. "There was such hurt in Audrey's eyes I decided right then I would ask her to play for us tonight after supper. But this morning I found I have no violin. So you see, Justin, it *is* an emergency. I came here in the hope you could tell me where I might buy one." She swept her gaze over the two of them. "Did I mention I want you to come for supper tonight?"

"We'd be delighted." Elizabeth smiled. "Abigail's violin, which no one uses, is in a cupboard in the drawing room. Why don't you take it until you can purchase one?"

Laina beamed. "That's a wonderful idea, Elizabeth!" She shifted her gaze to her brother. "Justin?"

He nodded. "Owen will get it for you. Keep it as long as you like."

"Thank you, dearheart. You're both so very generous." Laina smiled and lifted another piece of Justin's scone off his plate. "Perhaps your generosity would extend to your cook's recipe for these?"

"Come in."

Laina opened the door and stepped into Audrey's room, holding a large brown paper package in her hands. "Good afternoon, Audrey."

The girl rose from the writing desk and gave a polite bow of her head. "Good afternoon, Mrs. Brighton." She glanced down at the package, her lovely hazel eyes lighting with curiosity before they dulled again to indifference.

Laina waited, hoping, but the girl didn't ask any questions. She smiled and held out the package. "This came for you."

Curiosity flared again in Audrey's eyes, followed quickly by fear. She put her hands behind her back. "I didn't order anything, Mrs. Brighton—honest. I haven't been to any shops. I haven't been out of my room."

Laina tamped down her rush of anger at the people who had caused the girl such fear. "I know that, Audrey. I ordered it for you." She smiled and offered the package again. "Open it please."

Audrey looked at her for a long moment, then stepped forward and took the package. She placed it on the bed and began to undo the string that bound the paper.

Laina watched, her fingers itching to rip the paper apart and expose the dress Madame Duval had made. She clasped her hands together and stepped closer to the bed, where she had a better view of Audrey's face.

The girl removed the string, coiled it around her fingers and set it aside, then separated the double-folded seam and parted the paper. She gave a soft gasp.

Laina grinned.

Audrey darted a look up at her, then stretched out one small, delicately formed hand and touched the smooth bronze sateen fabric she'd exposed. In the next instant she lifted the dress out of the paper and held it against her, looking in the mirror. "This is for me?" Her voice was hushed, doubtful.

Laina nodded. "It is. I hope it fits. I had Madame Duval's seamstress take the measurements from your old dress that first night when I sent it to be mended. Do you like it?" It was a ridiculous question. Audrey's eyes were shining with pleasure.

"It's beautiful!" The girl ran her fingers along the brown satin piping that trimmed the collar and sleeves. "May I wear it to supper tonight?"

"I'll be very disappointed if you don't." Laina's long skirts rustled softly as she headed for the door. "I'm going to my room to dress for supper now. I'll send Cora to do your hair as soon as she finishes mine. When you're ready, please come down to the drawing room. I'll be waiting for you." She opened the door and hurried toward her bedroom, carrying the sight of Audrey's happy smile in her heart.

The faint scent of roses clinging to Laina's skin and hair formed an aura about her as she donned her chemise and corselet and stepped out of the dressing room. "I've changed my mind, Cora. I don't want the lavender silk dress—I'll wear the green linen." She started for her dressing table, paused and glanced at her maid. "No, the blue-and-white-striped satin."

"Yes, madam."

Laina frowned. What was wrong with her? Why couldn't she make up her mind? She tugged the front lacing of her corselet taut, then glanced up and shook her head as Cora pulled the striped dress from the wardrobe. "No, no. That's much too fussy. I can't imagine what I was thinking of, letting Madame Duval put those swags around the bottom of the skirt. And that stand-up lace collar…" She shuddered. "I want something soft, but elegant."

"Perhaps the gold watered-silk taffeta, madam? The new lower waistline style is most flattering to your slender figure. And the soft fabric drapes beautifully." Cora put the striped dress back and pulled the gold one from the wardrobe.

"Oh, I'd forgotten about that one." Laina swept her gaze over the dress. "Yes. It will be perfect." She continued to her dressing table and looked in the mirror. "Now, about my hair…" She sat on the bench seat and lifted the thick mass of still damp, softly curling brown hair off her neck and shoulders. "No dangling curls tonight. I want to wear it all up…I think."

Laina walked around the dining-room table, checking each place setting, making sure the flowers in the centerpiece were perfect. Everything was as it should be. She heaved a sigh and headed for the drawing room. Why was she so nervous? She'd given hundreds of dinner parties. Of course, it *had* been over a year. She hadn't even *attended* a dinner party since Stanford's passing. Still, this wasn't really a dinner party. The guests were all family, except for Thad.

Laina resisted a sudden temptation to go to the gilt-framed mirror on the wall of the entrance hall to check her hair, and entered the drawing room. The scent of fresh flowers greeted her. Flowers from her own gardens. She smiled and moved to the fireplace, checking the large bouquet on the mantel.

"Here I am, Mrs. Brighton."

Laina turned. "Audrey, you look lovely!" The girl's face flushed with pleasure. Laina smiled and made a small circle with her hand. "Turn about." The girl obliged. Light rippled over her thick, straight auburn hair caught back at her nape with a bow of the bronze sateen before flowing free to her waist. "You have beautiful hair, Audrey."

The girl finished her slow pirouette, looked at her and smiled, a true smile of pure pleasure that curved her lips and made her eyes shine. "Thank you, Mrs. Brighton. And thank you for the new dress. It's so pretty." Her delicate hands brushed the fabric of the skirt.

The smile transformed Audrey's face. Laina had never seen such a sweet smile—it brought a lump to her throat. How could anyone mistreat this child? She shook off the sour thought and turned to walk through the door beside the fireplace. "Come with me, please, Audrey. I've something to show you."

Laina's heart beat with excitement as the girl followed her into the music room. She picked up the violin she'd placed on the chair earlier and turned, holding it out in front of her. "I borrowed this from my brother. I hope it will suit until I can purchase one."

Audrey stood frozen, her gaze locked on the violin, her mouth forming a little O from which not a sound escaped.

"Audrey?"

The girl lifted her gaze, met Laina's, then collapsed onto her knees on the floor, covering her face with her hands.

"*Audrey!*" Laina put the violin back on the chair and knelt in front of the sobbing child, pulling her into her arms, holding her tight, stunned by the force of Audrey's reaction. "What's wrong, dear? Audrey, please don't cry. If it's not the right sort of violin I'll get another."

The girl began to laugh, hiccup and cry all at the same time. "It's a St-Strada-v-vari, like m-my father's." She rocked back on her heels and looked up, her eyes swimming with tears. "I never thought I would p-play one again."

Her father's? *Altman.* Laina's memory jolted. "Audrey, was your father Andrew Altman?"

Audrey wiped the tears from her cheeks. A smile quivered on her lips. "Yes." Hope flared in her eyes. "Did you know him?"

Laina hated to disappoint her. She shook her head. "No, I didn't know him. But I did hear him play once at a friend's house. He'd come home to collect his inheritance when his father died and was returning to Europe the following week." She covered Audrey's hand with hers. "I heard his ship was lost in a storm. I'm sorry."

Audrey nodded. "I don't really remember him. I was too young. I only know what my mother told me about him." She drew a shaky breath. "Mother gave me his violin, his Stradivari, and I took lessons, and then…well…" Her lips quivered. She looked down at her hands, drew another breath. "I feel close to my father when I play." Tears welled into her eyes again. She lifted her gaze to the instrument in the chair. "Thank you for borrowing the violin for me, Mrs. Brighton, but I know you didn't realize it's very valuable. You'd better return it."

Laina looked at the sadness in Audrey's eyes and shook her head. "I'll discuss it with my brother later. He and his wife are coming to supper tonight. Meanwhile, if it's possible—I don't know about such things—would you play for us tonight?"

Audrey caught her breath. Her gaze shifted back to the violin. "I haven't practiced for a very long time, but—but yes. It would be an honor." She burst into tears again.

Laina pulled her into her arms and held her close, her own eyes filling as Audrey's arms slid about her neck.

Thad whistled as he tied his silk cravat around his neck, pulled on his vest of gold-striped silk and shrugged into his black wool cutaway suit coat. They were his Sunday clothes, slightly out of fashion, but the best he had. At least he had trousers to wear instead of breeches. He frowned and reached for his watch. Perfect. The few minutes remaining would give him time to walk to Twiggs Manor. He started whistling again, tucked the watch into his pocket and stepped into his shoes.

"Doc! Are ya in there, Doc?" The muffled shout was accompanied by a pounding on his door. "Doc?"

Thad charged out of the bedroom and raced down the steps to open the door to a tall, wild-eyed man with straggly hair. "What is it?"

"My wife's been birthin' since early mornin' an' things ain't goin' right. The baby ain't comin', an' she's gettin' awful weak. Ya gotta come help her, Doc."

Thad nodded. "Start hitching my horse and buggy. I'll get my bag." He ran back upstairs to change his clothes as the man sprinted for the barn.

The last notes faded away. Laina stared at Audrey, her throat aching with the beauty of the music the young girl had coaxed from the violin she still held in her hand. She'd had the same reaction the one and only time she'd heard Andrew Altman play. *Audrey's father.* The thought broke the enchantment of the music.

Laina rose and rushed to the young girl. "I don't know what to say, Audrey. I haven't enough musical knowledge to comment intelligently on your playing. I only know what I felt in my heart. The beauty of your music made me want to cry." She smiled and cupped Audrey's cheek in her hand. "It was the same as I felt when I heard your father play. He would be so very proud of you."

Audrey nodded and blinked tears from her eyes.

"I'm also at a loss for words, Audrey." Elizabeth smiled as she and Justin joined them. "I can only repeat what Laina said. I, too, felt your music in my heart. It was absolutely beautiful!"

Audrey smiled at Elizabeth. "Thank you, Mrs. Randolph."

"That leaves me, young lady." Audrey moved closer to Elizabeth as Justin spoke. "I'm no music expert, either, but I doubt that violin has ever been played as well as you played it tonight. Your music *does* go straight to the heart." He lifted his gaze to Laina. "I think we shall have to look into lessons for this young lady. I'll make some inquiries about suitable teachers tomorrow."

Audrey gasped.

Laina laughed and hugged her, then went on tiptoe and kissed Justin's cheek. "Thank you, dearheart."

He winked at her and returned her kiss. "Time to go."

"Mr. Randolph?" Audrey straightened to her full height and held out the violin to Justin. "Thank you for your offer of lessons for me." Tears shimmered in her eyes, but she smiled up at him. "And most of all, thank you for loaning me your Stradivari to play tonight. It was a great kindness."

Justin cleared his throat. He reached out and closed his hand over Audrey's small one grasping the fingerboard and placed his other hand on her shoulder. "My dear child, you keep the violin. I can't imagine putting it back in that cupboard after hearing you play it." He smiled at her gasp. "I think it will be much happier in your hands. Now, good night." He tapped the tip of her small, finely molded nose, put his arm about Elizabeth and walked out of the music room.

Laina rose from the chair, walked to the window and looked outside. She couldn't see the road—couldn't see anything beyond the golden pool of light cast by the lamps beside the front door. She sighed, went back to the chair, then jumped up and hurried out of the parlor into the entrance hall.

The clock struck ten. Three hours late. He must be with a patient. Laina started for the library to get a book to read, and a moment later found herself standing at the front door. She gave in to her restlessness, pulled the door open and slipped outside.

So many stars! The sky was agleam with them. Laina moved down the porch steps, across the stone sweep and walked along the gravel drive. It had been a wonderful evening. Her lips rose in a happy smile at thought of the hug Audrey had given her when she went to her bedroom to tell her good-night. The girl was beside herself with happiness over playing the violin again—and *so* excited at the prospect of lessons. Audrey couldn't say enough good things about Justin. She'd been overwhelmed by his generosity in giving her the Stradivari. She treated the instrument as if it were made of the most fragile china.

Laina's smile widened. And then there were the warm, enthusiastic good-night hugs and kisses exchanged with Billy and Emma. A little worm of worry wiggled through her happy thoughts. She pursed her lips. What of tomorrow night? The carpenters, plasterers and painters were finally done, the cabinetmakers finished. The third floor had been transformed into a nursery. It was time to move Billy and Emma into rooms of their own, but they'd never been apart. How would they accept the move?

Laina frowned, pulled a leaf from a bush and absently shredded it with her fingers. She had tried to prepare them by moving Emma out of the bed onto the chaise, and by taking them to see the rooms that would be theirs as the work on them progressed. She would know tomorrow night if it had worked.

Laina sighed and glanced up, staring at the pillars at the end of the drive. She had walked all the way out to the street. She lifted her gaze and looked both directions. Empty. But of course it would be. It was getting late for people to be out and about. She should go inside. She tamped down her rising sense of disappointment, gave another quick glance up and down the street, then turned and started back for the house.

Why was she feeling so restless tonight? So…so…*dissatisfied* when things had gone so well? Laina looked up at the starry sky again, then lowered her gaze to the house. The lamps beside the door threw welcoming light across the porch. The downstairs windows glowed with candlelight. She smiled and quickened her steps. The house had come to life again. And so had she. Maybe that was why she felt these odd stirrings and vague discontentments.

The faint clop of a horse's hooves and the distant rumble of buggy wheels floated toward her on the warm night air. Laina turned back toward the street, listening. The sounds grew louder. The buggy was coming toward Twiggs Manor. Her pulse fluttered.

Thad. He was the reason she had come outside. She was looking for him. He was the reason she felt so— *Oh, no!*

Laina closed her eyes, willing away the knowledge of the truth that had just burst upon her. The buggy turned into the drive, the light from its sidelamps gleaming against her closed eyelids. She took a deep breath and stepped back to the edge of the drive.

"Hello."

Thad was only a dark form beyond the arc of light. Laina lifted her hand to shield her eyes and forced a smile. "You're late."

"I was with a patient."

She nodded. "I thought as mu—"

"Laina, forgive me for interrupting, but I have an injured boy in the buggy. May I take him inside?"

His voice made her shiver. "Of course." He nodded and urged his horse forward. She caught up to him as he stopped the buggy by the front steps.

Thad climbed down and handed her his black bag. "Will you carry this, please? I need both hands." He gathered a limp body into his arms and turned toward the house.

Laina gasped as the porch light fell on the boy in Thad's arms. He was bruised and swollen and bloody.

"He's been beaten."

Laina jerked her gaze to Thad's face. She had never heard him sound angry. Never seen his face taut with fury, as it was now. But she understood. She looked down at the young boy's cut, misshapen face and oddly bent arm and rage knotted her stomach and tightened her throat. She nodded, then hurried ahead to open the door.

Laina grabbed a clean towel, tossed the rag into the washbowl full of cold water and carried it back to the bed. "Here it is." She set the bowl on the nightstand.

"Good. I've finished stitching the cuts. A cold rag on his forehead will help with the swelling."

Laina looked at the little boy on the bed, at the stitches over his swollen black eye and on his puffed, purple cheek. Her stomach turned over. She swallowed hard and squeezed the excess water out of the cloth.

"Don't let the cloth touch the cuts. I cleaned them with alcohol." Thad put the needle and suturing thread back in his bag and looked up at her. "There's a theory that alcohol stops infection, and I'm finding it to be true. But you can't let anything that hasn't been washed in alcohol touch a wound once it's been cleansed."

Laina nodded. "I'll be careful." She leaned over, brushed the boy's soft, straight black hair out of the way and laid the cloth on his forehead. Tears threatened again. She'd been fighting them back with every new bruise and injury Thad discovered. And he'd discovered many after he'd bathed the boy.

She glanced at the bandage holding splints in place on the small broken arm, and anger drove the tears away. There was another splint on the boy's broken leg, covered now by a pair of Billy's soft cotton pantaloons. One of

Billy's undershirts hid the cloth strips wound around the boy's bruised—probably broken—ribs. She would never understand how someone could be so cruel, especially to a defenseless child. She took his small hand in hers. "How old do you think he is?"

"It's hard to say. These children don't eat enough to grow normally. I'd guess six, maybe seven."

"The same as Billy."

"A little older, I think. I'm sure Billy's no more than six." Thad looked at her, closed his bag and walked around to the other side of the bed.

"When do you think he will wake up?"

"It depends on how badly his head is injured."

Laina looked down and brushed the fingers of her free hand through the boy's hair. "So it's the same as it was with Billy. We can only wait."

"Yes." Thad pulled a chair up beside the bed, then lifted a hand to rub the back of his neck. "Look, I'm staying until he wakes up. Why don't you go on to bed? It's late. You should get some sleep."

Laina shook her head. "No. I'm staying. I want to be here when he wakes up." She looked up. "Have you eaten?"

"No. I was busy delivering twin boys at suppertime." He glanced at her, then looked down and pulled a blanket up over the boy. "I'm used to going without meals, but I'm sorry I missed supper tonight. I was looking forward to it."

"As was I." Laina's cheeks warmed. She turned and gave the bellpull hanging at the head of the bed two quick yanks, giving her cheeks time to cool. She mustn't let him guess how disappointed she'd been that he wasn't there.

"Audrey looked beautiful in her new dress. And she seemed different. I think the stained, mended appearance of her old dress is one of the reasons she stayed in her room. And when she played— I haven't had a chance to tell you about that."

Laina spun around and surprised Thad's gaze on her. The look in his eyes closed her throat on her words. Her knees went weak. She groped for the support of the night-stand.

"Oh!" Laina yanked her hand out of the cold water in the washbowl and grabbed the towel to wipe it dry, staring down at her hands as if they fascinated her, too disconcerted, embarrassed and horrified to look up at Thad. Had he guessed how she felt about him? Is that what that look was about? Hot blood flooded into her cheeks again. At least he was too polite to laugh at her. There was a soft knock on the door.

Laina heaved a sigh of relief, threw down the towel and rushed to the door to give orders for broth for the boy if he awakened and a supper tray for Thad. *Had Justin and Elizabeth guessed why she'd been so fidgety at supper?* Heat flowed into her cheeks again. She stepped out into the hall, pulled the door closed behind her and leaned against it, ignoring the quickly veiled look of curiosity in her maid's eyes.

Fool! Letting your feelings show like that. Now look what you've done! Thad plowed his fingers through his hair, scowling as his cowlick popped free. He swiped the hair off his forehead and stared at the closed door. His right knee began to jiggle. Should he apologize? No. If he apologized Laina would know for certain how he felt about her. Better to act as if that look had never happened. Yes. Better to simply ignore it. And never let it happen again!

Thad snorted. How did he do that? Every minute he spent in Laina's company deepened his love for her. His desire to have her for his own strengthened every time he saw her, heard her speak or laugh.

Thad glanced down to be sure the boy was still sleeping, then stormed to the window, tugged it open and looked up. "I need help, Lord. I'm trying my best, but I can't squelch my love for Laina. You've called me to be a doctor and I've been faithful to that calling even though it's meant a lonely, loveless life. But now, well, Laina's a wealthy society woman, Lord, and You know I have nothing to offer her. Please help me overcome my love for her, my longing to make her my wife. Please help me not to show by word or deed how I feel about her and—"

Thad broke off the furiously whispered prayer as the door opened. He gripped the window frame and stared at the night sky. *You've never failed me in the past, Lord. I trust You. Have Your way in this situation. Amen.*

"He's still sleeping." There was a soft rustle of fabric, the pad of satin slippers and the whisper of skirt hems brushing over the Oriental rug as Laina walked back to the bed. He watched her reflection in the window, his heart pounding against his ribs like a blacksmith's hammer against an anvil. "I wonder what color his eyes are?"

Thad cleared his throat. "Black—for the next few days." He gritted his teeth with determination. I can do this. I just have to focus on my patient. He sucked warm night air into his lungs, then turned and walked back to sit in the chair by the bed.

Chapter Thirteen

❧

"Another child! Laina—"

"I know, dearheart, I know." Laina put her hand on Justin's arm, silencing him. She gave a little tug. "Come with me." She led the way to the bed.

Justin's face tightened as he looked down at the battered little boy.

"It's not only his face, Justin." Laina's voice quivered with anger. She pulled back the sheet covering the small body. "He has a broken arm and leg, bruised—if not broken—ribs and perhaps injuries we cannot see, including his head. Which is why he doesn't wake up."

She looked up at her brother. "What would you have me do, dearheart? Turn him out?" Her eyes filled with tears. "Would you have me tell Thad not to bring any more of these starving, injured children to me?"

Justin shook his head. "No, of course not. Not after seeing this boy." His voice thickened. "It's hard to believe anyone would treat a child this way."

The sound of Billy and Emma laughing and playing on the back lawn floated into the room. Justin glanced toward the open window, then walked over and leaned on the sill looking down. After a few moments he straightened and walked back to stand beside her. "Laina, forgive me for trying to discourage you from taking these children into your home, for balking at your starting an orphanage. I wasn't thinking of their needs. I was thinking of you, and of myself. I was afraid you would be hurt, and that would hurt me. I hate to see you unhappy." He stared at her as if he'd never seen her before. "I never realized what a big heart you have—or how small and selfish mine is—until now."

"Dearheart, you're not—"

He laid a finger across her lips to halt her protest, shook his head and pulled her close. "I'm glad you have opened my eyes to the true state of my heart and the needs of these children. I pray the Lord heals this young boy and opens his eyes on the better, happier world you desire to make for him. I pray, also, that He will give me wisdom and show me how I can help as an adviser in this endeavor."

Laina was too choked to speak. She squeezed Justin about the waist, then stepped back and pulled the sheet over the boy again. When she finished, she cleared the lump from her throat and looked up at Justin. It was time to change the subject, to clear the air of all the soft emotion before she started crying. "What brought you here today, dearheart? What did you want to see me about?"

"Henry Rhodes."

That did it. Laina stiffened, any tendency toward tears gone.

Justin held up a hand. "Hear me out. Pastor Brown had his meeting with Henry. Now Henry wants to speak with you."

Laina lifted her chin. "I want nothing to do with that man!"

Justin placed his hands on her shoulders and looked down at her. "Laina, I know how you feel, but for the sake of these children it might be wise of you to curb that temper of yours and listen to what the man has to say. You need financial backing in order to start your orphanage and Henry Rhodes is a very wealthy—not to say influential—man. He could do the orphanage a great deal of good."

Her hands clenched. She shook her head. "No. I can't abide him. The man has a heart the size of a pea!"

"And a pocketbook the size of this room. Hear him out, Laina, for the sake of the children."

She stared at him, then looked down at the boy on the bed. A sigh rose from somewhere near her toes and exited her mouth. "Very well, but not until this boy wakes. I want to be here when he opens his eyes." She lifted the cloth from the boy's head, wrung it out in the bowl of cold water, then put it back on his forehead, being careful not to touch the stitched-up cut.

Justin gave a little shake of his head. She dried her hands and looked up at him. "What was that for?"

"I was thinking this isn't exactly the future you planned for yourself when you moved into this house." He grinned. "If I remember correctly, you were going to take Abigail's place as the leader of Philadelphia society." His grin widened. "You haven't given one party, and now half the bedrooms on the third floor have been turned into a nursery and the formal gardens into a play area."

She gaped at him for a moment, then burst into laughter. "I'd forgotten all about my plans. I guess I've been too busy to remember them. Anyway—" she wrinkled her nose at him "—I think Abigail would approve."

"I'm sure she would. She always wanted a houseful of children."

Laina's nerves tingled. Gooseflesh rose on her arms. "Abigail always wanted a houseful of children?" Justin's answering nod sent excitement zinging through her. "Dearheart, that's what an orphanage is." Her eyes widened with shock. She began to laugh. "What was I thinking? I don't have to buy another place. Twiggs Manor is the orphanage!"

Justin stared at her. "But this is your home!" He glanced at the boy on the bed, then looked back at her, ran his hand through his hair and rubbed his neck.

Laina giggled. "Poor Justin. You look as if you've been struck by lightning."

He shook his head. "No, only the hand of God, for the second time today."

That sobered her. Laina stopped laughing. She hated it when people said things like that. "I don't understand."

"I'll admit—I hate to say it, but I think you're right, Laina. I think Twiggs Manor is to be the orphanage and you are meant to start it. I think it's been the Lord's plan all along. I simply didn't recognize it."

Justin blew out a gust of air, rubbed the nape of his neck again and gave her a crooked grin. "*That's* why I felt so strongly I was to give you this house." His grin widened. "And that's not all. I'm going to turn everything I inherited from Abigail into a trust to help keep the orphanage running. It's enough for a good solid base we can build on."

Laina threw herself into his arms and hugged him so hard she thought her arms would break.

"He's sleepin' like Billy." Emma stared at the boy on the bed. "Did he get his head hurted, too?"

Laina rested her hand on Emma's shoulder to keep her from bouncing around. "Yes. He hurt his head. And his arm and leg, too. We have to be very careful not to bump him."

"I won't." Emma beamed up at her.

Laina leaned down and kissed her cheek. "Thank you, precious."

"How come Tom ain't got—I mean—"

"Tom?" Laina jerked her head toward Billy. "Is that his name? Do you know him?"

"I seen him sometimes." He flushed. "I mean—saw. How come he ain't—doesn't have a bandage? I did."

Laina smiled and put one arm around Billy's shoulders. She was so proud of him. He learned very quickly and was so eager to do the right thing. "He doesn't have a bandage because his cuts are on his face. Your cut was here." She touched the raised ridge on the back of his head.

"He opened his eye, Mama! Like this!" Emma tipped her head up with one eye slitted and the other scrunched closed.

"Truly!" Laina could see no change. Probably Emma had imagined it. She leaned closer. "Tom, can you open your eyes?" Nothing. She sighed her disappointment.

Billy tugged her hand, motioned her close when she looked down at him. She leaned down and he cupped his hand around her ear. "He's keepin' his eyes closed 'cause he's scared." His face flushed. "I know, 'cause I did."

"Oh, Billy." Laina hugged him tight, kissed his ear and whispered back. "What should I do?"

"I could tell him it's all right." His cheeks turned a brighter red. "You know…that you're nice and all."

Laina's heart melted. She kissed his cheek. "That's a wonderful idea, Billy. Here." She lifted Emma off the bedside steps and pushed them closer to the head of the bed, then took Emma into her arms.

Billy climbed the steps. "Tom, it's me, Billy. You can open your eyes. The lady won't hurt you none or chase you away." He leaned closer to the boy. "She's real nice. She's our mama now. Ain't she, Emma?"

"Yeah, she is, Tom! An' if you open your eyes she'll give you a cookie!"

Laina laughed at the memory and started down the stairs to the second floor. Billy's plan had worked—Tom had opened his eyes. And she *had* given him a cookie. He'd been eating them in prodigious amounts ever since—as did the rest of the children. It was one of the things all the children—including the ones who had arrived after him—had in common when they first came to Twiggs Manor. They couldn't seem to get enough food. Even Audrey.

Laina paused a moment at the bottom of the steps, listening to the soft sound of violin music floating up from downstairs. Audrey was practicing again. She practiced every day without fail. And she never had to be reminded or coaxed, unlike Becky. Becky was such a social little person she hated to be alone long enough to practice, though she loved to play the piano.

Laina smiled and stepped into the hall. Emma had solved that problem. She had appointed herself Becky's helper and sat on the piano bench beside her, happily chatting while Becky practiced.

Muted shouts and a faint stomping sound, followed by a burst of laughter, flowed down the stairwell from the third-floor nursery. Laina grinned. The tutor Justin had hired was playing a game with the younger children. He often taught them that way. It was very effective. Of course, her children were all bright and eager learners. Except for Michael.

Laina frowned and started down the hall toward the back stairs to the first floor. Michael was the newest addition to her growing orphanage family, and he was still quiet and withdrawn—wary. But that would soon change. They were all like that when they arrived, except Emma.

Laina's frown lifted into another smile. She always smiled when she thought of Emma. Everyone did. Emma had such a sunny nature. *Sunny. Sunshine.* That's what Thad called Emma.

Laina's smile faded once more. She saw him so seldom now—only when she summoned him because one of the children needed medical care. And he always left immediately after tending them. It had been that way ever since the night he had brought Tom to her and she had surprised that look in his eyes. The same look Justin's eyes held when he looked at Elizabeth.

Laina's pulse quickened at the memory, then slowed as she started down the stairs. It had never happened again, and sometimes she thought she had imagined it. Thad had become coolly polite and professional around her after that moment. Even their budding friendship had ceased.

It was for the best. She knew it was for the best. Thad deserved better than a barren widow, and so she treated him with the same cool politeness. But she couldn't stop missing him. Couldn't stop wishing things were different. That *she* was different. If she could only bear children, maybe he—

Laina drew herself up short and cut off the hurtful thoughts. There was no point in torturing herself with longing for something that could never be. She was barren. That was fact. The rest was only a lovely fairy tale. At least she had the memory of that one moment. It was more than she'd ever had before. And she had her children. They were enough. She would make them enough.

Laina drew a deep breath to try to rid herself of the hollow feeling that had become a part of her and crossed the hall to her study. She had to update Ellen's medical record—the girl had lost her other front tooth. She smiled and lowered her desk front, opened one of the small drawers and took out a penny, putting it in her pocket. She would hide it under Ellen's pillow after supper.

The work was progressing nicely. Laina walked around a pile of lumber beside the door, eyeing the partition that had been built that day. That was the last one. There was now the framework of eight new bedrooms in what was once the elegant ballroom. At two beds to a room, that would give her space for sixteen more children. That should do until the new wing was constructed. "Do you approve, Abigail?"

She smiled into the silence. Somehow she was sure Abigail was thrilled with every change that had been made to her home. That she was happy with the third-floor nursery, the library that was used as a schoolroom for the older children, the added bedrooms and the removal of the formal gardens to make way for play areas. She was positive Abigail smiled every time a child practiced in the music room or filed in to the elegant dining room to eat a meal amid chatter, giggles and laughter. How could she not be? Twiggs Manor was more alive than it had ever been as a gathering place for the social elite of Philadelphia.

Laina glanced around the room again, feeling a rush of satisfaction. But beneath it was the emptiness, the hollow space nothing filled. Tears welled into her eyes. She wiped them away and left the room.

She wasn't alone in the Twiggs pew now. Laina smiled and swept her gaze over the children walking ahead of her.

"You must be very proud of the children, Laina. They all sit so quiet and attentive through the church service. I never heard a peep out of any of them."

Laina laughed and shifted her gaze to Elizabeth. "Ah, but you couldn't see them behind you. Becky spent the entire time looking around at the other people in church, but she was discreet about it."

"Which is more than I can say for you." Justin grinned down at her. "You used to swivel your head around like an owl, trying to see what everyone else was doing."

"*Me?*" Laina tried to look offended, then gave up when her lips twitched. "Poor Father. I was a trial to him."

"You were the delight of his heart, and you know it." Justin's grin widened. "But Grandmother Davidson liked me best."

It was an old familiar childhood argument. Laina wrinkled her nose at him. "That's because you were such a *good* little boy."

"True."

She stuck out her tongue at him.

Elizabeth shook her head, joining in their laughter. "It's a good thing those children are in front of us and didn't see that, Laina. You're not supposed to teach them such things."

Laina laughed. "I don't have to. They all know already. Even Emma. I saw her stick her tongue out at Billy yesterday when they were playing on the swings."

"Really? What did you do?"

"Nothing. He stuck his tongue out back at her and she burst into tears. She adores him and it simply crushed her little heart to have him treat her that way. I figured that impressed her more strongly than any lecture I could give her."

Elizabeth nodded. "You're probably right." She gave a little tug at Justin's arm, then dipped her head in Laina's direction when he looked down at her.

Laina lifted her eyebrows. "Must you two have these secret communications about me? What was that about?"

Justin stopped walking as they reached the corner where they parted company to go their separate ways. "That's about your preoccupation with the children, Laina. Do you realize you haven't participated in any social events since you came to Philadelphia? It's been months since you've even left your house, except for church." He took a breath. "There's a new dramatization at the Chestnut Street Theater. It's based on James Fenimore Cooper's novel *The Spy*. I've heard it's very good.

Elizabeth and I are attending Thursday evening, and we want you to go with us."

She drew breath to speak.

Justin held up his hand and shook his head. "I can tell by the look on your face you're about to refuse, but this is not debatable. We'll come for you at eight o'clock." He took Elizabeth by the elbow and walked off toward Randolph Court, leaving her no choice in the matter.

The warm night breeze blew in the window, ruffling the pages on the Bible in her lap. Laina found her place again, and continued to read. "As for thee, O king, thy thoughts came into thy mind upon thy bed, what should come to pass hereafter: and He that revealeth secrets maketh known to thee what shall come to pass."

Laina's pulse leaped. *God* sent King Nebuchadnezzar a dream to show him the future? Had she read that right? Did God *do* that? She skimmed to the end of the verse and read it aloud. "And He that revealeth secrets maketh known to thee what shall come to pass."

I believe this is God's will for Laina.

Elizabeth's words surged from the recesses of Laina's mind into her consciousness. *Her* dream had come true. Did that mean God had given it to her? *Oh, surely not!*

Chills shook her. Laina lifted the Bible onto the candle stand and rose, staring about her bedroom, looking for she knew not what. She shook her head to rid herself of the questioning thoughts surfacing and hurried to the window. It was late. She was tired. That's why she was being so foolish. The excuses swirled in her head, but nothing could dislodge that one irrefutable fact. Her dream had come true. Every bit of it.

Laina wrapped her arms about herself and stared out into the night. Justin's hand *had* turned into a purse raining money down on the children. Not only had he turned the fortune he had inherited from Abigail into a trust fund for the Twiggs Manor Orphanage, he had persuaded his wealthy friends to donate money, as well—including Henry Rhodes. Combined with the proceeds from the sale of her house in New York it was enough to make the orphanage self-sustaining.

As for her, she had taken in every child that came to her, tucking them into her heart, loving and caring for them. And Thad continued to bring her children just as he did in the dream.

Thad's touch *did* make her breathless. Laina blinked tears from her eyes. Yes, it was true. The dream *had* come to pass. All of it. There was nothing more. She caught her breath at the finality of the words. *Nothing more.*

A sense of loneliness, of desolation, hit her, overwhelming in its force. Laina turned and ran to her bed, burying her sobs in her pillow.

Thad finished stabling Faithful and left the barn. His steps dragged. It was getting harder and harder to enter his empty house. He glanced at the dark windows. What would it be like to see welcoming light glowing there? To know someone was waiting for him?

Thad gave a disdainful snort and sat on the top step leading to the shed door. Who was he trying to fool? Someone. He didn't want *someone.* He wanted Laina.

Thad put his black bag down beside him, blew out a long breath and stared at the bricks in the walk. She was still awake. There had been candlelight glowing from her bedroom windows when he came down Fifth Street. He always looked. He tried not to, but he always did. And it just made everything harder.

A rabbit hopped out of the twilight shadow of the barn, stopped to nibble at some grassy treat, then continued on around the corner of the outhouse. In the distance a dog barked and another answered. A cat yowled. It all seemed to increase the yearning ache in his heart. Thad blew out another breath, picked up his bag and pushed to his feet. Time to bathe. Time to write the day's notes in his medical journal and go to bed. Alone.

His grip tightened on the handles of his bag. He was beginning to hate that word, to hate his bachelor life. He frowned and pulled open the door to his bathing shed, then paused and looked up at the sky. "Why did You let me fall in love with her, Lord? Why? It's hopeless. You know it's hopeless. I have nothing to offer a woman like Laina Brighton."

Chapter Fourteen

Ah—he was caught! Laina stared at the stage as the Loyalist spy, Harry Wharton, unable to deceive Captain Lawton of the Virginia Horse, took off his wig and eye patch. The theater erupted in a clamor as the audience on the main floor beneath the private boxes hooted and clapped and stomped their approval.

Laina swept her gaze over the jeering, cheering crowd, then glanced around the theater itself. She found it more interesting than the play. She liked the pink paper with dark spots that lined the boxes, and definitely approved of the crimson curtains with tassels. But then, with her love of color, she would.

She smiled and shifted her gaze to the elaborately ornate glass chandeliers. They were beautiful, as were the pillars representing bundles of gilt reeds bound with red fillets that supported the boxes. The entire theater was elegant—more so than the Park Theater in New York, in her opinion. Did Thad ever come to the theater?

Laina broke off her wandering thoughts as the audience again broke into applause. The dramatization was over. She rose and exited their box, nodding and smiling at acquaintances as she walked with Justin and Elizabeth to the stairs.

The voices of people chatting or calling out greetings created a continuous hum from the main floor as they descended. Laina crowded closer to Justin and Elizabeth as they moved into the small space created by the flow of people around the pillar at the bottom of the stairs. "Oh!"

The man who had bumped into her turned, hat in hand. "Excuse me, madam. I didn't mean to—" The man's face split into a smile. "Justin Randolph! It's been a while."

"Indeed it has, Simon. Well over three years." Justin placed his hand on Elizabeth's shoulder. "May I present my wife, Elizabeth—" he gestured toward her with his other hand "—and my sister, Mrs. Laina Brighton. Ladies, Simon Harper."

"Your servant, ladies." The man bowed his head, then lifted it, his gaze fastening on her. Laina acknowledged him with a polite smile. His lips curved upward. His gaze warmed. "How fortunate I 'bumped' into friends."

"Indeed, Simon. When did you get back from England?"

The man shifted his gaze back to Justin. "I came in Tuesday, on the *Cormorant*."

"Ah! An excellent choice. She's a good ship." Justin inched past the pillar, moving into the exiting crowd and creating room for Elizabeth and Laina to turn toward the door.

Elizabeth smiled at the man. "I hope you had a pleasant crossing, Mr. Harper."

"Very pleasant, Mrs. Randolph. Captain Darby is a good man and an excellent chess player. I enjoyed his company." Simon glanced at Justin and smiled. "I know the *Cormorant* is one of your ships, so when I booked passage I told Captain Darby I was your friend. He was kind enough to give me preferential treatment and introduce me to points of interest at our ports of call."

He stepped to Laina's side. "Did you enjoy the play, Mrs. Brighton?"

Laina nodded. "Yes, Mr. Harper, I did. I found it quite entertaining."

The crowd surged forward.

Simon Harper's arm brushed against hers in the tight space. He didn't move it. Was it a lack of manners? Or an indication of interest? Laina frowned and inched away from him as they flowed with the people out of the theater into the long outside entry lit with lanterns over the door.

The press of the crowd eased.

Laina sighed with relief. Perhaps now Mr. Harper would take his leave of them. He was pleasant enough, but his attention made her uncomfortable. She smoothed back a loose wisp of hair, adjusted her lace stole and moved to the brick walkway through one of the spaces between the columns supporting the front edge of the entry roof.

Simon Harper stayed glued to her side. "Have you become separated from your husband in the crowd, Mrs. Brighton? May I assist you in finding him?"

Laina shook her head, checking the twinge of irritation that spurted through her. It was most likely the man was only being polite because she was Justin's sister. She glanced at him. "I'm a widow, Mr. Harper."

"I'm sorry." He swept his gaze over her elegant gown of cherry-red watered silk. "I didn't know." He lifted his gaze back to hers. "My deepest sympathy."

He didn't look sympathetic—he looked *interested*. Her discomfort increased. Laina inclined her head and tugged at one of her elbow-length evening gloves. Time to change the subject. She glanced up at the sky. "What a beautiful evening." She moved toward the street, putting some distance between them.

"Indeed it is." He followed her.

The frown she'd been holding back broke free. Laina looked around for an excuse to leave Simon Harper's side. She couldn't simply freeze him with a look and walk away—the man was Justin's friend. "Oh, look, an oyster barrow!" She lifted her long skirts and took another step toward the street.

"Would you care to join us for some oysters, Simon?"

Laina whirled about and shot Justin a look, wishing she was close enough to give him a sharp jab in the ribs with her elbow. Couldn't he see she was trying to get away from the man!

"My pleasure, Justin. Be careful of the step down, Mrs. Brighton."

Simon smiled and took hold of her elbow as she stepped from the raised brick walkway to the cobblestone street. Justin's friend or not, Laina wanted to yank her arm from his grasp. She took a deep breath and counted to ten. The man had done nothing to warrant such aversion on her part. Still, she couldn't abide his touch. She would separate herself from him amid the people milling about the cart in the street, or perhaps she would use the press of people as an excuse to jab *him* in the ribs! Her lips twitched at the thought.

"Have you children, Mrs. Brighton?"

Laina glanced up, met Simon Harper's warm, intent gaze and stopped fooling herself. His interest had nothing to do with Justin. And her aversion to him had everything to do with Thad. She gave him a sweet smile. "Why, yes, Mr. Harper, I do. Twenty-three of them. I have an orphanage."

The warmth left his gaze. Shock rippled across his features. She was sure he would have turned and run if good manners and Justin's friendship hadn't held him glued to the spot. He made a visible effort to gather himself to a polite response. "So many. You've been…blessed with success." He gave her a weak smile. "Abundantly blessed."

"Yes." That took care of any interest Mr. Simon Harper might have had in her. A giggle bubbled up. Laina bit down on her lip and stared down at the street, entertaining herself with the image of Simon Harper's reaction as they waited their turn at the cart.

A hard shoulder bumped her off balance as the people squeezed closer together to avoid the carriages rumbling up to the theater to pick up their passengers. Simon grasped her elbow again to steady her. Laina's amusement soured when he didn't let go.

"Look at that old, hard-used buggy falling in line with the departing carriages. The man should have better taste than to bring it around where his betters are gathered for enjoyment."

Laina stiffened at the snobbish words of the jeering crowd and drew breath to speak. Justin laid a restraining hand on her shoulder. "The man who owns that rig is a doctor…."

Laina heard nothing more. She jerked her elbow out of Simon's grasp and spun about to step up onto the walkway where she could get a clear view of the street over the heads of the crowd around her.

It *was* Thad. Laina's heart pounded as her gaze met his. The smile that had started to her lips died. *Why was he scowling?* He doffed his hat, gave her a polite nod, then faced straight ahead as his buggy passed. Her heart sank to the level of her red satin slippers at his cool demeanor. She dug her fingernails into the palms of her hands, distracting herself from the horrible hollow feeling in her chest as she watched him drive away.

Who was the man holding Laina's elbow? Thad's hands tightened around the reins until his knuckles whitened. Whoever he was, he was a man of society, of obvious substance. His appearance shouted wealth.

Thad drew in a deep breath to ease the sudden tension in his stomach and guided Faithful around the corner. Laina deserved a man who could give her everything, who could keep her in the style she'd been born to. But that didn't make it easier to see her with one. He took another breath, blew it out slowly. He'd had only a brief look, but he knew the image of her standing in front of the theater in that red gown, with her dark hair piled atop her proudly lifted head, would never leave him.

Thad turned into the narrow alley that led to the Bauers' home and shook off thoughts of Laina as Faithful stopped by the front gate. He picked up his black bag and climbed from the buggy, his heart heavy with dread. He'd been expecting this summons. Martha had been steadily losing her battle with consumption, but knowing that didn't make facing her family less painful.

Lord, make Martha's transition from her husband's arms to Yours a quick and peaceful one, I pray. And give me grace and strength to help both Martha and her family through this time. I need Your wisdom, Your words and Your love to flow through me, Lord, for mine are not good enough. Amen.

Thad brushed his hand over the back of his neck, squared his shoulders and walked to the door. He hated this part of medicine.

"Yes?" Laina looked up from her desk, rubbing her eyes, grateful for the interruption. She hadn't slept well last night and she was tired, not to mention what Grandmother Davidson called "ouchy." She *hated* all this record keeping, but with so many children there was always something to keep track of.

Beaumont opened the door and stepped into the study. "There's a woman—a Mrs. Chandler—who wishes to speak with you, madam. She has three young children with her." A frown creased the butler's forehead. "They all look about starved."

"Oh, dear." Laina put the cap on the inkwell and hurried toward the door, her fatigue forgotten. "Is she in the parlor?"

"No, madam. I offered to show her to the parlor, but she refused. She's standing by the front door in the entrance hall."

"That's odd. Thank you, Beaumont." Laina rushed down the hallway, her mind whirling with speculation. Why wouldn't she wait in the parlor? Who was this woman? She'd never had anyone but Thad bring her children.

Laina turned the corner into the entrance hall and caught her breath. Her steps halted. It wasn't only the children who looked starved. The woman was rail-thin, her face attractive but pinched. She was leaning on the boy and seemed to be in pain.

Laina looked at the children huddled close to the woman's skirts. A little girl about Emma's age, another girl about Billy's age. The boy seemed about Tom's size and age. They were all spotlessly clean, but thin—much too thin. She glanced at the bulging drawstring bag resting on the floor at the boy's feet, then stepped back around the corner. "Beaumont!"

He stepped out of the butler's pantry at her soft, urgent call. "Yes, madam. I've already told cook to prepare a tea with sandwiches and cider for the children. I'll serve it immediately."

Laina smiled and nodded her approval. It had turned out that staid, stickler-for-convention Beaumont had a huge heart for these orphaned children. He was wonderful with them. She swept into the entrance hall and hurried toward the front door, smiling at the children, then lifting her gaze to the woman's face. "I'm Laina Brighton. You wished to speak with me, Mrs. Chandler?"

The woman drew herself straighter. A spasm of pain swept across her features. "Yes. Thank you for sparing me a moment of your time, Mrs. Brighton." She took a deep breath. "It's—it's about these homeless children."

Laina watched at they crowded closer to the woman, even the boy, who was trying so hard to look brave. Her heart ached for them. She nodded and fastened her gaze on the woman's overly bright eyes. Tears. Suspicion burst in her mind. "We'll talk in the parlor, Mrs. Chandler. Come with me, please." She turned to lead the way along the staircase wall to the parlor door, giving the woman no choice but to follow her.

"Ugh!"

"Mama!"

Laina whirled at the cry of pain. The woman was on her hands and knees on the floor, the boy tugging at her arm trying to help her rise. "Mrs. Chandler!" Laina rushed to kneel beside the woman. "What is it? What's wrong?"

The woman tried to look up, then clamped her teeth on her lower lip and hung her head. "It's…my back."

Laina's eyes filled at the woman's obvious distress. She looked up at the young boy. "Go to the end of the room—" she pointed behind her "—and call for Beaumont. Tell him I need him. Hurry!" She turned back and laid a comforting hand on the woman's bowed shoulders as the boy ran to do her bidding.

"Be careful not to bump her feet, Beaumont. You don't want to jar her." Laina opened the door for her butler, who was carrying Mrs. Chandler, and led the way into the spacious bedroom across the hall from her own. She glanced at the chaise along the wall to her left, then hurried on toward the bed draped with a white fishnet-weave tester and raspberry-colored curtains that matched the room's trim moldings and paneling. With quick, efficient movements she yanked the feather pillows from beneath the coverlet, propped them against the headboard and stepped back out of the way.

Beaumont lowered the woman to the bed and straightened. "Will there be anything else, madam?"

"Yes. Send John for Dr. Allen, then—"

"Forgive me for interrupting, Mrs. Brighton." The woman's pale face flushed as Laina looked down at her. "I appreciate your wonderful kindness in letting me rest, but a doctor is out of the question. I have no money."

Laina waved her objection aside. "Dr. Allen is a friend, Mrs. Chandler. There will be no charge." She smiled at the woman's look of amazement and shifted her gaze to the children clustered together at the other side of the bed. They looked frightened—and hungry.

She turned back to her butler. "Bring the children's tea up here, Beaumont. I think they'd like to stay with their mother." She looked back down at the woman on the bed. "They *are* all your children, aren't they, Mrs. Chandler?"

The woman bit her bottom lip and nodded.

"I thought so. They look like you." Laina smiled to put the woman at ease and walked around the bed as Beaumont left the room. Her long skirts billowed out around her as she crouched in front of the teary-eyed toddler leaning against her older brother. "Hello. I'm Mrs. Brighton. What's your name?"

The little girl pressed back against her brother's legs and reached for her sister's hand. "Heidi."

"Ohhh, that's a lovely name." Laina smiled. "Would you like to sit on the bed beside your mother, Heidi?" The toddler nodded. Laina rose, scooped the child into her arms, put her on the bed, then smiled down at the other little girl. Big, fear-filled blue eyes stared up at her. "And what's your name?"

The young girl glanced at her mother, then bobbed a curtsy. "My name is Louise. Louise Mae Chandler." Her voice trembled.

"How lovely! Louise is one of my favorite names." Laina shifted her glance to the boy. He straightened and gave her a polite bow.

"My name is Edward. Edward Tobias Chandler." He glanced at his mother, who smiled her approval.

"Well, I'm pleased to meet you, Edward." Laina turned and shoved the bed steps closer to the children. "You may climb up beside your mother if you wish." She turned at the knock on the door. "Come in."

Beaumont entered carrying a large tray holding a soup tureen surrounded with covered dishes. There was a maid, laden with a smaller lap tray, on his heels. He crossed to the tea table, put his burden down, then took the lap tray from Sally and dismissed her.

Laina glanced at the children. They watched with wide-eyed gazes as Beaumont set out dishes and flatware, filled the bowls with steaming soup from the tureen, placed a sandwich on each of the plates, then poured small glasses of cider. They tracked his every movement as he picked up the smaller tray, carried it to the bed and settled it over their mother's lap. Their eyes went wider still as he turned to them and bowed. "Your dinner is served. If you will permit me, miss?" He held out his arms to Heidi.

They all gaped up at him.

Laina fought back a grin. Beaumont was an imposing figure with his erect posture and impressive butler's livery.

"It's all right, Heidi. You go with the kind man." Mrs. Chandler kissed her youngest child on the cheek, then glanced at the other two. "Help Heidi, Edward. And both of you mind your manners."

"Yes, Mama." Edward and Louise answered in unison, then followed Beaumont to the tea table, where he placed a folded pillow under Heidi to make her tall enough to reach her dishes.

"I—I don't know how to thank you for your kindness, Mrs. Brighton. I didn't expect—" Mrs. Chandler dragged her gaze from her children and lifted it to meet Laina's. "The children...I thought—" Her voice broke. She covered her face with her hands, sobbing softly. "God bless you."

The whispered words lodged in Laina's heart. She placed a comforting hand on the woman's bony shoulder. "Everything will be fine, Mrs. Chandler. Now, please stop crying. You'll upset your children. You don't want to ruin their dinner, do you?"

It worked. Laina smiled as the woman shook her head, took a deep breath and wiped the tears from her face. "That's better. Now, why don't you eat your soup before it cools? We'll talk when you've finished." She walked over and sat on the window seat, her pulse picking up speed as she searched the street for a certain tall, dark-haired doctor.

"And then the step broke and I fell and hurt my back. I haven't been able to do the laundry work since." The woman looked up at Thad. Her lips were quivering. "I was dismissed from my employment, Doctor. I—I haven't any money to pay you."

"There's no charge, Mrs. Chandler." Thad blew out a breath and rubbed the back of his neck. His right knee began to jiggle. "As you're able to walk with assistance, even though it is very painful and at times impossible, I do not believe your back is broken." He frowned and plowed his fingers through his hair. Laina's hand itched to smooth back the lock of hair that fell onto his forehead. "Still, judging from the severe pain and the numbness you describe in your left limb, the vertebra could be cracked or damaged. However, a few weeks of bed rest should improve that."

"Bed rest." The words were soft, bitter. "I have no bed, Dr. Allen. I have no place to live since I was dismissed." Her voice trembling, she looked over at Laina, who was standing on the other side of the bed. "That's why I brought my children to you, Mrs. Brighton." She blinked tears from her eyes. "I know they're not truly orphans, but they are homeless. I can't work and provide for them any longer." Tears spilled down her gaunt cheeks. "Please take them. *Please*. I—I can't even feed my babies." She covered her face with her hands, her frail body shaking with sobs.

Laina swallowed hard and blinked away her own tears. "I certainly will *not* take your children from you, Mrs. Chandler!" She placed a comforting hand on the woman's arm as she sobbed harder. "However, they will remain here with you."

The sobs lessened. Doreen Chandler lowered her hands and stared up at her. "I-I don't understand."

Laina smiled. "It's quite simple, Mrs. Chandler. You *and* your children will have a home here. That way they won't have to be separated from you."

The woman's eyes widened with shock. "But—but I have no money to pay. And I can't work!"

"So you have explained." Laina patted her arm. "We shall come to some arrangement. Now, let me bring the children in so you may tell them the good news." She smiled and started for the door, pausing as her gaze fell on the writing desk sitting against the wall. Her smile widened. She spun back around. "Do you read, and write a good hand, Mrs. Chandler?"

Puzzlement spread across the pinched features. "Why, yes. I did the Stantons' accounts until the son…well, when he expressed unseemly interest I had to leave their employ without references. That's when I began to take in washing."

"Perfect!" Laina clasped her hands in front of her chest and glanced up at Thad. The look in his eyes almost made her forget what she was about to ask him. The look was quickly masked. He picked up his bag and started for the door.

Laina ignored the hurt spreading through her and forced a businesslike tone into her voice. "And may Mrs. Chandler write on a tray while she recuperates in bed, Doctor? Or would that be harmful to her?"

He turned and looked at her. "I see no harm in it."

She nodded and looked back at the woman on the bed. "Then if you agree, Mrs. Chandler, I will employ you as record keeper for the orphanage." Her smile returned at the woman's astonished look. "Room and board for yourself and your children will be included in your wage. But we can discuss that later." She kept her smile firmly in place as the door closed behind Thad.

The woman simply stared at her. She seemed to be rendered speechless. Laina turned and headed for the door to get the children. Surely their happy faces, when they heard the news, would chase this hollow feeling away.

Chapter Fifteen

"Is everything all right, Laina?"

"Why, yes. Why do you ask?" Laina gave Elizabeth an absent smile and stared after the wet nurse carrying baby James to the house. She would never hire a wet nurse. If she had a baby she would feed it herself. She would never willingly give up one precious moment with—

"I don't know. These past few weeks you seem quiet. Tired."

Laina forced a laugh. "Not surprising. I have forty-seven children now."

"Forty-seven?"

Laina nodded and focused her attention on Elizabeth. "Four more came in this week."

"I see." Elizabeth placed a careful stitch in the piece of needlepoint she was working on. "Where did Dr. Allen find these orphans?"

"Tha—Dr. Allen didn't bring them to me."

Elizabeth looked up at her and Laina suddenly felt as transparent as a window. As if the yearning sadness that filled her whenever she thought of Thad was clearly visible. She turned and reached over the gazebo railing, plucking a leaf from a lilac bush and shredding it into small strips with her thumbnail.

"Constable Peters brought them to me. He has a heart for the street children. He has eight children of his own." *That should distract Elizabeth.* She tossed the mangled leaf away and brushed her hands together to rid them of any clinging particles.

Elizabeth set her needlework aside. "Laina, is there a problem between you and Dr. Allen? Do you want to talk about it?"

So much for distracting her. Laina shook her head and reached for another leaf. "Wherever did you get such a notion, Elizabeth? There's nothing between Dr. Allen and I." That was the truth. Thad didn't even come around anymore except to tend one of the children. She held back the sigh that wanted to release the pressure in her chest.

"Then what is wrong?" Elizabeth came to stand beside her. "Are you working too hard?"

"Not at all." She slivered the leaf. "If anything, I haven't enough to do."

"With forty-seven children?" Elizabeth shook her head. "You'll forgive me if I find that hard to believe."

Laina laughed at her skeptical tone. "Nonetheless, it's true. Doreen has taken over all the record keeping and, since she has been up and about these last few weeks, manages all the special activities, like the children's music lessons. She does a wonderful job of it." She threw down the leaf. "And Mrs. Barnes and Beaumont keep the household running smoothly. He even oversees the gardeners. And then, of course, the tutors and nannies teach and care for the children all day."

She sighed and crossed her arms over her abdomen. "I seldom see the children, except in passing, until suppertime. There are so many now, not even Abigail's dining room can accommodate them all at once. I eat with one group and have dessert with the other."

"I see." Elizabeth studied her face for a moment, then glanced down. "It must be hard to feel really close to the children when there are so many."

She always *knew!* Laina unfolded her arms, which covered the emptiness she felt inside. "Yes. I thought…" She laughed at her own naiveté. "I thought it would all be like it was with Billy and Emma and Audrey. But the children come so rapidly now—sometimes two or three at a time— that I hardly know them. I try, but…well…it's difficult." She shot a look at Elizabeth. "I love them all. I just don't *know* them all."

"I understand."

That's what she was afraid of. Her sister-in-law was far too astute and understanding. If she didn't move away from her she'd most likely throw herself in Elizabeth's arms and blubber out the truth of her loneliness, of the horrible hollow place inside that nothing filled. Not even Billy and Emma and Audrey.

Laina headed for the table to pour herself another cup of tea she didn't want. Her first effort at distracting Elizabeth hadn't worked—she'd have to try another. "Speaking of Doreen and Beaumont…" She glanced over her shoulder. "Would you like more tea, Elizabeth?"

"All right." Elizabeth came and resumed her seat. She gave Laina one penetrating look, then picked up her needlepoint. "What about Beaumont and Mrs. Chandler?"

"I think they're in love."

"What?" Elizabeth gaped up at her. *"Beaumont?"*

Laina giggled and nodded. "Staid, proper Beaumont is acting like a love-smitten boy!"

Elizabeth laughed. "Well, I never! Tell me about it."

Laina started for home in the gathering dusk of the balmy late-summer evening, pausing as a yellowing leaf from the overhanging branch of a maple tree floated to the walk ahead of her. She stared at it for a moment, then moved forward and picked it up, turning it over in her hand. Autumn was approaching.

She tossed the leaf to the ground and walked on, then stopped and went back to pick it up. *Autumn.* That time of year when there was a last chance for flowers to bloom, for fruit to be produced. Laina twirled the leaf between her thumb and finger, studying it. She was at the edge of the autumn of her life. She had turned thirty a few weeks ago. Is that why she felt this way?

She sighed and turned onto Walnut Street, glancing at the wrought-iron fence that stretched along the edge of the walk. How angry she'd been that first day she walked here from Randolph Court and saw Abigail's house all closed up, cold and lifeless.

Laina glanced up, and a smile touched her lips. It wasn't lifeless now. Twiggs Manor Orphanage. The discreet, tasteful brass sign was attached to one of the brick lantern posts at the end of the gravel drive. A sense of satisfaction swept through her as she looked at it. It was done. The homeless children of Philadelphia had a place where they would be loved and cared for. The dream had come true. All she had set out to do had been accomplished. So why did she still feel unfulfilled?

Laina walked on toward the house, its windows ablaze with welcoming candlelight. Justin wanted her to name it Brighton Manor Orphanage, but she couldn't. It wasn't her home—she only lived here, like one of the orphans she cared for. Of course, she couldn't tell anyone she felt that way.

What had happened? In the beginning, that day on Market Street when she and Thad had rescued Billy and Emma...

Thad. A wave of desolation washed over her. The leaf was crushed as Laina clenched her hands against the loneliness, the ceaseless ache in her heart. She tried not to think about Thad. It made the emptiness inside unbearable. She paused at the bottom of the porch steps. It was here she'd crashed into him, had felt for the first time the breathlessness his touch caused in her. It was here she—

Laina slammed the door on her traitorous thoughts. She needed to submit to her fate. To grow up and stop railing against the inevitable. Why couldn't she simply be grateful for the children, for the opportunity to know how it felt to love a man, even if it was hopeless? Why did she have to *fight* everything?

She gave a disgusted sigh and threw the mangled leaf to the ground. She was a thirty-year-old barren widow.

This was her life. And she had come to believe, as Elizabeth had said, it was God's will for her. It was time she accepted it.

Laina took a deep breath and looked up at the dusky evening sky. "Forgive me, heavenly Father, for being so ungracious and willful. For always wanting more than I have. I do love the children. And I am so very thankful for them. And I know Thad deserves a whole woman, one who can give him children. So please take away this longing, this *love* I have for Thad. Take away this endless yearning and help me to be content with the life You have chosen to give me. I ask it in the holy name of Your Son. Amen."

Laina squared her shoulders, climbed the steps and crossed the porch to the front door. She could hear the beautiful sound of violin music as she went inside. Audrey was playing. Audrey, whose talent was beyond the capabilities of the local teachers.

A bittersweet joy flowed through Laina. In three days Audrey would be leaving to study in Europe. The arrangements had all been made. Audrey would travel on the *Cormorant* under Captain Darby's protection, with Justin's neighbor, Mrs. Springfield, to chaperone her. She was happy for Audrey, but she would miss her. Laina sighed, pushed aside the twinge of sadness and hurried toward the music room to listen.

Laina opened her eyes and lifted her head off her pillow, listening. The soft tap-tap on her door came again. Her stomach flopped. Something was wrong. She threw back the covers, slid from her bed and hurried to open the door. Nanny Tobin stood in the hall in her nightgown, her worried face lit by the candle in her hand. "Yes? What is it?"

"I'm sorry to wake you, madam, but it's the new girl, Anne, who we put in Emma and Heidi's room. She's complaining of her head hurting, and she feels quite warm to the touch."

"I'll be right with you."

Laina donned her slippers and dressing gown, fastening its ties as she followed the nanny up the stairs to the third floor. Candles burning in wall sconces at either end of the long corridor gave off dim light. She heard a child crying as they turned left into the young girl's section, and she quickened her steps.

What should she do? Should she send for Thad? Laina stared down at the flushed face of the little girl on the bed, wishing she had more experience at this sort of thing. She brushed back the russet curls clinging to the child's damp forehead, and heat from the girl's skin warmed her hand. The child definitely had a fever. That couldn't be good.

The child coughed, winced, coughed again. Tears spilled from the overly bright brown eyes staring up at her. "Does your throat hurt, Anne?"

"My h-head hurts."

"I know, dear. Nanny Tobin told me."

"I want my m-mama."

The words ended on a mournful wail that broke Laina's heart. Anne's mother had died three days ago—that's why Anne was here. She sat on the edge of the bed and pulled the little girl into her arms. "I know, Anne. I know. But your mama's in heaven with Jesus." Her arms tightened around the sick, feverish child. She laid her cheek against the perspiration-dampened hair and rocked back and forth. "But I'm here, Anne. And I'm going to take care of you. Heart's promise."

There was a patter of footsteps. Emma appeared, rubbing sleep from her eyes. She scrambled up onto the bed, placed her cheek against Anne's and patted her back with a small hand. "You don't gots to be afraid, Anne, honest. Mama will make you better."

That decided her. Laina kissed Emma's cheek. "Thank you, precious. I'm sure you make Anne feel better, but you need to go back to bed. I'm sorry if I woke you." She looked up at the nanny. "Tuck Emma back in bed, please." She smiled as the sleepy, softhearted daughter of her heart was carried off to bed, then pulled the coverlet closer around the small shivering body in her arms and rose.

Nanny Tobin glanced at her. Laina nodded toward the nightstand. "Bring the candle please. I'm taking Anne to my room, where I can care for her without disturbing the other children." She started for the door.

"You rang, madam?"

Laina peeked at Beaumont around the edge of her partially opened door, her eyes widening with shock. Her impeccably groomed butler's hair was mussed from sleep and the tails of his long nightshirt hung below his hastily donned jacket, stopping just above bony ankles leading to bare feet shoved into a pair of old, well-worn felt slippers. She fought back a grin. "Yes. Anne, the little girl who came in yesterday, is ill. Please send someone for Dr. Allen. Tell him she's fevered, her head hurts and she has a cough. Ask him to come immediately. Oh, and bring him here to my room. I have the child with me."

Laina closed the door as Beaumont hurried off down the hall, then pulled off her nightgown and tossed it aside, shrugged into her blue-and-white-striped gown and fumbled to fasten the buttons in back. Why didn't they design gowns with the closure in the front? She would have to order some made that way for emergencies such as this.

Anne moaned and threw off her covers.

Laina glanced at the fretful child, scooped up her shoes and hurried to the bed. Poor baby—she was so hot! Should she put a cold cloth on Anne's head or wait for Thad? She leaned down to comfort the little girl, frowning as her long, thick hair fell forward over her shoulders. What could she do with her hair? There was no time to ring for Cora.

Laina dropped her shoes, pulled the cover back over the restless child and ran barefoot to her dresser. There had to be something... Ah! She snatched a length of white satin ribbon from her drawer, slid it under her free-falling hair, then knotted it at her nape. That would have to do. Her hair still flowed down her back, but at least it was restrained. Now for her shoes.

"Mama."

Laina spun around. Anne had thrown off the cover again.

"Where are you, Mama?" Anne flopped over, trying to climb from the bed.

Laina rushed over and lifted the little girl into her arms. "It's all right, Anne dear, I'm here." She sat on the edge of the bed, holding her close and rocking back and forth, praying Thad would be at home and not out on some emergency.

* * *

He could hear her soothing the child through the door. Thad lifted his hand and rapped softly. Laina Brighton was a natural mother. It was a shame she was barren. She should have children of her own. Of course, that would involve a husband. He shoved that thought away and rapped again.

"Come in."

Thad opened the door and stepped into Laina's bedroom. His heart knocked hard against his ribs at the sight of her sitting on the edge of the bed rocking the child in her arms back and forth.

She smiled up at him and he lost track of why he had come. "I'm so glad you're here, Thad." The relief in her voice brought him back to his purpose. "Anne is sick and I don't know what is wrong or what to do for her."

Thad shifted his gaze to the child in Laina's arms. "Put her down on the bed and I'll have a look at her. Maybe I can figure it out." He strode to the bed and put his black bag down on the nightstand.

The child coughed and whimpered. Laina moved forward out of his way, bent close to Anne's head and took her hand. "It's all right, Anne. I'm right here." She glanced up at him. "Her mother died a few days ago. The housekeeper brought Anne to me yesterday." She stroked the little girl's hair. "I think the fever has made her delirious and she thinks I'm her mother, because she quiets when I hold her."

Thad nodded and tried unsuccessfully to ignore the warm compassion in Laina's eyes. Every time he saw her his admiration for her grew. Admiration? *Hah!* Who was he fooling?

Thad stepped closer to the bed, leaned over and placed his hand on the toddler's moist, hot forehead. She had a fever, all right. A high one. He gently pulled back the lid of one closed eye. Glassy. Not surprising with the fever. He brushed her hair aside, looked behind her ears, then placed his fingertips on the inside of the small wrist and looked up at Laina. "Beaumont said she's complained of her head hurting?"

"Yes. I thought of putting a cold cloth on her head, but I didn't know if I should."

Worry clouded her eyes. Those beautiful dark blue eyes. He looked away. The child coughed again. Thad frowned, lifted the candle from the nightstand and held it out to Laina. "I need you to hold this for me. I want to look in her mouth." His gaze met hers. "You'll have to come closer."

Laina nodded and broke the eye contact. She took the candle and moved to stand beside him, keeping her gaze fastened on Anne.

Thad put his hand over hers and moved the candle down. "Hold it right here." Her hand was trembling. *Because of him?* The errant thought made Thad's heart pound. He jerked his mind back to his patient, leaned down and looked in her mouth. There were spots on the insides of her cheeks, just as he'd suspected. He straightened. "Well, the mystery is solved. Anne has the measles."

"The measles!" Laina glanced from him to Anne, then back. "But she has no spots." Her eyes filled with hope. "Shouldn't she have spots?"

He nodded. "If I'm right in my diagnosis, she'll break out with them any time now. The fever usually brings them out." Thad leaned forward again and covered Anne, gently tucking the blanket beneath her little chin. "The rash most often starts behind their ears or on their forehead and spreads from there." He straightened again. His arm brushed against Laina's shoulder. Awareness sizzled through him.

The candle in Laina's hand flickered violently. She stepped back and set it down on the nightstand. "What am I to do for her?"

Her voice sounded strained and she didn't look at him. Why? Had that touch jarred her as much as it had him? Thad cleared his throat and focused on the business at hand. "Keep her warm and quiet. Give her plenty to drink to help the cough and fever, and keep the room dark. Light will hurt her eyes. When she's feeling better give her light foods to eat."

"All right. May I put a cold cloth on her head?" Laina glanced his way. Her cheeks flushed as their gazes met again.

Thad's heart started tripping all over itself. He shook his head. "No. I believe the heat of the fever brings the rash out. Children get very sick if they get chilled and the rash goes inward."

"I see." She turned and looked down at Anne, who was mumbling in her sleep. "I'll be careful to keep her warm. I'll close the windows. The nights are turning cool."

"No. I believe fresh air is beneficial to the ill. Covers will be enough." Thad yanked his gaze from the silky mass of softly curling brown hair streaming down Laina's back and picked up his bag. He had to get out of there! He started for the door. "You'll have to keep Anne here in your room, separated from the other children, until the disease runs its course. And you must stay here, too. Don't leave the room. And don't let *anyone* else in. Measles spread very quickly."

"Oh, dear."

He didn't like the sound of that. He turned back to face Laina. "What's wrong?"

"Anne has been upstairs with Nanny Tobin and the other young children since yesterday afternoon." Her panicked gaze locked on him. "She was sleeping in the same room as Emma and Heidi when Nanny Tobin discovered she was ill. That's why I brought Anne to my room—so I could care for her without disturbing the other children."

"I see." There was a silent plea for reassurance in Laina's eyes. Unfortunately, he had none to offer her. Thad blew out a breath. "Well, then…it's too late to stop the spread of the disease among the other children. Some are bound to be infected—especially Emma and Heidi, as Anne shared their room. And probably Billy, as he and Emma are so close—and that means Tom, also, because he's in Billy's room."

"Oh, my. So many?" Laina looked completely dismayed.

"I'm afraid so." Thad scrubbed the back of his neck with his hand and threw her a ray of hope. "Perhaps we can stop it there if we isolate them all."

"*Perhaps?*"

So much for his good intentions. There was something close to horror in Laina's voice. Thad nodded. His right knee began to jiggle as he worked on a plan to contain the spread of the disease. "We can't put them here in your room. I don't want them close to Anne, in case—by good fortune—they *haven't* picked up the infection."

He snapped his fingers. "We'll use Emma's room. Nanny Tobin can care for them there, as she has already been exposed and might carry the disease to others." He frowned. "Of course, we'll still have to isolate the entire third floor. The maid and tutor can care for the rest of the children there. But if contact has already been made…" His frown deepened. "I can't risk it. I'll have to quarantine the orphanage."

"Quarantine us?" Laina's eyes went wide with shock.

"Yes. This could start an epidemic."

"But a quarantine means…"

"No one comes in or goes out."

She stared at him. "No one?"

She looked a little stunned. Perhaps she'd had the same thought that had just struck him with the power of a lightning bolt. Thad shook his head. "No one—including me."

She looked away. "For how long?"

"Until two weeks after the last child to come down with the measles is well."

Laina's gaze shot back to meet his. "But that could be— Oh, my." She clamped her teeth down on her lower lip and reached out and gripped the bedpost so hard her knuckles whitened.

Thad wasn't sure what prompted such a reaction in her, but he felt the same way. He could use some support himself. The thought of being in Laina's company for an indeterminate amount of time robbed him of his strength, not to mention the ability to form a coherent thought.

Anne coughed again. Whimpered. Laina tore her gaze from his and leaned down to comfort the little girl.

Thad plowed the fingers of his free hand through his hair. *I don't understand, Lord. I've been doing my best to stay away from Laina, and now this has happened! I'm forced to stay here! There's no choice. If this has come to pass as a test of my resolve to serve You as a doctor, or a test to measure my love for Laina, to see if I love her enough to deny myself my own heart's desire for her good, how can I not? I've only to look about this elegant room to know I'm not worthy of asking for her hand. I—*

"Thad."

He blew out a breath, yanking his mind away from his discourse with the Lord. "Yes."

"You must be right about the measles. Look. Spots." Laina lifted a damp curl off Anne's forehead as he walked back to the bed.

Thad stared down at the telltale red spots, then placed his bag on the nightstand and leaned forward to again check behind Anne's ears. The spots were appearing there, as well. "It's measles, all right."

He straightened, ran his hand through his hair again and glanced around the large room. "Since you've already brought Anne here, we'll use your room as the infirmary. We can move that chaise and the writing table to one side and set beds up along that wall." He frowned. "Hopefully, some of your grooms and gardeners have had the measles."

"Why hopefully?"

"Because they will be immune to the disease and can help move the beds in. Otherwise I shall have to move them myself." He looked at her. "The quarantine isn't only to protect the other children, Laina. If an adult comes down with the measles it can be very serious. They often become more ill with them than a child—" Thad stopped, his stomach tightening with a dreadful suspicion as Laina turned away from him. *Please, Lord, let me be wrong.* "Laina."

"Yes?"

Please, Lord. "You *have* had the measles?"

"I don't know." She took a breath, turned back to face him. "I don't remember having them."

The tightness in Thad's stomach turned into a knot that felt the size of his fist.

Anne began to whimper and thrash about. Laina reached down to comfort her.

Thad darted his hand out and grabbed her wrist. She shot a startled gaze to his face. He jerked his head toward a door in the wall behind them. "Is that your dressing room?" The words came out more terse than he intended.

She stared up at him. "Yes, it is. Why? I don't understand what—"

"I want you to go into your dressing room, take off everything you are wearing and put it into a pile, then bathe and wash your hair. When you're through, put on all clean garments. *Don't touch the others.* Then I want you to go to another bedroom and stay there. I will—"

"I'll do no such thing!" Laina lifted her chin. Her eyes flashed with anger. "Anne is four years old. She's just lost her mother and been put into a home with strangers! Now she's ill and frightened. I will not abandon her!"

"Laina—"

"No."

He tried another tack. "I'll be here to tend Anne. I'll—"

"No, Thad. She's only a baby. She needs me." Laina looked him full in the eyes. "Don't you stay with your patients when they need you, in spite of the risk to yourself?"

"That's different! I'm a doctor, Laina. It's my job to…"

She shook her head.

Thad stopped, blew out a breath and released his grip on her wrist. "I never realized you were so stubborn."

"I'm only stubborn when I've good reason to be." Laina reached down and took hold of Anne's small hand.

Thad wanted to grab her and carry her bodily from the room to keep her safe. The problem was that if she hadn't had the measles, it was probably already too late. His doctor's mind knew that, but his heart refused to calmly accept the fact. He sucked in a breath and headed for the dressing room to wash his hands. "If I'm to stay here I have to go home and get my things. I'll be back shortly."

Laina lifted her head and looked at him. "I thought you couldn't leave."

"Ordinarily, I wouldn't. But it's the middle of the night and I'm not likely to run into anyone on my way home and back, and there's no one at my house for me to infect." He reached for the doorknob.

"Thad."

"Yes?"

"If you're going home, will you take Audrey to Elizabeth and Justin? She's going to Europe to study the violin and she's to leave in three—no, two—days. Her trunks are all packed and ready." Laina's eyes pleaded with him. "Please let her go. She hasn't been near any of the young children."

"How can you be certain of that?"

"Because she's been busy in her room all day." Laina stepped toward him, her hand raised in supplication. "She even had her meals on a tray. The only time Audrey came out of her room was to practice in the music room this evening, and the young children were all in bed."

Thad stood for a time, rubbing the muscles at the back of his neck, weighing her words. "All right. As long as you're sure she hasn't been exposed, I'll take her."

"Oh, thank you, Thad! I'll have Cora wake Audrey immediately." She gave him a smile he felt clear to the soles of his feet and reached for the bellpull.

"Don't ring!"

Laina yanked her hand back from the pull and swept a startled gaze to his face. "Why? Cora will help her—"

Thad shook his head, stopping her words. "If anyone in this house touches Audrey, she has to stay. Tell me where her room is. I'll wake her, then I'll get your groom to harness up and come for her trunk. She'll have to prepare herself to leave."

"Oh, I see. All right. It will be as you say." Tears shimmered in Laina's eyes. "I won't be able to see her to tell her goodbye. Will you…" Her lips quivered. She took a deep breath. "Will you tell her I love her and I'll miss her? Tell her I'll write and—" Her voice broke. She covered her face with her hands and turned away.

Thad clenched his hands into fists to keep from pulling her into his arms. "I'll bring Audrey to stand beneath your window, Laina. You'll be able to tell her goodbye."

Justin sat up in bed, looking around their moonlit bedroom, listening. Hooves clattered against bricks, wheels rumbled. He tossed back the covers and slid from bed.

"What is it, Justin? Is something wrong?"

He glanced at Elizabeth, who was looking up at him through sleepy eyes, and shook his head. "I don't know, dear. Someone is coming to the house."

"Coming to the house?" She sat up. "It's the middle of the night."

"I know. Go back to sleep." He hurried to the window, staring down at the chaise coming up the drive.

"Who is it?"

Justin shook his head. "It's Laina's rig, but I can't see…" He stopped, staring in disbelief at the tall man exposed to his view as the rig entered the curve of the sweep below. "It's Dr. Allen! He's walking beside the chaise."

"Dr. Allen?" The words were a startled gasp. "Oh, Justin, what's wrong?"

"I don't know, but I'll soon find out!" He raced to the bed, grabbed his dressing gown and headed for the door.

"Wait! I'm going with you." Elizabeth swirled her own dressing gown around her shoulders, stepped into her slippers and rushed up beside him. He took a protective grip on her arm as they hurried along the hall and down the stairs with only the glow of moonlight to guide them.

"Measles." Justin scowled.

Thad hurried to offer reassurance. "There's no chance Audrey is infected, or I never would have brought her here."

"I know that, Doctor." Justin glanced after Elizabeth, who was leading Audrey upstairs, then stepped around Audrey's trunks and out onto the brick portico. He pulled the front door closed as Laina's chaise drove away.

Thad backed up. "Don't come any closer—I've been with the patient."

Justin nodded. "Is there anything I can do to help?"

"Yes, inform Dr. Gibbon of the problem. My patients will be calling on him when they find I'm unavailable. I'm going home to get my things and then I'm going back. I'll stay until the quarantine is lifted."

Justin shook his head in disbelief, rubbed his chin and shot Thad a dark look. "I don't like this, Doctor. I don't like Laina's health being at peril. And I don't like feeling helpless to do anything about it!"

Thad gave him a rueful smile. "I know exactly what you mean." He started down the steps.

"Doctor."

He looked back at Justin.

"If I can't come to Twiggs Manor and no one from there can come off the grounds, how am I going to know what is going on, or if there is anything Laina needs?"

Thad ran his hand through his hair, considering. "Send one of your servants to stand on the walk outside the fence by the pillar at the end of the drive at ten o'clock every morning and at five o'clock every night. I'll get word to them. But be sure they don't touch the fence or come on the grounds."

Justin nodded. "A feasible plan." His face tightened. "But we're talking about my sister. I will be the one outside the fence."

"Very well, Mr. Randolph. Until ten o'clock tomorrow." Thad gave him a polite nod and walked off toward the street.

Thad stepped inside his dark, empty house, lit a candle, then climbed the stairs to his bedroom, threw his necessaries in a bag and hurried to his office. He would need the journal he kept his medical notes in. He lifted it off his desk, tucked it under his arm and walked to the front door to hang his Out sign in the window. That was everything. Except for Faithful. Faithful would be stabled at Twiggs Manor for the duration.

Thad shook his head in disbelief at the turn of events, then stepped out into the moonlit night and headed for the barn to get his horse.

Chapter Sixteen

✦

Thad slid his chin to the left, pulled his skin taut and skimmed his razor down over his cheek, shaving the last of yesterday's beard stubble from his face. That was it. He was finished. He rinsed and dried the straight edge, put it away in its case, then leaned forward and splashed the remaining soap from his face. The silence as he grabbed the ends of the towel hanging around his neck and dried his face was deafening. Where was she? It was getting late.

He dampened his toothbrush, shook on some tooth powder and scrubbed his teeth. Nothing. The silence continued as he grabbed his brush and dragged it through his damp hair. He hung his towel on the brass rod to dry, straining his ears to catch any sound from Laina's dressing room on the other side of the wall. At last a door opened and closed.

Thad froze like a dog on point, listening. A pipe rattled

as water rushed through it. Relief relaxed the taut muscles in his stomach. The scowl left his face. She was all right. He donned his shirt, tied his cravat around his neck, then shrugged into his suit jacket and left the dressing room.

"Thank you, Lord, for keeping Laina well." Thad murmured the words he'd said every morning and every evening since the measles outbreak had occurred, and walked to the chair by the open window. His Bible waited for him. Lately he'd had the luxury of reading it without interruption at the start of every day. There were no fists pounding on the door, no scared voices calling for him here. The quarantine took care of that.

He glanced out the window. Dawn was dragging light into the night sky. There's always a battle between darkness and light, and the light always wins. A smile lifted the corners of his mouth at the thought. He stood for a few moments watching the brightness of day arrive, then picked up his Bible and settled himself in the chair. "Lord, I pray You will open the 'eyes of my understanding' and reveal the truth You wish to show me today through Your word. Help me to grasp it, Lord, and cause the light of it to lead me to the path of Your choosing for me that I might better serve You. Amen."

His marker was in the book of Psalms. Thad glanced down the page to where he had left off reading yesterday. Psalm 41. He read the entire psalm, then returned to read the beginning aloud. "'Blessed is he that considereth the poor: the Lord will deliver him in time of trouble. The Lord will preserve him, and keep him alive, and he shall be blessed upon the earth.'"

He sat back in the chair pondering the powerful words. It was quite a promise. He set the Bible on the stand beside the chair and rose. Laina should be ready for the day by now. It was time to go check on his patients. He tugged his jacket to straighten it and headed for the door, bracing himself for the rush of love that hit him every morning when he first saw her.

"Papa Doctor! Come see! I've got spots!"

The name tore at Thad's heart. Emma had called him "Papa Doctor" ever since the day she had decided they were all a family because he and Laina took care of her and Billy. *If only it could be true.* He smiled at her and closed the door. "Is that right?"

"Yes!" Emma popped up on the bed like a jack-in-the-box. "Heidi and Billy gots spots, too!"

"Really?" He grinned and strode to Emma's bed. Obviously it would take more than a case of measles to dampen her exuberance.

"See?" Emma jumped to her feet, sinking almost to her knees in the feather mattress, and lifted her gown to display the red patches on her tummy, then dipped her head forward, tugging her hair out of the way so he could see behind her ears.

"Well, so you do!" Thad lifted her into his arms, gave her a hug while he checked her back and legs, then laid her down, pulled the covers over her and tapped the tip of her tiny nose. "People with spots have to stay quiet and warm so they don't get sick. Will you stay under the blanket for me, Sunshine?" Where was Laina?

Emma nodded. "Mama already told me, but I forgotted."

"Well, you need to remember." Laina was always with the children when he came in. He fought down a surge of apprehension and glanced toward the closed dressing-room door.

"I will, Papa Doctor. Heart's promise." Emma took a breath. "You gots—"

"To do a heart's promise." Thad smiled down at her as he spoke the words with her, then tapped her nose again, leaving her giggling as he stepped to Heidi's bed. She didn't look quite as jaunty as Emma.

"Hello, Heidi." Thad smiled down at Doreen Chandler's four-year-old. "How are you feeling today?"

"It hurts here." Heidi's lower lip pouted out as she pointed a pudgy finger at her throat. Tears welled into her blue eyes. "I want my mama."

"I know you do, sweetie." Thad lifted the little girl into his arms and cuddled her against him as he checked behind her ears and on her back and legs. "But if Mama comes to see you she might get sick. You don't want her to get sick, do you?" He smiled as Heidi shook her head against his shoulder, then lowered his head and kissed her soft, warm cheek. "I'm going to give you some special tea to make your throat feel better. Will you be a big girl and drink it for me?"

She lifted her head and nodded.

"Good." He laid her down in her bed. "Now, you stay under your covers." He tucked them around her. There were footsteps behind him. *At last.* Relief washed over him.

"Good morning."

The words ended in a small cough. Thad's stomach muscles clenched. *No! Please, Lord. Not Laina. Please don't let her have the measles*. He turned to look at her, his doctor's eyes taking note of the flush on her cheeks, the unnatural glassy shine of her beautiful eyes. A shiver shook her, rippling the water in the large bowl she held in her hands.

She lowered her head and turned away. "It's time for the children's morning wash."

"No, Laina, it's time for you to go to bed." Thad stepped forward, blocking her path as she moved toward Emma's bed.

She looked up and shook her head. "The children need…" Her words dissolved into a fit of coughing. Water sloshed over the edge of the bowl, dampening the front of her gown.

Thad's face went taut. He took the bowl from her trembling hands, set it on the small table between the beds, then lifted the towel off her shoulder. "I'll take care of the children. I want you to go to your dressing room, put your nightgown on and get back into bed." It was his doctor's voice. At least that hadn't deserted him along with his professional detachment.

Laina opened her mouth to speak—to protest, judging by the look in her eyes—and another fit of coughing took her. Another shiver shook her body.

Thad clenched his hands into fists to keep from grabbing her and carrying her to her bed. "It won't help the children if you get sick, Laina. They need you well."

He could see her resistance crumble before his logic. She nodded, then turned and headed for the dressing room.

Thad forced his mind back to the business at hand and walked over to check on Billy.

* * *

"I'm coming in there!" Justin stalked to the end of the farm wagon parked sideways to block the entrance to Twiggs Manor Orphanage.

Thad moved with him on the opposite side of the wagon. "No, Mr. Randolph, you're not. That won't help Laina, or anyone else." He took a deep breath. "Laina is all right. She's more worried about the children than anything. The orphanage can't keep running without your help in supplying us with food and other needs. You can't do that if you're quarantined along with the rest of us."

Justin glared at him. "Don't give me your reasonable arguments, Doctor! My sister—"

"Told me to tell you she loves you—and then send you home to your wife and children." Thad braced himself. Justin looked ready to come over the wagon after him. "Laina's right, Mr. Randolph. You need to go home." He held up a restraining hand as Justin started toward him. "Think, sir! If you had been with Laina when she took ill, what would you do but send for a doctor?"

Thad took a relieved breath as Justin halted—he didn't have time for a physical altercation. "I'm already here, Mr. Randolph. And I promise you, I will do everything possible for Laina. If you come in, all you will accomplish is to put yourself in danger and bring worry on your wife."

Justin stared at him for a long moment, then scrubbed his hand over the back of his neck and took a long breath. He turned his back, walked away a few paces, then returned. "All right, Doctor, you win. I'll go home. But I'll have a servant posted here day and night, and I expect you to keep me informed of Laina's condition."

Thad nodded. "You have my word, sir, as long as I have yours that you'll honor your sister's wishes and not enter these grounds."

"What choice have I?" The words were bitter, fraught with helplessness.

Lord, grant him Your peace. "None, Mr. Randolph. You have a wife and children who need you."

Justin sucked in a breath. "Yes. Because of them, you have my word, Doctor." He pivoted on his heel and strode away.

Thad's heart went out to him. He knew exactly how Justin Randolph felt. He hadn't wanted to leave Laina even long enough to come outside, but she had refused to go to bed until he promised to come tell Justin she had contracted the measles and elicit his promise not to come in to see her.

He turned and hurried to the house. Laina had been right to make him come—Justin Randolph would never have listened to a servant. He shook his head, pulled open the front door, then headed for the stairs. Thank heaven the man wasn't as stubborn as his sister!

Thad pulled the drapes in front of the open windows to block out the bright afternoon sunshine, then glanced around the bedroom. That was everything. The children were settled in. Laina had wanted them to stay in her room, but he'd turned a deaf ear to her pleading. It wasn't wise—for two reasons. Laina would never rest with the children there, and if he was right about that cough—

Thad broke off the thought, not wanting to put the other reason into words even in his mind, but all the same, he was moving into her room. *Please, Lord. You know what can happen. Please protect Laina.* He lifted his Bible from the table at his side, put it on top of his other personal belongings and carried his bag to the door. "I'm leaving now, Sally. Are you clear in your instructions?"

The maid looked up, pausing in her chore of making up the bed she would be sleeping in. "Yes, Dr. Allen. I understand what I'm to do."

Thad nodded. "Very well. The children should be fine, but I'll be in Mrs. Brighton's room if you need me."

Thad swept his gaze over the children in the beds. "I want you all to rest quietly and stay under the covers." He stepped to the bed closest to the door and leaned down to whisper in Billy's ear. "You keep Emma quiet for me, all right?"

The boy nodded. "I will, Papa Doc."

Thad squeezed his shoulder. "That's a good man." That earned him a grin. He gave Billy a conspiratorial wink and left the room.

Laina woke when the door opened. Thad entered, carrying blankets, a pillow and his doctor's bag in one arm and a large scuffed leather bag in his other hand. He looked over at her, smiled and lifted the bag in a sort of salute. "I've been dispossessed."

Her eyes widened. "You put the children in *your* bedroom?"

He nodded. "There's no other choice if we're to contain the spread of the disease."

It was true, but it didn't make her feel any better. "I'm sorry—" she coughed "—for the inconvenience."

"No need to apologize. You didn't cause the measles. I'll make a pallet for myself in the hall."

His smile made her heart skip. Laina watched him carry everything over to the chaise along the opposite wall. He was somewhat taller than Justin and every bit as broad-shouldered, yet he moved with a quiet economy of motion her brother didn't possess. He had probably acquired it from his years of tiptoeing around sickrooms.

She looked up at Thad's thick dark hair and a smile tugged at the corners of her mouth. He must have run his fingers through his hair, dislodging his cowlick, for that stubborn lock of hair hung down on his forehead. Her fingers twitched. How wonderful it would be to have the right to smooth it back in place.

Laina frowned and turned her mind from such thoughts. "How is Billy?" The effort of speaking made her cough. She winced at the pain it caused in her head and forged on. "His head was still hurting him last night—" Another cough took her. She wiped her mouth with her handkerchief.

"Billy is fine. The rash has come out and his head has stopped hurting. Now, stop talking." Thad came to the bed and stood looking down at her. "I want you to stop concerning yourself with the children and rest, Laina." He laid one hand on her forehead and took hold of her wrist with his other hand, sliding his fingers to the inside to take her pulse. A frown creased his forehead.

Not surprising. Even in her present state of illness, his touch stole her breath and made her pulse race. Laina turned her head away so Thad couldn't read her feelings in her eyes. The movement made her cough again. Her head throbbed. *Did the children feel this miserable? Poor little ones.*

Laina closed her eyes and snuggled deeper under the covers. She was cold and tired—very tired. She stole another quick peek at Thad. *I know I must get over my love for Thad, Lord. I know he deserves a whole woman. But thank You that he's with me now. His presence...makes me...feel...better....*

The front door slammed. Rapid footsteps clattered against the polished wood floor of the entrance hall.

"Elizabeth?"

Elizabeth dropped her needlepoint, jerked to her feet and rushed across the drawing room to the door. "I'm in here, Justin. What is it?"

"Laina has the measles!"

"Oh, no! Oh, Justin, I'm so sorry." Elizabeth ignored the icy chill spreading through her and ran to him, putting her arms around his waist as he pulled her into his embrace. "How is she?"

"Dr. Allen says she's all right. But I can't go in to see her."

The words were a pained murmur against her hair. His arms tightened around her. Tears filled her eyes. Elizabeth pushed back her fear and concentrated on Justin's need. *Lord, help me to help my husband. Give me strength and wisdom, Lord.* "I'm sorry, Justin. But it must comfort you that Laina knows how much you love her. That she knows you would come to her if you could."

His arms almost crushed her. "She told Dr. Allen to send me home to you and the children, and to make me give him my word I wouldn't come to see her."

Bless you, Laina! Relief made Elizabeth weak. She lifted her head, her heart squeezing painfully at the look of helpless despair on her husband's face. "We have to trust the Lord, Justin. We must pray and trust the Lord to keep Laina safe, to heal her and restore her to us."

"I know. But I keep remembering some of the people from church—Adam Greening and Elmer Westfield, Donald Smith and Mrs. Forbes. They all died of measles." A shudder passed through him. " I may never see Laina again."

Elizabeth took a breath. "You may not be able to see Laina, Justin, but you could do the next best thing. You could write her a letter. Dr. Allen has no objections to things going *in* to Twiggs Manor, only to things coming out. And I'm sure hearing from you would cheer Laina."

She watched the shadow of hopelessness leave Justin's eyes as she spoke. "An excellent idea, Elizabeth! I'll do it right now." His gaze warmed as he looked down at her. "Whatever would I do without you?"

"No, dear. What would the children and I do without you?" In spite of her best effort, the fear had crept into her voice. It was probably in her eyes, also. She laid her head against his chest, listening to the steady, solid beat of his heart. *Please, dear Lord, grant us many, many more years together.*

"Elizabeth…" Justin cupped her chin in his hand and raised her head until their gazes met again. "You don't have to be afraid. I love you and the children. I won't go in to Laina—" His voice caught. "She understands." He cleared his throat. "Now…I have a letter to write." He kissed her soundly on the lips and hurried off toward his study.

Elizabeth braced her hand against the wall, weakness overcoming her now that she needn't be strong for her husband. "Dear gracious heavenly Father…dear Father—"

Her throat closed. She couldn't say more. Couldn't force a prayer from her quivering lips. All those people Justin knew who had perished from measles. Her mind stalled on the memory of her childhood friend Charlotte—her parents had both died from the dreadful disease.

What if—? A fit of trembling overtook her. Elizabeth sagged against the wall and covered her face with her hands, sobbing softly. *Please, Father God, spare Laina. Please spare Laina!*

"'Elizabeth sends her love. Sarah sends the enclosed picture.'"

Laina swallowed her spoonful of soup and glanced at Thad. "May I see it?"

"Of course. It's only the reading that might strain your eyes." Thad laid down Justin's letter and lifted the candle, holding it and the picture in front of Laina.

A smile curved her lips as she studied the stick figure beside a large black, somewhat shapeless form. "It's Mr. Buff—" A spasm of coughing choked off her words. She sagged into the pillows propped against the headboard.

Thad put the candle and picture on the stand and rose to hold a cup of medicinal herbal tea to her lips. "This will help that cough."

Their gazes met. Laina's heart fluttered. Oh, how silly she was to react so. She loved him so much she was imagining he cared for her, too! She looked away, gazing down at Thad's hands—his strong hands that were so gentle when they touched a child. *Dear God, I know it's pride, but please don't let Thad guess I love him.*

Laina laid her spoon on the lap tray beside her bowl of soup and forced her hands up to take the cup. "I can do it." She swallowed and grimaced, offered the tea back to him.

Thad shook his head. "Finish it. A fever demands that you drink a lot of fluids."

She stared up at him, telling herself there was only warm compassion for a patient in his eyes, that it was the foolish longing of her heart that made her misread it as something more. "I thought—" she took another swallow as a cough threatened "—this was for the cough." She drank the rest of the tea, shuddering as her lips puckered. Poor children. She'd been making them drink this vile stuff.

Thad took the empty cup from her hands. "It serves both purposes." He grinned down at her. "It will take the taste out of your mouth if you eat more soup." His grin faded. "You need to eat to keep your strength up, Laina." He put the cup on the nightstand and picked up the letter. "Let's see, where was I?"

She loved his voice. It was deep and calm and soothing. Laina forced herself to eat another spoonful of soup, then broke off a small bite of bread, chewing it as she leaned back against her pillows. Why did she feel so weak? The measles didn't seem to affect the children that way. Maybe she'd feel better once the rash was out. She pushed aside her thoughts to listen as Thad continued the letter.

"'Can you tell what Sarah drew? I confess I had to ask her. She told me it is you playing with Mr. Buffy when you are restored to health and come to visit us again. Alas, I'm afraid Mary has no such offering to send you. She ate her charcoal stick.'"

Laina burst into laughter, drowning out Thad's chuckle. It was followed by a fit of coughing that left her trembling and gasping for air. Tears burned her eyes. She wiped her mouth with her handkerchief, then clenched her hands in helpless anger and blinked the tears away.

Thad poured out more of the horrible tea and held it to her lips. She swallowed and shuddered. "Shall I continue reading?"

She nodded. "But please take the tray first." She leaned back, weary from the effort of eating and coughing.

Thad carried her tray to the table by the door, stacked it on top of his own, then came back and picked up the letter again. "'I shall close now and write more tomorrow. Please know, Laina, that I wish I could be there with you. I love you, my dear sister.'" Thad cleared his throat. "'Elizabeth and I are praying for you. You will be well soon, Laina. All will be well soon. Heart's promise. Your loving brother, Justin.'"

Heart's promise. You can't break a heart's promise, dearheart. Laina smiled. How blessed she was to have a family that loved her and prayed for her. And Justin was right—she would be well soon. After all, Anne was much improved already.

Anne. Who would care for little Anne, who so wanted her mama? Laina closed her eyes again and tried to take a deep breath. It made her cough so hard tears seeped from under her lashes and overflowed the corners of her eyes.

"What is it, Laina?" Soft material gently touched her temples. Laina's breath caught. Thad was blotting away her tears. Oh, how she loved this wonderful, gentle man! "Are you in pain?"

"It's not…" She paused and bit down on her lip, waiting for the tightness in her throat to ease so she could talk.

She took a breath and tried to push out the words. "Anne doesn't…she needs—"

"Anne is fine." Thad's hand touched her forehead and rested there. "Sunshine is making sure of that. She's 'taking care of her' while you get better."

Emma. Her own sweet Emma with the big, big heart. Laina smiled. She didn't have to worry. Little Emma would make sure Anne was all right.

Laina sighed. Being sick was so enervating! She stole a quick look at Thad as he resumed his seat in the chair beside her bed, then closed her eyes again and gave in to the weariness.

Thad rose, lifted Laina's wrist and checked her pulse before tucking her arm back under the covers. He rested his gaze for a moment on the long, damp lashes so dark against her flushed skin, then raised it to the red spots visible along her hairline. If it was only the measles the fever should break soon.

He lifted his hand and gently brushed a stray hair from Laina's cheek as she slept, then let his hand linger there, resting against her heated skin. He loved her so much. *Please, God, let my suspicions be wrong. Let her be well.*

Laina coughed, stirred. Thad jerked his hand away from her cheek. It was pride, he knew, but he couldn't bear for her to know he loved her when he had nothing to offer her. A woman of Laina's social position had only the best. He frowned. The next time he was tempted to allow outward expression of his love for her, he should look around first. The furniture here in her bedroom was worth more than his entire house.

Thad took a deep breath, grabbed the candle and headed for the dressing room to wash his hands while Laina slept. At least with this measles outbreak in the orphanage he had an excellent opportunity to test his theory that lack of cleanliness had much to do with the spread of disease. And it would serve him well if he concentrated on the medical aspects of this situation and left his heart out of it.

Chapter Seventeen

"Laina. Laina!"

Who was calling her? Why didn't they let her sleep? She was tired. And her chest didn't hurt when she was sleeping.

"Laina!"

She frowned and forced her eyes open a slit. Daylight stabbed knives of pain into them. She closed them again, but not before she saw Thad bending over her. Her irritation fled. She loved Thad. And he was a doctor. He'd make her feel better.

"Laina, I know you can hear me. I want you to drink this." His arm slid behind her shoulders, raised her off her pillow. Cold china touched her lips. She shivered. She didn't want to drink anything. She wanted to sleep, but she swallowed the warm liquid to please him. A fit of coughing overcame her, making her chest hurt more and her head throb.

"Good!"

Good? It didn't *feel* good! She wanted to tell him he was wrong, but was too tired to make the effort. Fabric brushed against her skin as Thad lowered her to her pillows, setting off another spasm of violent shivers. Heat radiated from his hands as he tucked the covers under her chin and around her shoulders. A second later his palm rested lightly on her forehead. It felt wonderful there. Laina smiled and let herself drift back into sleep.

Thad went to wash his hands again, then walked to a window and pulled back one of the curtains, staring out at the branches of the maple tree that grew beside the house. The remaining leaves were yellowed, brown and sere around the edges. He studied them closely, then turned his attention to the fading glory of the flowers planted along the path to the playhouse. Anything to keep from dwelling on his growing fear for Laina.

He frowned, made his thoughts veer away from that direction and focused on the coming winter. It was only a matter of weeks until snow would cover the ground. He made a mental note to get the runners on his sleigh sharpened soon. It wouldn't do for him to be caught unprepared and unable to get to a sick patient.

Thad's stomach muscles tightened. He blew out a breath to relax them and ran his fingers through his hair, then lowered his hand to massage the tense muscles at the nape of his neck. Would he still be here caring for Laina and sick children when the first snowfall occurred? He hoped the answer to that question was no. That his orders for strict isolation and cleanliness would prove successful in stopping the measles before they swept through the entire orphanage.

"Take therefore no thought for the morrow: for the morrow shall take thought for the things of itself. Sufficient unto the day is the evil thereof."

The words of Jesus, recorded in the book of Matthew, slid into his mind. Thad wasn't sure if they comforted him or frightened him. He ran his hands through his hair again and looked up at the blue afternoon sky. "All right, Lord. I yield to Your wisdom. I won't think ahead. I'll take this situation one day at a time." He took a deep breath, let the curtain fall back into place and went to check on Laina.

Laina turned onto her side and broke into a spasm of coughing. Thad laid his Bible aside, slid the candle closer to the bed and reached out his hand to touch her forehead. She was burning up! And her cough was harsher…deeper.

He took a firm grip on his fear and rose to pull the stethoscope from his bag, sliding the pieces together. He pulled back the blankets and placed the end of the wooden tube on Laina's chest, lowering his ear to the other end. The crackling in her lungs confirmed his suspicion and sent fear racing through him as the memory of every patient he'd lost to pneumonia rushed to the surface of his consciousness.

Thad slammed the door of his mind to the memories and shoved the stethoscope back into his bag. He didn't dare remember. His professional detachment was already shattered. He covered Laina, who was shivering so hard she was shaking the bed, and dropped to his knees.

"Lord, please…*please* touch Laina with Your healing power. She's slipping beyond my ability to care for her, but You are the great physician. Your word says You healed *all* who came to You. Please, Lord, I lift Laina to You now. *Please* heal her. I ask it in Your holy name. Amen."

Thad blew out a breath and forced himself to leave Laina's side, to go wash his hands before he yanked the bellpull to summon Beaumont. He couldn't delay any longer. He had to convey the news of Laina's condition to Justin Randolph. He had given him his word.

Elizabeth took one look at Justin's face as he came back into the drawing room and a silent prayer for mercy rose from her heart. "What was the message?"

"Dr. Allen says Laina's not doing well—" His voice broke. "She has pneumonia." He paced the length of the room and back again, then stopped pacing and faced her. "I'm frightened, Elizabeth. I'm frightened for Laina."

"I am, too, Justin. But we mustn't give in to our fears." Elizabeth hurried to his side. "We have to have faith that God will hear our prayers and heal her."

"He hasn't so far."

The hurt in his voice brought tears to her eyes, and the anger underlying the hurt brought an ache to her heart. "I know, Justin…I know. But we still must cling to our faith in Him. We still must believe in His mercy and goodness and love."

"I suppose. What else have we?" His face went taut. He spun away from her. "I feel so helpless! Of all the riches I have, there's nothing that can help my sister."

Tears spilled from Elizabeth's eyes. She stepped forward and wrapped her arms around Justin's waist, placing her cheek against his back. He was rigid with hurt. His hands closed over hers, pulled them away from his body. He stepped forward out of her arms. Fear snaked through her. "Justin?"

"It's all right, Elizabeth. Don't worry. It's going to be all right. I'm not turning my back on God. I learned the hard way the folly of doing that. It's only—I don't understand…." He sucked in a breath. "I need to be as close to Laina as I can be right now. I'm going to go stand on the walk outside Twiggs Manor and pray. Don't wait up for me." He strode out of the room without a backward glance.

Elizabeth's knees gave way. She sank to the floor, staring after Justin, then wrapped her arms about herself and rocked back and forth. "'What time I am afraid, I will trust in Thee…. What time I am afraid, I will trust in Thee…. What time I am afraid, I will trust in Thee.'" She repeated the words over and over, wresting comfort and strength from the Scripture verse she had learned to live by.

"Stanford, sorry…so sorry…barren…"

She was dreaming again. Or hallucinating because of the fever. Thad laid his hand on Laina's forehead and she quieted. He lifted her off the pillow and held a cup of broth to her parched lips. She needed liquid and nourishment. She turned her head away. "Laina, you must drink this. Please drink it for me." He was begging, but he didn't care. *Let* his love for her show. What did it matter? Nothing mattered but that she get well!

Thad set the cup aside, drawing in a deep breath, trying to help Laina breathe as she struggled to pull air into her congested lungs. Four days! *Four days* she had been like this! "God help her! You're the breath of life! *Breathe* for her! Almighty God in heaven, *breathe* for her!"

His voice reverberated off the walls and ceiling, the anger and fear in it echoing in his ears. *Who was he to order God!*

Tears welled into Thad's eyes. He drew Laina's limp, un-resisting body close against his chest and buried his face in her hair. "Forgive me my anger. I'm so afraid, Lord. I'm so afraid. Please give me wisdom to know how to help Laina."

The curtains he'd drawn in front of the open windows to block the light during the day and keep out any breeze fluttered. Thad lifted his head, staring at them. A sudden gust of fresh night air rushed in the window, parting the curtains and filling his lungs. *Life-giving* air. His nerves tingled. He glanced down at Laina, lowered her to her pillow and pulled the covers up over her. She mumbled something incoherent. His hands clenched into fists. For-get the conventional medical practices! If he didn't do *something* she would die.

Thad ran to the windows and yanked down the cur-tains, throwing them in a heap on the chair by the hearth. He tugged open the windows as far as they would go, then hurried to the chaise along the side wall and pushed and pulled until it sat parallel to the window.

Fresh, cool night air flowed over top of the chaise, rif-fling his hair as he spread a sheet. He tossed his pillow on the upward sloping end of the chaise, pulled a table over to stand beside it, then hurried to the dressing room for a basin of cold water and a facecloth.

Everything was ready. Thad lifted Laina into his arms and carried her to the chaise, covering her with a blanket, then went back and grabbed the blanket from her bed. He wanted her cool, not chilled. He spread the second blanket over her, then wrung out the cloth in the cold water and placed it on her forehead. That was all he could think of to do. He stood staring down at her, feeling helpless, useless, *desperate,* praying that nothing he had done would harm her.

"Baby…can't have…baby…" Laina threw the covers off, opened her eyes.

"Shh, it's all right, Laina." Thad leaned down and smoothed the covers back over her, lifted her shoulders and tucked the second pillow beneath them, then held another cup of broth to her mouth. This time she swallowed some of the nutritious liquid. She broke into a fit of coughing.

Thad held her until the paroxysm passed, then lowered her to the elevated pillows as she slipped back into fevered sleep. He tucked the covers close about her so not a whisper of the cool night air could chill her, replaced the cool, moist rag on her forehead, then sat in the wooden chair he'd pulled to the side of the bed and reached under the covers to hold her hand. It felt small and fragile in his. Small, fragile and hot. His stomach knotted with fear.

"'Blessed is he that considereth the poor: the Lord will deliver him in time of trouble. The Lord will preserve him, and keep him alive….'" He whispered the words of the psalm looking at Laina, who had turned her home into an orphanage for the poor street children of Philadelphia, and he grabbed the ray of hope. "Make the promise in Your word real in Laina's life, Lord. Make the promise of Your word real in her. Preserve her, and keep her alive—"

A sob choked off his words. Thad's throat closed. He leaned forward, resting his head on the bed beside their clasped hands, and let his heart pray while the night air flowed over them.

"Children...help me...catch them!" Laina twisted and turned in the bed, the hand that rested in his opening and closing in convulsive movements.

"It's all right, Laina." Thad rose and leaned over her, stroking her hair with his free hand. "The children are all right. Sally is taking care of them."

"Stranger...help me...children..." She coughed, shivered. "Who...stranger? Who...?"

She *was* hallucinating. She didn't know who Sally was. Thad laid his hand on Laina's forehead, wincing at the heat that seared his hand. The facecloth was dry again. He wrung it out in the water and replaced it. "It's no stranger caring for the children, Laina. It's Sally, your maid. Everything is all right."

She turned her head away. "Breathless...his touch... makes...breathless..." Her eyes opened wide, and she stared up at him. "Thad!"

She recognized him! "Yes, Laina, it's me."

"Thad...stranger!" She twisted her head back and forth on her pillow. "No...*no!*" She convulsed in a fit of coughing. "Can't love Thad...can't...barren..."

Thad's heart lurched wildly, then settled. She was delirious. She didn't know what she was saying. He stroked her temples to calm her. "Shh, Laina, it's all right. Everything's all right. You rest quietly." He lifted Laina, cradling her in his arms, holding her close, rubbing her back and soothing her. The heat from her fevered body poured through the fabric between them, scorching his skin.

He grabbed the blankets and yanked them over her, then lowered his cheek to rest against her hair and rocked back and forth, struggling to pull air into his own lungs that were squeezed tight by the band of regret and dread that girdled his chest. What a fool he was! She loved him! *Loved* him! And he had let his pride keep them apart. Now…

Thad's heart slammed against his ribs. It couldn't be too late! He jerked his head up to look at the dark night sky.

"God, have mercy! I've been a fool, Lord! Forgive me my foolish, overweening pride that has kept us from sharing the love you've placed in our hearts, and spare Laina! Heal her, dear Lord. Honor Your promise and preserve her to life and I vow to You I will cherish her forever." He choked on the lump in his throat, swallowed back a rush of tears. "I love her, Lord. I love Laina. Please give me another chance to build a life with her. Have mercy, dear Lord, have mercy…."

Elizabeth opened her eyes, her heart jolting at sight of the empty space beside her in the bed. She sat up, sweeping her gaze around the room searching for her husband. He was standing at the window that faced toward Twiggs Manor, his hand braced against the frame as he looked out into the night. She slid out of bed and hurried to him. "Are you all right, Justin?"

He nodded, then draped his arm around her shoulders, pulling her close against him as he turned back to look out the window. The tension was gone from his body. She searched his face, looking for a clue as to what had happened to change him. She was afraid to question him for fear it would bring back his angry despair.

"Look at those stars, Elizabeth. And the moon! Look at the trees and the earth. How did He do it? How did God create all of these things? And then, to make a man…" Justin's voice trailed off on a note of wonder. "How powerful and mighty God is! How loving and wise."

He dropped a kiss on top of her head, then pulled her around in front of him. Elizabeth leaned back against him, reveling in the gentle strength of her husband's arms as he held her.

"Laina's going to be all right, Elizabeth." Justin's voice was a soft murmur of quiet conviction against her hair. "I woke up a little while ago, feeling an urgent need to pray for her, and then, while I was praying, I suddenly knew she was going to be all right." His voice was filled with awe. "I don't know how I know, but I know. Laina's going to be all right."

Chapter Eighteen

⚜

Their joined hands were pressing into his cheek, making the side of his face numb. He'd dozed off! Thad forced his gritty, sleep-deprived eyes open, squinting them against the bright sunlight pouring through the branches of the tree outside the window. Silence pressed against his eardrums, sending terror surging through him. *Laina wasn't struggling to breathe!* Panic jolted him fully awake.

The chill that raced through him stopped his heart, congealed his blood. Thad jerked his head up off the bed, the fingers of his hand holding Laina's automatically sliding upward to seek a pulse as he looked at her face. The flush was gone.

Her pulse throbbed steadily beneath his fingertips.

Thad's heart jolted to life, thumping out a wild dance of thanksgiving, sending his blood roaring through his veins. The crisis was past! Laina was breathing more easily, sleeping normally. She was going to live!

"Thank you, Lord Jesus!" The shout ripped from Thad's throat as he vaulted to his feet, spreading his arms wide and looking up toward the ceiling.

Laina jerked and opened her eyes. Light stabbed into them. She closed them to mere slits and stared up at Thad. He was unshaven and unkempt, his head was thrown back and he was staring up at the ceiling laughing like a madman. "Thad?" His name came out as a hoarse croak. She started to cough.

"Laina!"

In an instant Thad was bending over her, his hand touching her forehead, brushing her cheek. He snatched a cup from a small table, slid his arm beneath her shoulders and lifted her, holding the cup to her lips.

She didn't want any more of that horrid tea, but her mouth was so parched she swallowed, anyway. It was tea—*real,* delicious tea, even if it was cold. She drank it all, enjoying the feel of it moistening her mouth and sliding down her throat. Why did her throat feel so sore and raspy? "Do I—" Her voice cracked. She tried again. "Do I have the measles yet?"

"Do you have—? Oh, Laina—"

He was laughing again. And was he *hugging* her? The empty cup fell onto the bed as Thad's hand slid up to the back of her head. He drew her close and laid his head against her hair, murmuring her name. Laina stiffened with panic. She must be horribly ill. She was hallucinating!

Thad's arms immediately relaxed their grip. He looked down at her. "I'm sorry. I didn't mean to hurt you. I forgot myself. Are you all right?"

Laina nodded, relieved she wasn't hallucinating, but too nonplussed to speak. Why was Thad acting this way? She turned her head and glanced across the room, then squinted up at him. "Why am I not in my bed?"

He stroked her hair. "I moved you by the window so the fresh air could help you breathe easier. You've been very sick." His fingers brushed against her jaw.

"I have?" Maybe that accounted for the tingles streaking along her nerves. Maybe it wasn't his touch.

"Yes. You frightened me." She looked adorable! Squinty-eyed, mussed, tousled, confused and absolutely adorable! Thad sucked in a deep breath, reining in his emotions. More than anything in the world he wanted to crush her to him, claiming her lips in a kiss that would give vent to his overwhelming love for her, but that would have to wait. She had to be well—truly well—before that could be. For now, he would have to content himself with holding her. His arms tightened.

Laina's eyes widened. She stared up at him. "Wh-what are you doing?"

"Something I've wanted to do from the moment I first saw you standing in the street over Billy, demanding Henry Rhodes take him to a doctor. I'm holding you in my arms." His control broke. "Laina, have you no idea how much I love you?"

Her mouth gaped open and she went completely slack in his arms. "What did you say?"

"I said I love you." He held her astonished gaze with his. "Now and forever, I love you." In her eyes he saw her confusion, saw the very instant that she understood. To his horror, she burst into tears. She began to shake, sobbing and coughing until she gasped for breath and went limp.

"Laina, don't cry! Please don't cry! You're too weak. You'll make yourself ill again." Thad could have cut out his tongue. He drew her close against his chest, tucking her head beneath his chin. "I'm sorry, Laina. Please forgive me. I'm a clumsy oaf, speaking about my love when you've been so sick. Please don't cry. Everything can wait until you're strong and well. Shh…shh, my love, shh…"

Exhaustion overtook her. He sensed her trying to fight it, trying not to succumb to the seduction of sleep, but she was too frail. She gave a long sigh and fell asleep in his arms.

"Thank You, Lord. Thank You for bringing Laina through the crisis. Help her to become fully well and strong again, I pray." Thad whispered the words against Laina's hair, then reluctantly lowered her to her pillow. He had a lot to do before she woke again. He lifted the cup from the bed and set it on the table, then picked up the basin of water and headed for the dressing room. His steps slowed. He paused beside Laina's bed, frowning. His cleanliness theory was proving true, and he wanted to change the linens, put Laina back in her clean bed and set the sheets and blankets on the chaise outside the door with his pallet for laundering. But what about Laina herself?

Thad strode to the head of the bed, yanked the bellpull, then hurried on to the dressing room to get rid of the bowl. When Beaumont arrived, he would send him for Laina's maid to wash her and change her gown. He would also have him order some nourishing soup made and send news of Laina's recovery to her brother. As for him, he would set the room to rights, and when all was done, bathe and shave.

Thad glanced in the mirror over the washstand and lifted his hand to scrub at the five days' accumulation of stubble on his chin. A smile curved his lips. It felt good to think about ordinary, everyday things again.

Something was tickling her cheek. Laina frowned and brushed back the strand of hair that was fluttering in the warm autumn breeze coming in the window. The simple movement tired her. Why was she so weak? She rested quietly a moment, then summoned the strength to open her eyes.

"Good afternoon. How do you feel?" Thad smiled at her from his chair beside her bed. A neatly dressed, clean-shaven Thad.

So it had all been a dream. Laina stared up at the tester overhead and swallowed back a rush of tears. It was for the best that Thad not love her, considering her barren condition, so why did she feel like crying? How selfish a person she was! She faced back his way and forced a smile. "I feel thirsty. And tired." She frowned. "Why is my voice so raspy?"

"It's from the cough." Thad laid aside what looked like a journal he'd been writing in and went to the fireplace, pouring tea from a kettle resting on its iron trivet over a pile of hot coals. He stirred in some honey, then came and slid his arm under her shoulders and held the cup to her lips. "It's not hot, only nicely warm."

She took a tentative sip. The tea tasted wonderful, and felt even better going down her throat. But it couldn't compare to the comfort and strength of Thad's arm about her. She pushed away the thought and took another swallow of tea. "That's enough."

Tears welled up when he nodded and removed his arm. Laina blinked them away. If only she felt stronger she wouldn't be so weepy! She took a breath, coughed, then sagged into the pillows behind her, feeling like a wrung-out rag. "When will I be over the measles?"

"They're already fading away."

Thad reached for her hand, his fingers sliding to her wrist as he took her pulse. How warm and strong his hand was. Laina resisted the impulse to curl her fingers up to touch his. "Fading away? How can that be? I've only been ill—" she flushed at thought of the two days when she'd hidden her symptoms from him "—a short while."

"No, Laina. It's been several days." His gaze held hers. "You should have told me when you became ill. If you'd gone to bed right away you might not have developed pneumonia."

"Pneumonia!" She wasn't sure if her heart was fluttering because of the startling news or because of the look in Thad's eyes, but she knew her breathlessness was caused by his hand sliding down and enfolding hers.

"You frightened me."

There was a tremor in his voice. Laina fought to keep hers steady. "I did?"

He nodded, sat on the edge of her bed. "I thought I was going to lose you."

She cleared her throat. "I'm sorry. I know how you hate to lose a patient."

"Not a patient, Laina. You." He lifted their joined hands, kissed hers. "I love you. I've loved you from the day I first saw you standing over Billy, demanding care for him."

It wasn't a dream after all! Laina's heart thudded. Joy flooded her soul, followed immediately by despair. She blinked back tears. For once she would be grateful for what she had instead of demanding more. *Thank You,*

Lord, for this moment. Thank You for allowing me to experience what it feels like to be loved by this wonderful man. She drew in a breath. "I'm honored, Thad, truly. But you mustn't love me."

"Because you're barren?"

His voice was soft, warm, loving—but oh, how those words hurt. Laina nodded and looked away, too choked up to speak.

Thad took her other hand. "Look at me, Laina."

She blinked away the tears and turned her head back toward him. He drew both her hands to his chest. "Do you feel that, Laina? That's the steady, solid beat of a heart that loves you." His eyes held hers. "I don't care if you're barren. I don't want you for any reason other than I love you and want to be with you for the rest of my life."

Tears overflowed her eyes, running down her cheeks. "But Thad, you—"

"No, Laina. I want *you.*" A slow smile spread across his face and twinkled in his eyes. "And you already have forty-seven children. That's enough for any man." His heart thudded beneath her hands as his smile faded away. "Laina Randolph Brighton, I love you. And though I have little in the way of worldly goods to offer you, will you do me the honor of being my wife?"

Chapter Nineteen

❧

"So what is your answer going to be?"

Laina looked up at Justin. "I don't know, dearheart. I don't know what is the right thing to do. That's why I came over seeking advice. All I know is the love in Thad's eyes when he asked me to marry him made it impossible for me to say no to him. But I couldn't say yes, either."

Laina stirred on the garden bench and glanced at her brother and Elizabeth. "Am I being selfish to want to marry him? I know Thad *says* he doesn't care if I'm barren, but in a few years…"

"Laina, listen to me." Justin reached out and took her hand in his. "You know how much I love James, but I love Sarah and Mary every bit as much. And I would want Elizabeth for my wife if we never had a child." He let go and reached for his wife's hand. "I love her. I need her. I want to be with her forever. It's that simple."

"Truly, dearheart?"

"Truly." His gaze held hers. "Thad isn't Stanford, Laina. If you marry it will be because you love one another, not because of mutual respect only. And unlike Stanford, Thad's not going to distance himself from you because you can't produce an heir for him. He's asked you to be his wife *knowing* that's impossible."

Tears stung her eyes. Laina rose to her feet, pulling her fur-trimmed velvet coat close against the crisp October air. Thad had made her promise not to get chilled. Thad. He'd been so patient these past few weeks, saying everything could wait until she was well again, but he was coming tonight for her answer. *Oh, Lord, don't let me hurt Thad. I love him. Help me know what is right to do for him.*

"I think we'd better go inside, Laina."

Laina glanced down as Justin rose and took hold of her elbow, turning her toward his house. He must have seen her shiver. He was so protective of her since she'd been ill. Her heart swelled. She no longer took the blessing of his brotherly love for granted. "All right, dearheart."

"Why don't you turn the situation around, Laina?" Elizabeth moved over to walk beside her. "It might help you to understand Thad's feelings and clarify your own."

Laina frowned. "I don't understand what you mean, but I'm willing to do anything that will help me get rid of these feelings of guilt and doubt so I can make a decision."

"All right." Elizabeth smiled at her as they climbed the steps to the back porch. "Tell me this. If you weren't barren and had no children and you knew Thad was unable to father any for you, would you marry him?"

"Well, of course I would!" Laina all but sputtered with indignation. "I *love* him! And I— Oh." Her eyes widened.

Elizabeth and Justin grinned at her. She burst into laughter and hugged her sister-in-law. "Elizabeth Randolph, you are the wisest woman I know."

Justin laughed. "I've been telling her that for the last two years. Now, let's get inside, Laina. Thad will have my hide if I let you catch a chill." He pulled open the door and ushered her into the house.

He was here!
At the sound of Thad's voice in the entrance hall, Laina jumped to her feet and hurried to the mirror hanging on the wall of the parlor. A faint scent of roses was released as she gave a light pat to the dark brown curls piled atop her head and skimmed her gaze over her face. She looked slightly panicked. She inhaled deeply to calm the nervous quivering in her stomach and turned from the mirror.

She should sit down. No! She should stand by the window, looking casual….

"Good evening, Laina."

Her legs made her decision for her. They lost all strength as Thad walked into the room. The long skirt of her cherry-red watered-silk taffeta gown poofed out around her as she collapsed into a chair. A flush climbed her throat and warmed her cheeks as she smoothed the skirt into place. "Good evening, Thad. I see no emergency has detained you." *What an inane thing to say!* The heat in her cheeks increased.

Thad stopped a few steps away, looking down at her. "Yes. No emergency tonight." His gaze fastened on hers. "Red suits you, Laina. You look beautiful in it." He took a step closer. "But then, you always look beautiful. Inside and out, you're the most beautiful woman I've ever known."

Warmth rushed through her. Laina clasped her hands in her lap as they began to tremble.

Thad took another step, leaned down and took her hands in his. Her lungs stopped functioning. The insane thought that she had survived pneumonia only to die because she went breathless at Thad's touch flashed through her mind as he knelt in front of her.

"Let's get to the purpose of my visit, shall we? I didn't come here for polite conversation, Laina. I came for your answer." His voice was soft, mesmerizing. She got lost in the love glowing in his eyes. "Will you marry me?"

Laina struggled to gather her disjointed thoughts, to find her voice. It was only fair to give him one last chance to change his mind. "I'd come to you barren, but with fifty-three children attached." A whisper was the best she could achieve. She finally managed a breath. "If that's acceptable—and I'll understand if it's not—then…yes, I'll marry you."

Flames flickered deep in Thad's eyes. He rose, gently pulled her to her feet and slid his arms around her. "Fifty-three now, is it?" A delicious shiver of anticipation tingled through Laina as he lifted her chin and lowered his head. "So what *is* our newest child—a son or a daughter?"

She couldn't remember. But it didn't matter. Thad's mouth hovered over hers, awakening emotions she'd never before experienced, and her ability to speak had disappeared altogether.

"I love you, Laina."

Tears of happiness welled up. "I love you, Thad."

Joy flashed in his eyes the instant before his mouth descended, claiming her lips in a kiss that made her head whirl.

Laina closed her eyes and grabbed the lapels of his jacket, holding on for dear life as she answered his love with her own.

"Judge, thank you for coming, for making the journey to Philadelphia. Having you here made this day even more wonderful." Laina hugged her portly surrogate father.

The elderly man chuckled. "Did you doubt that I would come?" He leaned back and looked down at her, his gray eyebrows lowering as he gave her a mock frown. "Surely you didn't think I'd let anyone else perform your wedding ceremony?"

Laina tilted her head, slanting a look up him, and patted his jacket over the area of his heart. "Not really." She stretched up and kissed his chin. "You love me too much to allow that."

Justin hooted. Laina was truly restored to health after these long weeks of her recovery. She was her teasing, saucy, forthright self again. *Thank You, Lord.*

Laina turned and wrinkled her nose at him, then smiled and stepped into his arms, giving him a big hug. "I love you, dearheart. Thank you for letting us borrow your drawing room for the ceremony." She whirled and hugged Elizabeth. "And thank you so much for the lovely wedding supper." She took a deep breath and looked at Thad.

He smiled at her. "Are you ready to go?"

A wholly unaccustomed shyness struck her dumb at his question. She felt like a bride, not a thirty-year-old widow. She nodded and moved to his side, into the welcoming comfort of his outstretched arm. He drew her close and held out his free hand. "Thank you for coming, Judge

Braden. You've made Laina very happy. And I'm honored to meet you."

The elderly man nodded. "And I'm honored to meet you, young man. Thank you again for taking such good care of Laina when she was so ill." Tears misted his faded blue eyes. "I've no doubt the Lord used you to restore her to us, and it comforts me to know she's in such loving, capable hands." He cleared his throat. "God's richest blessings on you both."

"Thank you, sir." Thad turned and extended his hand to Justin. "And thank you, Justin, for standing with me and for allowing us the use of your home for our wedding." A smile curved his lips. "It's a little crowded at Twiggs Manor."

Justin grinned. "That's an understatement if ever I've heard one." He cleared his throat. "I echo the judge's sentiments, Thad. It comforts me to know Laina is in your care. And I *know* God's hand has been upon you both. May He continue to bless you through all your years together."

"And that is my wish for you both, as well." Elizabeth stepped forward, kissed Laina, then went on tiptoe and laid her cheek against Thad's as she squeezed his free hand. "Welcome to the family, Thad." She stepped back and smiled up at him. "I've always wanted a brother."

"You're sure you don't want the use of the carriage?"

"No, dearheart. It's only a short distance. We'd rather walk."

"All right, then." Justin gave her a last hug. "God bless, and good night." He closed the door.

Laina glanced up at Thad and promptly went tongue-tied at the look of love in his eyes. Her cheeks warmed.

Thad raised his hands, brushed back her fur-trimmed hood, cupped her face, then leaned down and lightly brushed her lips with his. "Shall we go home, Mrs. Allen?" He pulled her hood back in place, tucked her gloved hand through his arm and started down the stairs.

Big, soft, fluffy snowflakes started to fall as they strolled down the drive to the brick sidewalk. Thad smiled down at her. "I think God is showering us with His blessings."

"What a beautiful thought." Laina snuggled closer to his warmth and returned his smile. "I didn't know you had a whimsical side to your nature."

With his free hand Thad covered her hand resting on his arm. "It only sounded whimsical, Laina. I'm serious. I'm a thirty-two-year-old orphan bachelor who has suddenly acquired a beautiful, loving wife, children, a brother and sister, and nieces and a nephew. I've always wanted a family. How could I not be aware of God's hand of blessing?"

Laina stopped walking. Snowflakes caught on her eyelashes as she tipped her head back to look up at him. "Thaddeous John Allen, you're the most wonderful man I know. I love you." She lifted one gloved hand to the back of his neck and tugged his head down. Her lips met his in a brief kiss of promise.

Thad sucked in his breath, tucked her hand back through his arm and continued walking.

"How much farther is it?"

"The middle of the block. Are you cold?"

Laina shook her head and looked up at him. "No. Are you?"

"Not after that kiss."

Heat rushed to her cheeks. Thad chuckled and guided her onto a stone walk. She looked up, seeing his house for the first time. "Oh, Thad, it's lovely!" She swept her gaze over the small two-story brick home with a one-story clapboard addition on the right side. Warm candlelight glowed from the multipaned downstairs windows and formed golden pools of light on either side of the centered door. She glanced at him in surprise. "Who lit the candles?"

"Mrs. Harding, my housekeeper. I asked her to come over at dusk and light the candles and start the fires." He kissed her forehead. "I didn't want you coming to a cold, unwelcoming house."

Tears welled in her eyes at his thoughtfulness.

He squeezed her hand. "Shall we go inside?" He pushed open the door and stepped back for her to precede him.

Laina walked through the door into the small entrance hall and the oddest feeling hit her. She stopped dead in her tracks, looking around, suddenly sure she was exactly where she was supposed to be. All doubt was gone. She had come home. She sighed, turned and stepped into her husband's welcoming arms.

"There you are, boy." Thad poured the feed into the manger, gave Faithful a last pat and left the barn, hurrying along the path to the house. He climbed the steps to the shed, washed up, stepped out of his boots, then walked on stocking feet through the door into the kitchen. A thumping, scraping sound issuing from the front of the house greeted him.

Heart pounding, Thad ran down the hall toward the parlor, stopping short as he spotted Laina standing in the middle of the room with her arms crossed over her ribs and her head tilted to one side as she studied the settee that now sat facing the fireplace. That explained the scraping noise—she'd dragged the piece of furniture from its place along the far wall.

"Laina, what are you doing? You shouldn't—"

"Thad!" Laina spun toward him, brushing back a strand of hair that had fallen free. Her cheeks colored. "I wanted—" the color deepened "—that is, I thought it might be more cozy on these cool nights if the settee was closer to the fire." She took a breath. "But if you don't care for it here, we can put it back."

"No." He shook his head. "I like the look of it there."

She beamed. "Do you truly?"

"Yes." He walked toward her. "But I want you to promise me you won't move furniture by yourself. You're too frail to do such things."

Laina waved away his objection. "I only look frail because I've always been pampered. I'm really very strong." She gave him a beguiling smile. "But if you would care to pamper me, you could bring that green brocade chair over and set it here." She indicated a spot at right angles to the settee and fireplace. "And then if you would place the two Windsors under the windows, and put the piecrust table between them."

She clasped her hands in front of her, tapping her forefingers together as she studied the room. "And I believe we should bring in the Chippendale desk that's hidden away in that nook under the stairs. It will look wonderful on that far wall." She gave a deep sigh.

Thad's heart sank. He sucked in a breath and stepped up behind her, circling her with his arms and kissing the warm, silky skin just below her ear as she leaned back against him. "I'm sorry, Laina. I was thoughtless to bring you to a house so small and without amenities when I know you're accustomed to so much more. I only did so because I thought perhaps you'd prefer to be alone these first few days. I was wrong, and I'm sorry. But I'll make it up to you. You don't have to try to make this house into something it's not, and you don't have to wait for the week to pass. We'll go to your home immediately."

"Thaddeous Allen!" Laina twisted out of his arms and spun about, her eyes flashing angry sparks up at him. "How dare you say such a thing to me! I *love* this house."

Thad gaped at her. "But I thought—"

"Well, you're wrong! And Twiggs Manor is *not* my home. It's Abigail's, and it always will be. At least to me." Laina squared her shoulders and lifted her chin. "Please sit down, Thad. We have to talk." She sat on the edge of the settee and turned to face him, then promptly rose to her feet again and walked to the fireplace.

Thad stood beside the chair, watching her, puzzled by her agitated state. "Laina, whatever is bothering you…"

She lifted her chin. "Thad, I know we planned to live at Twiggs Manor, and I don't want to disappoint you, but things have changed. Doreen and Beaumont have been running the orphanage since I was taken ill, and when they marry next week they're going to need privacy. My rooms would be perfect for them."

She took a breath and fastened her gaze on his. "Twiggs Manor is only a short walk from here and…well, I was wondering…" She took another breath. "Would you be horribly disappointed if we bring Emma and Billy and Anne here to live with us? If we make this our home?"

"If we— But I thought—" Thad blew out a breath and raked his hands through his hair, dislodging his cowlick. "Laina, you astound me."

She walked over and reached up, satisfying her long-held desire to smooth his stubborn lock of hair back in place. "Does that mean yes?"

Thad pulled her into his arms. "That means nothing would please me more." He lowered his head.

"Wait! There's more."

He stopped, his lips an inch above hers. "What is it?"

She glanced around the room, sighed and looked into his eyes. "May we paint the walls? Everything's so white!"

Thad burst into laughter. "How could I say thee nay, my love?" He lifted her up until their mouths were level, then wrapped his arms around her and kissed her until they were both breathless.

"And you're really *truly* my papa?"

Thad grinned at Emma. "I really truly am."

"Oh, goody!" Emma threw her little arms around his neck and squeezed so hard Thad had to put his hand down on the floor to keep his balance. The next instant she spun to face her brother. "Billy, we gots a papa! A *real* papa, not a pretend one!"

"Yeah!" Billy flushed. "I mean, yes. And I'm gonna be a doctor like him!" He grinned from ear to ear as Thad reached out and tugged him into his arms for a hug.

"And we gots a new sister!" Emma danced around Laina, who was holding Anne in her arms.

"I know." Billy leaned close to Thad's ear. "Anne's sorta little, but I'll take good care of her, Papa."

Thad swallowed the lump in his throat and ruffled Billy's hair. "We'll take care of her together, son. We'll all take care of each other—that's what you do in a family." He lifted his gaze to Laina and his chest ached with his love for her. She was so beautiful, standing there with Anne in her arms. *Oh, Lord, please let me give Laina a child.*

He rose, dropped a kiss on Anne's soft warm cheek and lifted her from Laina's arms. "I'll carry Anne down the stairs. She's heavy for you." He settled the toddler in one arm, wrapped his other arm around Laina and smiled. "Let's take our children home."

Chapter Twenty

Laina laid two thick chunks of wood on the pulsating red coals in the brick fireplace and turned to survey her daughters' bedroom. The flickering light of the greedily feeding fire threw lacy shadows from the testers of the two small beds against the pumpkin-colored walls and warmed the bright colors in the matching quilts. There all resemblance stopped.

Laina smiled. Anne's bed was smooth, every cover in place. Even her small body, cradled as it was in the feather mattress, didn't break the bed's even plane. Only her russet curls, barely visible above the edge of the quilt, gave testimony to her occupancy. Emma, on the other hand…

Laina's smile widened. Emma's blankets were askew. Her quilt hung over the edge of the bed, partially covering a small, dangling, flannel-clad arm and leg before ending in a thick puddle of folds on the floor—beside her pillow.

Laina crossed to the bed and picked up the pillow, then gently rolled Emma into the center of the mattress and pulled the covers over her. She leaned down and kissed her soft warm cheek, then moved on to Anne, who was burrowed in so deep she contented herself with dropping a kiss on top of the silky russet curls. The little sweetheart didn't even stir. But then, she never did. Trying to keep up with Emma's boundless energy all day quite wore the toddler out.

Laina's heart swelled with thanksgiving. *Thank You, Lord, for giving Thad and me these beautiful children. For making us a family.* She stood watching her daughters sleep for a moment, then turned and left the room. Her long skirts whispered softly against the wide plank floor as she crossed the hall to Billy's bedroom. She glanced in the direction of his bed, tiptoed to the fireplace and bent to pick up a piece of wood.

"Will Papa come home soon?"

Laina almost dropped the wood. She placed it on the fire and turned toward the bed. "I thought you were sleeping."

Billy shook his head against his pillow. "I want to tell Papa good night."

Sweet, sweet Billy, who adored Thad. He was fighting to keep his eyes open. Laina smiled. "I know you do, honey." She tucked the deep blue woven coverlet under his chin and perched on the side of his bed. "But I think you'd better go to sleep now. Papa had to go see a patient and I don't know when he'll be home." She reached out and smoothed back the soft blond curls that had fallen on his forehead. "When Papa comes home, I'll have him come wake you and say good night."

Billy's mouth gaped in a wide yawn. "Heart's... prom...ise?" His eyelids slid closed.

Laina smiled and leaned down to kiss his cheek. "Heart's promise."

Bells jingled outside. Laina rose and hurried to the window, pulling aside the blue curtain and opening the louvers of one of the shutters to peer out into the night. Sidelamps from a sleigh flickered in the darkness on the street below. The bells grew louder. It was Thad. He was home safe. *Thank You, Lord.*

Excited anticipation tightened Laina's stomach as she watched the sleigh turn into the drive leading to the barn. He'd soon be coming in the door. She smiled and tiptoed from Billy's room, then hurried down the stairs to poke up the kitchen fire and warm Thad some of the soup Mrs. Harding had made for their supper.

"Hmm, something smells good."

Laina turned from stirring the soup. Thad stood by the door, the towel draped around his neck testifying that, as always, he had bathed and changed into the clothes he kept hanging in the shed dressing room before coming into the house. The hint of soap, herbs and spices that hovered around him tantalized her nostrils. Billy called it his doctor smell. She smiled. "Yes, it does, Doctor."

He caught her meaning, grinned and started toward her. "It is such a blessing not to have to pump pails of water for my bath. I believe having that water piped directly into the house is the smartest thing I've ever done—

second to marrying you, of course." He smiled down at her. "Hello, Mrs. Allen. Do you have any idea how wonderful you are to come home to?" He took her in his arms.

Laina dropped the spoon and lifted her face to receive Thad's kiss, letting out a started squeal as water dripped into her eye from the lock of hair hanging on his forehead. She grabbed the ends of the towel, dabbed her eye and scrubbed at his hair. "That's better." She gave him a saucy smile. "Now, where were we?"

Thad gave a low growl and claimed her lips.

"How are things at Twiggs Manor?"

"Wonderful! They placed three children in homes this week." Laina glanced at Elizabeth and shook her head. "Whoever would have thought that staid, proper Beaumont would one day run an orphanage?" She turned her attention back to James, who was using the bodice of her dress for leverage to pull himself erect. She placed her hands under his pudgy little arms to steady him and kissed the tip of his tiny nose. "Aren't you getting to be a big strong boy?" The baby bounced up and down, waving his arms and giving her a wide smile. "Elizabeth, he has a new tooth!"

"Yes." Elizabeth glanced with pride at her son. "It came in yesterday."

The familiar yearning ache—stronger and more painful than ever now that she was married to Thad—rose in Laina's heart. Not only would she never have the joy of having a baby and watching him grow, but she had robbed Thad of that joy, also.

"He maketh the barren woman to keep house, and to be a joyful mother of children. Praise ye the Lord."

The verse of Scripture she'd read a few weeks ago slid into her mind. Laina glanced over at Anne, who was seated on the floor rolling a ball with Mary, then shifted her gaze to Emma and Sarah, busy with their dolls. Billy was seated in the rocker on the hearth looking at a book. *I do praise You, Lord! And I thank You for Thad and the children You have given us. Please forgive me the selfish desires of my heart and help me to be content with my barren condition. You know what is best for me, Lord. I yield to Your will.*

Laina sent the silent prayer winging heavenward from her heart. When she'd read that verse, she'd vowed to be thankful for the blessings the Lord had showered upon her and to stop longing for what could never be. She did quite well—until she held James. And that was another blessing. *Thank You, Lord, that Elizabeth is unselfish and is willing to share James with me. I shall be content with holding my nephew.*

"Laina."

She looked over at Elizabeth. "Yes?"

"Justin and I are entertaining tomorrow night. Would you and Thad be free to join us for dinner?" She gave her a twisted smile. "Before you answer I feel it's only fair to warn you that Mr. Henry Rhodes will be among our guests."

Laina stiffened. Her gaze shifted to Billy, her fingertips tingling with the memory of the raised scar on the back of his head. "Thank you for the invitation, Elizabeth, but no." She looked back at her sister-in-law. "I have no desire to be in the same room with Mr. Rhodes—let alone break bread with him!"

Elizabeth gave her one of those penetrating looks that made her want to squirm. "You know you have to forgive him eventually, Laina. It's in God's word."

She wrinkled her nose at her. "Yes, I know. And I will forgive him...eventually." She laughed. "I'm doing my best to follow God's ways, Elizabeth, but I only seem able to manage one lesson at a time."

Laina brushed her hair, gathered it on top of her head, twisted it into a thick coil of brown curls and shoved in the combs to hold it in place. A smile of satisfaction curved her lips. She was getting quite good at styling her hair. She wound the wine-red silk ribbon that matched her dress around the base of the coil and tied it in place. There! She was ready for the day. Now to wake Anne.

Laina opened the bedroom door and walked out into the hall. The smell of cooking greeted her. She smiled. Mrs. Harding was frying bacon and eggs, Billy's favorite breakfast. Her smile faded as her stomach churned. She took a deep breath to quell the sudden spate of nausea and her eyes widened. The eggs! She clapped her hand over her nose and mouth and ran for the dressing room.

"Mama."

Laina rinsed her mouth, wiped her face with a cool, moist rag and went into her bedroom. Anne was standing in her long ruffled flannel nightgown in the middle of the room, rubbing her sleepy eyes.

"I'm here, sweetie." Laina lifted her youngest child up in her arms and sat down on the side of the bed.

"Me hungry, Mama."

Laina's stomach turned over at the thought of food. "I know you are, Anne. Mama will take you downstairs in a moment, but first we have to get you dressed." She carried her into the dressing room and closed the door. That was better. She couldn't smell the eggs in here. She washed Anne's face and hands, then brushed her hair.

"Go see Mary?"

Laina smiled. "Not today, sweetie. Today we're going to Twiggs Manor. Mama is going to visit with the nice people who adopted Tom." She put stockings on Anne's small feet, then tugged pantalettes on over them. "They want a sister for Tom. Isn't that nice?" *What was wrong with her stomach?* She took a deep breath, pulled the green gingham dress over Anne's head and tied the sashes on the matching apron.

"Laina?"

"I'm in the dressing room with Anne." She looked up as Thad opened the door. The smell of eggs assailed her nostrils. Her stomach heaved. "Take Anne!" She shoved the toddler into Thad's arms, slammed the dressing-room door and spun toward the washbasin, gagging.

"Stay right here a moment, sweetie." Thad put Anne in the middle of the bed and closed the bedroom door so she couldn't go down the stairs. "Papa will be right back. Here, look at this." He gave her his pocket watch, opened the dressing-room door and stepped inside.

Laina was sitting on the wood chair by the window she'd tugged open. She made pushing motions with her hand. "Close the door, please!" She put the moist cloth back over her nose and mouth.

"Laina, what's wrong?" Thad went on his knees in front of her, his eyes searching her pale face as he took her hand in his. It was trembling. His fingers slid upward to her wrist.

She opened her eyes and shook her head. "I don't know. I was fine, and then I smelled the eggs." She shuddered. "I got sick twice." She shuddered again and handed him Anne's shoes. "Will you take Anne down to breakfast, please? I don't want to get near her again. I think I must have the ague that's going around." She leaned her head back against the wall and closed her eyes.

Thad set Anne's shoes aside and laid his palm on Laina's forehead. "You have no fever, and you're not shivering. Are you chilled?"

"No."

"Do you ache anywhere? Does your skin hurt? Your head?"

"No. It's only my stomach."

"And you were fine until you smelled the eggs?"

She shuddered and nodded. "Don't talk about them."

Lord, can it be? Excitement coursed through Thad. He fought to keep the grin from his face. He could be wrong. It *could* be the winter ague. Several children at the orphanage had it. He mustn't build her hopes, but he was almost positive… The grin spread his lips wide. He couldn't stop it. He lowered his head.

"Why are you *grinning?*"

He hadn't been fast enough. He looked up. Laina was staring at him, a mixture of hurt and confusion in her beautiful eyes.

"You find my taking sick amusing?" Tears welled into her eyes.

"No, Laina! Never." Thad rose and took her in his arms.

She stiffened and leaned back to look up at him. "Then why were you grinning? *Something* was amusing you."

The hurt was still in her eyes. He'd have to tell her. He slid his hands to her upper arms and took a deep breath. "I was grinning because I don't believe you're sick, Laina. I don't think you have the ague. I think you're going to have our baby."

The color drained from her face. She stared at him a long moment, then shook her head and stepped back out of his grasp. "That's quite impossible, Thad." Her voice broke. He reached for her, but she moved away. "I didn't know you were hoping for such a thing to happen. How can you— How can you even *say* such a thing to me? You know I'm barren."

She sounded hurt...wounded. He took her by the shoulders and turned her to face him. Her face looked frozen with pain. "Laina, listen to me. If you never have our child it won't matter. I love you now, and I'll love you forever. But I don't *know* that you are barren, and neither do you."

He searched her eyes, looking for some sign that he was reaching her through the fear and hurt she'd carried for so many years. "You told me your first husband was a childless widower twenty years older than you." He wiped a tear from her cheek. "I don't *know*, Laina, but it's possible that Stanford was unable to father a child."

For an instant hope blazed in her eyes. A hope so fervent, so pure it seared his heart. She took a breath and turned away. "Please don't ever say that again, Thad. I've finally accepted what God has willed for my life. I read a verse a few weeks ago that says it perfectly. 'He maketh the barren woman to keep house, and to be a joyful mother of children.' It's true." She turned back to look at him. "You and Emma and Billy and Anne are my joy and my blessings from the Lord. I'll not hope or ask for more. Not ever again."

Chapter Twenty-One

Laina frowned and fastened the ties on her nightgown. Why couldn't she get over the ague? She was so tired of the alternate spurts of boundless energy and bone-weary fatigue. And her stomach still wasn't normal.

Laina picked up her brush and stroked it through her hair, using the steady rhythm to calm her nerves. Tears were far too ready to fall these days, her emotions far too touchy. But that was understandable. Thad treated her like a piece of fragile china and walked around with a proud grin on his face. Oh, if only he would stop *hoping!* It was forming a chasm between them she didn't know how to bridge. She couldn't bear to disappoint him, but it had taken her too long to come to the place where she could accept God's will for her life to go back to the place of hope and despair. It would destroy her.

At the sound of Thad's footfalls on the stairs Laina took a deep breath and blinked away the hot tears stinging her eyes. She grabbed a ribbon and busied herself tying her hair back at the nape of her neck as he came into the bedroom.

"Umm, you look delicious." He leaned down and kissed that tender spot under her ear. "How do you feel?"

She *hated* that question. "I'm fine. No reason I shouldn't be." Laina rose and went to turn down the bed. "How is Mrs. Ferguson?"

"She's doing fine, now that I managed to talk her family into opening the windows a bit to give her some fresh air to breathe." He came and put his arms around her. "I owe that bit of knowledge to you, my love. I was so terrified of losing you I was willing to try anything, even if it went against conventional practice." She felt him shudder. "I never want to go through anything like that again!"

"Well, you won't have to." She put her arms around him and smiled, trying to tease away the bad memory. "I've had the measles now."

"So you have." He kissed her and went to the dressing room.

Laina climbed into bed, aching with love for Thad, hating the distance his stubborn belief in his diagnosis was causing between them. Why couldn't he simply accept her barren condition? *Oh, Lord, help us. Please do something to help us be as one again. Please send an undeniable sign so—*

Laina jerked to a sitting position. A sign! She'd been so upset she hadn't considered… When had she last… She stared down at her fingers, counting the weeks. Of course, with her irregular—

"I had to cover Emma again when I went to their rooms to bank the fires." Thad climbed into bed, put his arm around her. "What's wrong?"

"Nothing." *Could it be?*

"You're shivering, Laina."

"I'm fine. A little chilled." *Lord?*

"Come here." Thad lay back against his pillow and pulled her close against him. "Is that better?"

"Yes. Thank you."

"My pleasure, Mrs. Allen." He turned his head and brushed her lips with a soft kiss.

Laina went rigid.

"What's the matter?" Thad lifted himself up onto an elbow and looked down at her. Her eyes were wide, startled. "Laina, what is it?"

"Something *moved*. In my stomach. Like—like butterfly wings brushing against me. *Oh!*" She sucked in a breath. "There it is again. Oh, Thad, we're going to have a *baby!* God truly does answer prayer!" Laina threw herself into his arms, laughing and sobbing as he crushed her against him.

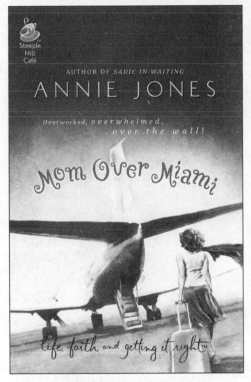

From *USA TODAY* bestselling author Deborah Bedford comes BLESSING

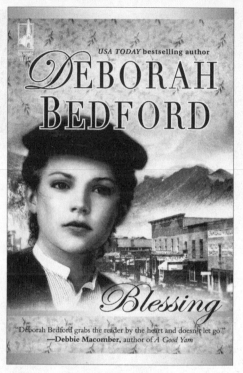

USA TODAY bestselling author

DEBORAH BEDFORD

Blessing

"Deborah Bedford grabs the reader by the heart and doesn't let go."
—**Debbie Macomber**, author of *A Good Yarn*

The secret beneath Uley Kirkland's cap and mining togs is unsuspected in 1880s Tin Cup, Colorado. She longs to hide the clothing of deception and be honest about her feelings for handsome stranger Aaron Brown. But while Uley dreams of being fitted for a wedding gown, the man she loves is being fitted for a hangman's noose, and she is the inadvertent cause of his troubles.

The truth will set them free, and Uley will do whatever it takes to save Aaron's life—even risk her own.

It was a story to put Hideaway, Missouri,
in the national headlines...

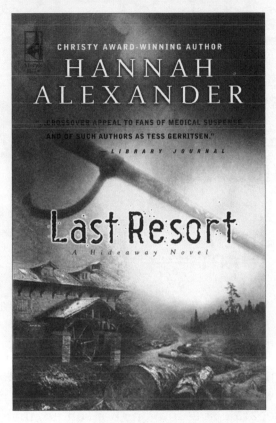

CHRISTY AWARD-WINNING AUTHOR

HANNAH
ALEXANDER

"CROSSOVER APPEAL TO FANS OF MEDICAL SUSPENSE
AND OF SUCH AUTHORS AS TESS GERRITSEN."
— *LIBRARY JOURNAL*

Last Resort
A Hideaway Novel

A missing child...
A woman in crisis...
A man of faith...

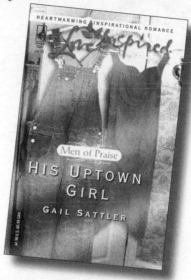

Love Inspired

GIFT FROM THE HEART

BY

IRENE HANNON

Adam Wright needed some divine intervention.
The widowed doctor was juggling a bustling practice
and a willful daughter. Enter Clare Randall. She
needed to fulfill the condition of her inheritance—
to be the nanny for her beloved aunt's friends, the
Wrights. Deep in his soul, Adam hoped that the
blond beauty could be the one to breach the
walls around his family's battered hearts.

Don't miss GIFT FROM THE HEART
On sale July 2005

Available at your favorite retail outlet.

Love Inspired

THE PATH TO LOVE

BY

JANE MYERS PERRINE

Francie Calhoun found God when she was touched by the words of "Amazing Grace." The former con artist was determined to be wretched no longer. But first, she had to convince her stiff-necked parole officer—the very handsome Brandon Fairchild—that her conversion was real...as real as her growing feelings for him!

Don't miss THE PATH TO LOVE
On sale July 2005

Available at your favorite retail outlet.